PRAISE FOR BETSY

Swim

"Poignant and at times rollickingly hilarious in its treatment of family ties and losses, as well as finding one's own personal journey, this engaging story, set in the 1970s, never flounders." —*Miami Herald*

"A delightful escape . . . a sweet, laudable fantasy of good-hearted upward mobility. BUY IT." —*New York* magazine

"[A] sweet story of self-reinvention . . . satisfying." —*Publishers Weekly*

"Warm, appealing." —*Booklist*

"A wonderfully indulgent read . . . it transports you to a sweet dream world." —*Glamour*

"[A] wild and wonderful summer novel." —*OK!*

"A sweet coming-of-age story." —*Florida Today*

"A keeper . . . The author's ability to communicate characters' complexities with more tenderness than judgment underscores her faith in crucial second chances." —*Louisville (KY) Courier-Journal*

The Orange Blossom Special

"A tender yet wickedly funny novel about people hoping for—and getting—second chances." —*People* (4 stars)

"Affecting... Instantly engaging. A light, funny read that offers a distinctive sense of place." —*Booklist*

"The appeal of this story is in its well-developed characters.... Though [they] confront issues such as death, racism, and war, the tone of the story is consistently bright and optimistic, making it a perfect summertime read." —*Roanoke Times*

"With an insightful and compassionate touch, Carter depicts a mother and daughter who create family from the people living at the crossroads." —*Harper's Bazaar*

"A terrific debut." —*Ms. Magazine*

"A sweet debut novel...an endearing portrait of a place and time." —*Kirkus Reviews*

"Engrossing...[a] warm, wise book." —*Elle*

"[A] high-energy debut novel."—*O, The Oprah Magazine*

A Note on the Author

PAT WILLARD is the author of *Pie Every Day*, *A Soothing Broth*, and *Secrets of Saffron*, which was nominated for an IACP award for the Best Literary Cookbook. She lives in Brooklyn.

Also by Betsy Carter

The Orange Blossom Special

Nothing to Fall Back On: The Life and Times of a Perpetual Optimist

Swim to Me

Betsy Carter

A Bantam Discovery

SWIM TO ME
A Bantam Discovery Book/September 2008

Published by Bantam Dell
A Division of Random House, Inc.
New York, New York

Previously published in 2007 by Algonquin Books
Cover photograph courtesy of Weeki Wachee Springs

Image, *Swim 1942*, from Wiki Media Commons
Book design by R. Bull

Library of Congress Cataloging-in-Publication Data

Carter, Betsy, 1945–
Swim to me / Betsy Carter.
p.   cm.
ISBN 978-0-385-33977-3 (trade pbk.)
1. Teenage girls—Fiction.   2. Weeki Wachee (Fla.)—Fiction.
3. Amusement parks—Fiction.   4. Mermaids—Fiction.   5. Adolescence—
Fiction.   I. Title.

PS3603.A7768S85 2008
813'.6—dc22
2008013059

Printed in the United States of America
Published simultaneously in Canada

www.bantamdell.com

BVG 10 9 8 7 6 5 4 3 2 1

For Miriam Brumer

$\mathcal{S}$HE WAS TWO YEARS OLD when her mother dropped her into the shallow end of a lake. Her mother insisted that instinct would prevail and that instead of sinking, she would paddle like any dog in over its head. Delores Walker always claimed she had a vivid memory of this incident. She remembered the cold and how she suspended her breath, and how she waved her hands and kicked her feet. Things got calmer when she realized that the water was carrying her. She stopped being scared. Her body moved with the flow of it, the most natural thing in the world. From then on, the water was where Delores felt most at home.

Twelve years later, over the Christmas break of 1970, Delores and her parents drove from their apartment on the Grand Concourse in the Bronx to Winter Haven, Florida, where they went to see the famous water ski show at Cypress Gardens. Delores watched with gape-mouthed attention as the skiers in their great plumed tiaras climbed on each other's shoulders to form pyramids, twirled in the air, and danced on one leg, all the while skittering above the water like flies. That night, her mind filled with all she'd seen, Delores lay awake in the room she shared with her parents at the Slipaway Motel. At one in the morning she was still fidgeting in her canvas cot when her mother sat up. "You having trouble sleeping, hon?" Her pin-curlers twinkled in the moon-filled room.

"Those skiers were the most beautiful thing I've ever seen," said Delores. "Can you imagine wearing those costumes every day? I swear I could do that for the rest of my life."

Her mother switched on the reading lamp and lit a cigarette. Next to her, Roy Walker was sleeping, making sounds like a little animal that's just been stepped on. "It was pretty enough. But as they say in the movies . . ." and her mother talked through the side of her mouth, affecting a gangster accent, "you ain't seen nothin' yet. Tomorrow we're going to Weeki Wachee."

The next morning, they got into the old Pontiac and followed a curlicue highway eighty miles northwest to the tiny town of Weeki Wachee Springs. They drove on tar roads made soft by the sun. On either side of them were swamps. Now and then, a gator would rear its head—not ready for a showdown, just checking the weather. Hot fish air filled the car. Roy had on the kind of wraparound sunglasses that Elvis wore, and a Hawaiian shirt that he'd bought for the trip. He held the wheel with one hand, and took off his Yankees baseball cap to wipe away the sweat. "What a stinkhole," he said. Delores and her mother ignored him. They were too busy passing a vanilla Bonomo's Turkish Taffy bar between them, biting off large hunks of the candy. "That one," said Gail Walker, pointing to a yawning gator and dangling the candy wrapper out the window. "Look at the brown hide on

him. He would make me a nice handbag and pair of shoes."
She let the wrapper fly.

They pulled into a gas station, where there was a big old
Florida bear caged up next to the cans of car wax and
Texaco Motor Oil. Behind the station was a hand-painted
sign that said: LIVE ALLIGATOR WRESTLING. For three dollars,
they watched a Seminole Indian wrestle a worn-out gator
until the animal rolled over on its back. Then the wrestler
rubbed a spot on its scaly stomach, and the gator went out
like a light. It looked easy enough, but the guy who took
their money said that only the Seminoles knew where that
sleep-inducing spot was. Just before they got to Weeki
Wachee Springs, they drove past an orange grove, where
the air was sticky and the smell was as sweet as if it had
rained honey.

This was Delores's first time away from New York City.
She'd never seen an animal in the wild, if you didn't count
pigeons. The white egrets with their long ballerina necks
filled her with wonder. The limber palm trees, the gnarled
mangrove swamps, even the way the heat forced itself on
her was new. And then there was the water: the blue Gulf,
brown swamps, green lakes. And somewhere, the ocean.
Delores swam in the turquoise pool at the Slipaway Motel,
a dingy little square whose bottom was slimy with algae.
Still, it was water, and she had the whole thing to herself.

They drove into the nearly filled parking lot at Weeki
Wachee Springs and followed the other families to the
park's entrance. In front of the gates to the park was an
obelisk in the center of a fountain. On top of the obelisk
was a statue of two mermaids who appeared to be spinning

underwater. One held the other over her head, with one hand holding the heel of her foot and the other resting under her arched back. There was a seat shaped like a clamshell in front of the obelisk, and people, mostly women, lined up to sit on it. The women would twist and turn in the clamshell seat, then strike pinup-girl glamour poses as their husbands took their photographs. Roy grabbed Delores by the arm and pulled her into the line. "Let's show 'em what a real mermaid looks like, eh?"

Roy Walker was a chunky man, five feet eight inches and 190 pounds. He worked at a wholesale grocery store, and his arms were thick and ropy from hauling cartons of canned beans and lard out of the trucks and onto the shelves. "Watch this," he said, heaving Delores over his head, one hand under her back, the other holding her foot, just like the statue above them.

"Dad, quit it," she shouted. "Put me down." Her father shouted back. "Go on, Delores, show 'em what a real mermaid looks like." Instinctively, she threw back her head, arched her back and splayed her arms. She could almost feel the water around her as she forgot her embarrassment and floated in the air above her father's head. Word rippled through the crowd, so that even the people at the ticket booth turned to see the man who had, for the moment, turned his daughter into a mermaid. Her mother stared at the two of them, her mouth slack with disbelief. She appeared to be the only person in the crowd without a camera. "That's my daughter and my crazy husband," she began telling the people around her. There was an elderly couple beside her. The husband kept nudging the wife with his elbow and saying, "Get a load of this," as he shot frame after frame. The woman turned to Delores's mother: "Don't you have a camera of your own, dear?"

"No," she said. "There was nothing much to photograph, until now." The woman asked her where she lived, pulling a pen and an envelope from her purse. Gail told her they were from the Bronx.

"We're from Baltimore. That's not too far from New York City. If you write down your name and address, I'll be sure to send you a print. What a nice family," she said, smiling at Roy, whose arms were beginning to shake by now.

Finally, he lowered Delores to the ground and back to earth. "How'd you like them apples?" he asked her.

"Dad, I know I will never forget this," she answered gravely.

Even as they walked to the amphitheater, little kids pointed and grown-ups smiled at them. One man with a wooly beard winked at Delores and said, "You looked like the real thing up there." By the time they took their seats in the bleachers, Delores's heart was tap dancing in her chest. Then the lights went down and the music started to play. It was "Moon River," the jelly-sweet theme from the movie *Breakfast at Tiffany's*. As the music oozed into the amphitheater, the black velvet curtain rose slowly. There was a collective intake of breath from the audience as one of the mermaids, already in the limpid blue water, swam to the edge of the aquarium. She had long blond hair that floated like a nimbus around her, and wore a pink halter-top and pink Lycra fin that flapped to the rhythm of the

current. She carried a sign that read: MERMAIDS GO TO THE
MOON.

A year earlier, the Apollo 11 space mission had brought
the first men to the moon. As they touched down, Neil
Armstrong and his crew had played Frank Sinatra's brisk
version of "Fly Me to the Moon." In Weeki Wachee's hom-
age to this historic event, the show began with a rocket
blasting into space. A mermaid with long red hair and a silver lamé tail hung on to the wing as the tape recorder sput-
tered a scratchy rendition of a takeoff. Then came Frank
and his jazzy anthem. The lady in lamé lip-synched without appearing to swallow any water, while behind her, another mermaid, also in silver, played backup, snapping her
fingers and thrusting her shoulders in time to the music.
Two mermaids in cobalt-blue tails and white helmets did
somersaults and pirouettes around some Mylar stars and
planets. A turtle floated by.

Delores could feel what it would be like to be underwater with them: the weight was gone from her arms, her
body felt buoyant. She felt herself lulled by the soft,
rolling rhythm. Time slowed down, as it does in that moment between waking and dreaming. Every second was
filled with different colors, depending on where the sun hit
the water. Things happened: one mermaid drank from a
bottle of RC cola, another blew wet bubbly kisses to the
audience. When one of the mermaids peeled a banana and
then ate it, her father whispered something to her mother,
who then giggled. Her father could be so funny at times.
Her mother had rolled her eyes and whispered back: "Roy,
you old turd, get your mind out of the gutter." But maybe

because the words of the lady from Baltimore were still fresh in her mind—"nice family"—she'd also squeezed his arm and held on to it.

The images melded with the harmony of colors; mermaids and water became one. Delores saw the mermaids occasionally suck air from the air hoses that were hidden behind the scenery. Even so, she was dizzy with the illusion that what she was seeing was real.

For their grand finale, all the mermaids gathered around a moon rock. One pulled an American flag from beneath her fin and planted it in the ground. A tinny version of "God Bless America" rose up through the amphitheater as the mermaids stood on their tails and saluted the flag.

Delores hoped nobody noticed the tears sliding down her cheeks. She stayed fixed in her seat, worried that if she stood up, she might break into pieces. There was no name for what she was feeling, only this certainty: whatever she had to do, wherever she had to go, one day Delores Walker would become one of those mermaids.

After the show, they checked into the Best Western motel across the street. Her father seemed so strong and robust that night and her mother was more flirtatious than she'd ever seen her. They decided that, this being their last night in Florida, Delores would stay in a separate room next door. There was a bolted door between them. "Just knock if you get scared, hon," her mother had said. But by the way her father raised his eyebrows, and her mother turned away with a smirk, Delores knew that unless someone broke into her room and put a rope around her neck, she was to stay as far away from that door as possible.

That was a happy time.

It turned out her parents would never forget that magical day either, partly because on that magical night, another Walker was conceived. Nine months after their trip to Weeki Wachee, Delores's brother West was born. Named after the motel in which he was conceived, West Walker was thick and stubby, just like his dad. He slept in Delores's room, and at night, she would sing to him or talk to him as though he understood what she was saying. He never complained, even when she dressed him up in old doll clothes and wheeled him around in a toy baby carriage that she'd kept from childhood. She started calling him Westie.

For a while, the Walkers seemed like any other happy family. Her father would toss West in the air and say things like, "How's my buddy boy?" He'd tuck him under his arm like a football and run across the room shouting, "It's the great halfback from the Grand Concourse, WEST WALKER." As fast as he could, West would wriggle away from him until Delores's father would give up and pass him off to her mother. Eventually, her father stopped treating him as a football. "He's a real mama's boy," he'd say to Delores. "Too bad it didn't turn out the other way. You shoulda been a boy, he shoulda been a girl."

On winter afternoons, particularly on Sundays, Delores would get a hollow feeling inside her. It was a gnawing ache, as if her insides were concave. She knew it best by its absence, the times when she did not feel like the loneliest person in the world.

A little more than two years after the Weeki Wachee

trip, on a late Sunday afternoon, Delores, Westie, and their parents were holed up in their Bronx apartment. Outside, the low March clouds were the color of dirty sheets. Inside, the smell of liver covered every inch of the house like fresh paint. After reading in *Teen Girl* that bangs "were a pick-me-up for any kind of face," Delores locked herself in the bathroom and took a pair of scissors to her brown, straight hair. She needed a pick-me-up.

She wet her hair and combed it down in front of her face. The scissors made a snipping noise as dark brown ribbons filled the sink. In the background, she could hear her father say something in a gruff voice. Her mother yelled back: "Liver, what'dya think it was?" West was playing on the floor of their room. Delores didn't hear what her father said, only the sound of a door slamming. Often when her parents fought, Delores would run a bath and lie there with her head underwater so she wouldn't hear them screaming. Now, the pounding on the door made that impossible.

"Delores," her mother shouted. "You and me and West might as well eat dinner. Your father has picked this moment to lock himself in the bedroom. I swear, that man is dumber than a slotted spoon."

"Ugh, liver again?" Delores asked her mother.

"Liver is a delicacy, Miss Snotnose," her mother shot back. "Not everyone knows how to prepare it so well."

Liver stuck in Delores's throat like a wad of mud. She was sure her mother cooked it just to be spiteful. Delores and her father would watch with disgust as her mother would cut her liver into jewel-sized pieces, then say to her family, "Liver is a specialty in France. The way I have a natural taste for it, it wouldn't surprise me if I had some French blood in me." Then she'd stab a piece of the meat with her fork, shove it into her mouth, and make smacking noises as she chewed out loud.

There was no use getting into a fight about it. If Delores or her father refused to eat her liver, her mother would cry, then rush into the bathroom, where she would make loud retching sounds. Delores knew what her father meant when he said he felt "like a trapped mutt." Sometimes it seemed to her that her life would never get any bigger than this; that she would never get out of here.

When her father finally did come out of the bedroom, his fists were clenched at his sides as though at any second he might reach for a gun. He walked toward the kitchen, never taking his eyes off the piece of liver lying on his plate. He stood over the table and in one sweep, picked the piece of liver off his plate and chucked it against the kitchen wall.

The history of the Walkers' marriage was written in food stains. "Cockroaches eat better than this," he shouted. "I'm going out to get some real food." Westie started bawling. Her father grabbed the car keys and his Yankees cap and headed out the door. Delores was left at the table with West as her mother ran to the bathroom. Part of her wished she could leave with her father. West's eyelashes were lacquered with tears; there were puddles of strained carrots on his bib. He looked fenced in and miserable in his high chair. Poor kid, at eighteen months old, he was even more trapped than she was. She pointed to the plum-colored stain that the liver had left on the wall. "Look,

Westie, isn't that pretty?" Then she crouched down next to where the liver had landed on the floor. It lay there curled like a glove.

She picked Westie up out of his high chair, and showed him the shriveled piece of meat. "How do you like that?" she said, holding him on her knee as she wiped the snot from his nose. "Liver bounces."

"*Ous*," said Westie. The word came out in little bubbles.

Just then, her mother came back into the kitchen. Water was dripping from her chin.

"I try so hard to please. And this is the thanks I get," she said, pointing to the meat stain. "I don't deserve this." She started to cry.

"Mom," said Delores, still on the floor with Westie. "Do you know that liver bounces?"

"*Ous*," shouted West. "*Ous*," he said again, kicking his legs.

Her mother cried harder. "Do I deserve this?"

"No, Mom," said Delores, staring ahead at the flesh-colored walls and the balding shag rug. "Nobody does." Delores hated her mother in the way only a teenage girl could hate her mother. She hated her for being whiny and self-pitying. She hated herself for not being more sympathetic and felt guilty about envying her father's ability to up and leave.

"Why don't you go watch *Glen Campbell*?" Delores said. "I'll feed Westie and clean up."

Her mother blew her nose, then went into the living room to watch her favorite TV show. Delores put Westie back into his high chair and sang the "Ugly Duckling" song to him as she cleared the table. West loved it when she came to the quacking part: "*...and all the birds in so many words said* QUACK, *the best in town,* QUACK QUACK, *the best,* QUACK QUACK, *the best,* QUACK QUACK, *the best in town...*" He would spit, thinking he was quacking as well, and laugh as if it were the funniest thing in the world.

West and Delores joined their mother on the couch, and they were well into *Bonanza* when her father came back. He was carrying a grease-stained carton of Chinese food. Because he had been drinking beer, his words came out like mashed bananas. "This is real food. Taste it," he said, scooping out a clump of chow mein and holding it up in front of them. Her mother smacked his hand away, and the food flew into the armrest of the worn lime-green sofa. West wailed as she sponged away at some water chestnuts.

"The two of you are nuts," said Delores.

"Believe you me," said her mother, "if I could afford a lawyer, I'd call one tonight."

Her father threw a dime at her feet. "Whatcha waitin' for? Call one."

Her mother lobbed the dime at his head. "I wouldn't waste this precious money on you." Westie was shrieking now, and even Delores began to cry. Again, her father reached for his Yankees cap and shoved the car keys in his pocket. "Gotta get out of this insane asylum," he said, stepping over the pool of soy sauce and cornstarch that was spreading on the beige broadloom.

Delores lay on her bed next to Westie in his crib. She tried singing the "Ugly Duckling" song to calm him down. He was hiccuping in between his sobs. She sang "Thumbelina," and used her thumb to act out the words. She pulled Otto, a little white hand puppet she'd had for years, out of the shoebox and held him up in front of his face. "Hi," said Otto in a funny squeaky voice. "Please don't cry. Delores and I will take care of you." Finally, the hiccups subsided. He tried to keep his eyes open, but soon he grudgingly fell asleep. His fist lay balled against his cheek and his curly blond hair was matted from all the tears. He looked angelic and at peace. Delores gently moved a damp curl from his forehead. She closed her eyes and did the thing she did when she wished that she were somewhere else. She lay as still as possible and willed herself underwater. After a while, she could feel the water undulating around her, feel her foot brushing up against a wisp of sea grass and the blast of fish scuttling past her. She could even hear the lapping sound of it. She imagined she was swimming without needing to take a breath. On this night, Westie swam beside her, his chubby legs moving as slowly as a turtle's. "Swim, Westie," she shouted. "Swim away."

She was talking in her sleep, and the effort of it rocked her awake. She looked over at Westie, who was sprawled on his stomach. Outside, she could hear the sound of the TV. According to her alarm clock, it was after eleven. She went into the living room, where she found her mother sitting on the couch smoking a cigarette. Her mother studied the floor as she exhaled: "You might as well go to bed, Delores. He's not coming home tonight."

She was right about that. Her father didn't come home that night or any night after that.

Part One

One

THE AIR IN THE BUS smelled like the inside of a suitcase: stale and used. Delores got on the bus early to make sure she had a window seat. Through the opaque windows she could see her mother waving. She didn't wave back, and when the bus pulled out from the station, she kept her eyes forward until she was on the other side of the Lincoln Tunnel. Alone in her seat, she pulled out her suitcase and unpacked Otto, who was wrapped carefully in a pair of her pajamas. Otto was a puppet with a white ceramic clown head that her father bought her the time they went to the Barnum & Bailey Circus in Madison Square Garden. It was one of the few times she and her father ever went anywhere alone.

At intermission, when he told her she could buy anything at the circus that didn't cost over five dollars, Delores chose the puppet with a bald white head because, even though he had a red dollop of paint on his nose, he also had a rhinestone teardrop under each eye and the sad demeanor of someone pleading, "Get me out of here." Delores recognized him as a kindred spirit, and she picked him with the intention that one day they would be able to help each other.

On days when she felt particularly lonely, she'd take Otto out of the shoebox where he lived and occupy his frumpy puppet's body with her fingers. She'd tell Otto things about school or her parents—things she wouldn't tell anyone else. Then she'd twist her voice into a high pitch and listen as Otto told her how pretty she was. "Someday, Delores," he'd say, "you and me, we'll live by the ocean. You'll swim all day. You'll be tan and beautiful and the most popular girl anyone ever knew."

She would have liked to keep Otto on her lap, liked to hold on to something that was hers, but it was weird enough being alone on the bus. A bald puppet with rhine-stone teardrops would only call attention to her. So she packed up Otto again, this time between her suede fringed jacket and the satin green miniskirt her mother had given her. Delores had stuffed her money, along with a return ticket and the letter inviting her to Weeki Wachee, inside Otto's hollow head—a small comfort. His sad eyes were looking down on her. "We'll be okay," she wanted to call out to him. "This is what we've always wanted. You'll see." She tried to contain her thoughts, knowing that if she al-lowed herself to think about Westie she would cry. Better to stare straight ahead, holding on to the brown paper bag that her mother had packed with sandwiches and other food that she promised would keep overnight.

The world slid by, turning from the buds of early spring into the soothing green pines of Virginia and the Carolinas. She ate one of the sandwiches along with an ap-ple and some Chips Ahoy! from the bag. The stack of sand-wiches wrapped in wax paper and the individual packages of cookies, four to a packet, made her homesick. There was a dull tugging in her heart. She kept reminding herself that she wasn't doing to Westie what her father had done to them. She wasn't abandoning him. He'd always know where she was. She'd call him once a week. And one day he, too, would swim away.

The bag was heavy on her lap. It would be a long time until anyone else would know what her favorite foods were. As the bus put distance between them, Delores thought about her mother differently. She thought about how she'd hugged her tight at the bus stop. "Honestly, hon," she'd said, "I didn't think you'd have the nerve to go through with it." She'd smelled of cigarettes and Mum deodorant. Delores thought about how, when she was little, her mother would wash her hair, brush it, then wrap it around her fingers while it was wet to curl it. In her absence, her mother was becoming more of a mother than she had been at home. If Delores cried now, she'd reveal herself to be the frightened sixteen-year-old girl she was instead of the mermaid she was about to become. She pushed the sad thoughts out of her mind.

By leaving home now, Delores believed she wouldn't turn out like her mother, who had never left home or tried anything new. Her mother had been only a few years older than Delores was now when she'd had her. Her mother never talked much about her childhood, other than about her mother, Audra. Audra, she always said, "could have been an Olympic swimmer." Audra was thirty-four when she learned she had an untreatable blood disease. She left her two-year-old daughter and her husband to spend whatever time she

had left with the man she'd begun having an affair with a
year earlier. The man was rich, and they moved to a house
in Westchester.

Audra was a beauty, judging from the one surviving photograph of her. Every now and then, her mother would say
to Delores, as if for the first time: "Have I ever shown you a
picture of your grandmother?" Delores would sit next to her
on the bed and watch her mother pull a yellowing envelope
from the back of her drawer. She'd open it carefully, as if the
Constitution were inside. Then she'd pull out a fading photograph with serrated edges and hold it up with both hands.
"That's her," she'd say, her voice lifting. Delores would look
at the picture of a woman with a thick pageboy and high
cheekbones. Her head was tilted to the side and she had
a small smile on her face, as if the person taking the picture had just whispered something vaguely shocking. Each
time, Delores studied the big almond-shaped eyes, hoping
that this time they would give something away, but they
were cast downward, and whatever they were trying to
conceal remained locked there forever.

Delores thought how it must have been for her mom and
her grandfather, the rejected ones, licking their wounds together after beautiful sloe-eyed Audra swam out of their
lives. If your mother leaves you when you are two years
old, there is a whole part of your story that will never be
finished. A girl with no mother must learn to be her own
mother. It made Delores sad to think of her that way.

Leaving certainly ran in the Walker family.

A little more than two years after their trip to Weeki

Wachee, Delores's father had left the family. Now she was going, too.

Her mother was husbandless and daughterless.

Westie would always be a fatherless child.

No, that wouldn't have to be so.

Even though she was far away, Delores would try to be a father to him. She would support him and do for him all the things a father should do. She would be a good daughter and make her mother proud.

Alone on the bus now, Delores realized she had no witness to her vow, only herself. But this was a promise born in love and sadness, and they were witnesses enough.

Across the aisle, a young couple was making out. They were both long and slender, and their bodies moved together like wheat in a breeze. She had large blue doll-eyes and straight blond hair down to her waist. Her red, orange, and green striped bell-bottoms hung low on her hips, and, as her mother would say, they were so tight they looked as if they'd been painted on her. He had long, dirty black hair and hatchetlike sideburns. Occasionally, he'd lean over and plant feathery kisses on her forehead. They were whispering, so Delores couldn't hear what they were saying, only that they called each other "honey." Sometimes she'd slap his arm and say, "You are too much." Every now and then they would sing. Her voice was like spun sugar, sweet and airy. His had more of a twang to it. They went in and out of song, and Delores closed her eyes, soothed by their happy sounds. She pretended that they were her parents and they were singing her a lullaby. She thought about how her life would be different with parents like that. Maybe they were in show business. Maybe she would be in show business, too. She'd be popular. They'd travel all over the world, a rich and famous happy family.

Delores knew that the Walkers were not really a happy family. She could spot happy families a mile away. They were always bumping against each other, like puppies in a crate. They told stories about each other that never added up to much, but were constant reminders that they all spoke the language of the family. The dads didn't slouch and snap, "Now what?" whenever the moms called their names. The moms didn't roll their eyes and say, "Ha-ha, so funny I forgot to laugh," when the dads made jokes. Happy moms didn't hold on too tightly to their daughters' arms and tell them, "When it comes your time, marry for money. There's nothing sexy about a man who can't afford to buy you a steak once a week." Happy dads didn't talk about feeling "like a trapped mutt."

Westie's family would be happy someday, she would certainly see to that.

The last thing Delores remembered before she fell asleep was thinking how Westie would like it if she would learn to play the guitar. When she awoke, the sky was misty lavender, as it is at sunrise. Instead of the pine trees, there were palms: the bold royal ones that always look as if their hands are on their hips and their chests are round and puffy. As the morning sunlight blazed its way into the af-ternoon, Delores grasped her situation. *I am on my own now,* she thought. *If I eat, if I sleep, if I stay alive—it's all in my hands.* The truth of those thoughts was strangely familiar to her. It mirrored the way she felt when she was underwater: alone, propelling herself forward, utterly unafraid.

Twenty-three hours earlier, when she'd stood at the Port Authority bus station in New York, there had been dozens of buses lined up, like horses in stalls. Now her bus pulled in to a small yellow building with only one other bus. The young man across the aisle pulled a guitar case from the overhead rack. Then he pointed to Delores's valise. "This belong to you?" She nodded yes, and he swung it over his head and put it by her feet. "All yours, little lady." He smiled. The girl in the striped pants smiled, too, and said, "Have a good time now, ya hear?"

"Thank you," said Delores, her lips sticking together from not having spoken for nearly a day. She got a good look at the man and woman. How ridiculous to fantasize that they could be her parents; they were only a year or two older than she was.

Delores waited until everyone left the bus station. She went into the ladies' room and opened her suitcase. She pulled out her suede jacket, then unwrapped Otto, running her fingers around his head. No cracks. What a relief. He would stay with her for a while. She reached inside his skull and pulled out the letter inviting her to audition at Weeki Wachee. She plucked a coin from the bathing cap in which she had stashed her treasured silver dollars and closed the suitcase. The man at the ticket counter seemed surprised when she asked for change, but handed her ten dimes, smiled, and said: "Anything else I can do for you?"

She wasn't used to people being this friendly: the man who lifted her suitcase, the girl who told her to have a good time, and now this man who wanted to know if he could do something else for her.

"Thank you, I'm fine," she said.

"You take care," he said, winking at Otto.

Delores found a phone booth. She closed the door and dialed the phone number on the letterhead.

"Weeki Wachee, how may I help you?" It hadn't even rung twice.

Delores asked for the director, Thelma Foote, the woman who had signed the letter.

"Hello, this is Delores Walker. You sent me a letter saying I could try out to be a mermaid if I came here," said Delores. "Well, I'm here."

"Delores, sweet thing," said Thelma Foote. "Where's 'here'?"

Delores read from the sign in front of her. "The Tampa bus depot."

"Are you by yourself?"

"I am."

"Hang on a moment, will you?

"You stay right there," she said. "One of my girls will come get you. It'll take about an hour. How will we know you?"

"I'm tall with long, brown hair and I'll be carrying a fringed suede jacket."

Delores sat on the concrete bench outside the depot and started to reread her copy of *Teen Girl* magazine. The sun made her head pound. She moved inside the stuffy building and sat on a backless wooden bench, too distracted to read. She put her suitcase and the brown paper bag next to her. Otto flopped on her lap. She unwrapped the last of her sandwiches. It was cold sliced liver on Wonder bread with ketchup. And now, here Delores was, eleven hundred miles away from home, eating liver and already missing it. A little touch of France in Tampa. She polished off the sandwich and decided against buying a drink to go with it. Best to save her money. Who knew where she'd wind up sleeping tonight?

When she was sure no one was looking, she slipped her hand into Otto's flaccid body. "Hey, kiddo," he said in his squeaky voice. He cocked his head, then looked around in the darting way that pigeons do. "We're here. We made it."

"Otto," she whispered, staring at the return ticket in her other hand. "What am I going to do if they don't take me as a mermaid?"

Otto leaned his cool face against hers. Then he pulled back and looked her in the eye. "With your looks and talent? It's in the bag, kiddo. Would they drive an hour one-way to pick up just anyone? I don't think so." With Otto still alive on her right hand, Delores curled up on the bench and fell asleep. She awoke to the sound of a honking car horn. They were here. She gave Otto a quick peck on the cheek, wrapped her pajamas around his head, and shoved him into the suitcase. She ran her hands through her hair, squeezed her eyes open and shut a few times, then walked outside. There was a white pickup truck with the blue letters WEEKI WACHEE and a drawing of the two mermaids in front of the clamshell.

"You the girl from New York City?" asked the young woman who was driving.

"That's me," said Delores.

"C'mon then, let's go."

The girl behind the wheel was named Molly Pouncey. She was seventeen, just eleven months older than Delores. She had long blond hair, bluish-green eyes, with no whites showing, and there was a tiny crook in her thin, long nose. Molly Pouncey had come from Philadelphia only six months earlier. She swallowed her *l*'s, so that "please" came out "plgease" and "delicious" as "deglicious." When she said to Delores: "You'll love the girls, and the springs. The water is so unbelievably blue and clear, you don't even need goggles," it sounded to Delores as if she were talking underwater.

They drove by the swamps and marshes that had capti-vated Delores a little more than two years earlier. They passed a church with a marquee outside. BY SORROW OF THE HEART, THE SPIRIT IS BROKEN, it said in high, bold letters. Had something changed, or, back then, had she not noticed the fried-chicken joints and Jesus billboards that lined the road?

"The food is out of sight," continued Molly. "Great pizza, corn dogs. We get to eat whatever we want."

Molly talked as if Delores was already one of them. Delores had read in *Teen Girl* that appearance was a matter of self-esteem. "When you feel insecure, put a smile on your face and a bounce in your voice, and no one will be able to tell," it said. "After a while, even you will begin to believe that the day's getting brighter." *Teen Girl* had never let her down; it certainly wouldn't now.

Delores and her best friend, Ellen Frailey, used to spend hours reading *Teen Girl*. Once, they sat in the sun for two hours with wax paper on their arms after reading: *Give yourself a suntan tattoo. Cut out a small diamond or flower shape and paste it on your shoulder while you sunbathe. Small beauty spots are best. Avoid large shapes or complicated designs—you don't want to look like a sailor. Teen Girl* was where Delores learned that "popular people are enthusiastic." According to her score on the "Are You an Extrovert or an Introvert?" quiz, she was somewhere in between, with a tendency toward "keeping to herself and shying away from others." By now, *Teen Girl* had become Delores's personal guidebook. She turned to it for advice on how to look and act like other girls her age.

Because she had teeth that stuck out ("braces are a luxury for people like us," her mother had said), Delores normally kept her lips together and smiled in the shape of a canoe. But as Molly rattled on about the routines and about the hot room where the girls went to warm up after swimming, Delores flashed the most luminous, toothy grin she could muster. "Gosh, that sounds so exciting," she said. "I can hardly wait to get there." Molly gave her a sidelong look: "You look like that actress from *Gigi* that my mother's always going on about," she said. "Oh, you know, the French one."

"Well, I have a little French in me," said Delores. "From my mother." It wasn't a lie exactly. She had, after all, grown up on liver.

Delores studied Molly's profile: a thin, white scar ran down the side of her neck. She wanted to ask Molly if she'd been stabbed and also how she got the money to come

from Philadelphia, but she didn't think it was appropriate
to ask those kinds of questions so soon after meeting her.
Molly, it appeared, did not have the same problem. "How
does a girl from New York City make her way down to this
part of Florida?" she asked in her gluggy accent. "Did you
run away from home?" "Oh no," answered Delores. "My
parents—they're in the entertainment business—have always encouraged me to do my own thing."

"Are they famous?"

"Is who famous?"

"You know, your parents. Are they famous?"

"Well they travel a lot," said Delores, startled at how
easily the words were leaving her lips. "They play the guitar. They sing. You've probably seen them around."

Molly fell quiet, realizing that she might be in the presence of greatness, or at least someone related to greatness.
She took in Delores's outfit—a red-plaid miniskirt, a short-
sleeved black knit sweater, and white vinyl boots. High
fashion for 1972. There was a sudden shift as if, by Delores
introducing the possibility of famous parents and glamour,
Molly was the one who would now have to try to please
Delores. Delores let the silence linger before asking a
question of her own.

"Is that scar a stab wound?"

Molly put her fingers to her neck. "Oh that," she
laughed a little falsely. "I forget that it's there half the
time." Then, in a hurry to change the subject, she said,
"What's your sign?"

Delores checked herself up and down. "What sign?"

"Your birth sign, you know, your sign of the zodiac."

It was as if Molly was speaking Swedish.

"I don't know if I have one."

"Of course you do—everyone does. When's your birthday?"

"May fourth."

"Taurus. Your sign is Taurus. People born under the sign of Taurus are determined and stubborn. They can also be lazy and greedy." She made a sad clown face. "Are you stubborn and lazy?" She quickly brightened. "My birthday's in June, so I'm a Gemini. We're very sociable and good communicators. People like to have us around." She made a happy face.

Delores had assiduously avoided the horoscope section of *Teen Girl*. With its weird drawings of animals and planets, she had assumed it was some column about religious stuff. So Molly spent the rest of the trip explaining astrology to Delores. By the time they arrived at Weeki Wachee, Delores's head was filled with images of bulls and twins and rising moons and waning tides. Westie, she'd learned, was a Sagittarius (cheerful but restless). Her dad had bought Otto at the circus in mid-September, she remembered, which made Otto a Virgo (shy and fussy).

Molly led Delores to the dormitory where the mermaids slept at night. The room was sparsely furnished and overheated. Eight girls, wearing identical white terry-cloth robes and with towels tied like turbans around their heads, sat on a modular couch in front of a fireplace.

"Everyone," shouted Molly, clapping her hands. "There's someone new I want you to meet. She's from New York City." She put her arm around her new friend's shoulder. "Say hello to Delores Taurus."

Two

$\mathcal{T}$HE NAME STUCK. Since all of the recruits except for Molly came from the area, Delores Taurus was the only name on the list for tryouts the following morning. That night, she stayed across the street at the Best Western—the same motel where she had stayed with her parents two and a half years earlier.

Molly walked her to her room. All afternoon, she'd been giving her tips for her tryout: smile while you lip-synch; if you get water in your nose, just blow it out; play to the audience, not just one person; and, most important, don't panic if you get disoriented.

"Get a good night's sleep," she said now, tentatively patting the suede fringe jacket draped over Delores's arm. "Tomorrow is your big day."

Alone behind the closed door, Delores noticed that the room was the color of overcooked peas. It was small, with a low ceiling and a stained bedspread that had a poinsettia print. The smell of Lysol cut through the old cigarette air. Next door, a bunch of men were laughing in that deep, hollow way that men do when they drink. What she felt dug deeper than any Sunday night loneliness in the Bronx. Delores propped Otto up on the peeling chest of drawers;

his head fell against the mirror. Even he looked sallow in the low-wattage light overhead. She waited to hear his quacky, reassuring voice, but he had nothing to say. She put her return ticket next to her on the nightstand.

The last time she had been in this motel was right after she and her parents had seen "Mermaids Go to the Moon." She remembered how, when the show was over, the men in the audience had been the first to jump to their feet and cheer while the women and children sat in their seats and clapped. Someone whistled. The mermaids took mock curtsies and blew kisses. They were so beautiful and teasing, safe behind their Plexiglas wall.

Delores longed for the time when the Walkers were a whole family, for the safe feeling of having her parents on the other side of this motel wall. The sulfurous taste of fear caught in her throat. She unpacked only her pajamas and toothbrush, since she had no intention of spending another night in this place. Then she pulled back the poinsettia spread and got into bed. "So this is how it is," she said to no one in particular. Grateful to be sprawled out on a mattress instead of scrunched up in her seat on the bus, she pictured Westie lying in his crib and how she would wiggle her fingers across the fat of his belly like some creepy crawly thing, and how he would try to swat her away with his spongy fist. She tossed and turned and knocked the poinsettia bedspread to the floor. Exhausted, she finally fell asleep hugging her pillow.

Sunlight jutted through the window shades the next morning. Delores jolted awake as if one of them had rapped her on the head. Where was she? Why was her heart flip-flopping so? In daylight, the room seemed even smaller than it had the night before. Best to get up and out of here as soon as possible. She took a quick shower and dropped the tiny bar of Camay soap a half-dozen times. Remembering the laughter of the men from the night before, she wrapped herself in her towel as she rummaged through her suitcase for the bathing suit that her mother had brought home from her cleaning job at the office of a fashion magazine. It was a bright, iguana green, nylon Speedo, cut high on the thigh and low in the back. Her mother said it must have been the latest thing. She'd found it in a bag marked "Photo shoot" that was way in the back of a closet. "No one will want it now," she had reasoned. "It's already been used." Delores put on the suit and spun around in front of the small mirror in the bathroom.

"Kiddo, you look stunning"—Otto was back—"like the princess of the sand castle. You're going to be the most popular girl in the place." Delores slipped on a pair of cut-offs and a men's white T-shirt (also from the "Photo shoot" bag) over her suit. She stepped into a pair of platform shoes and clopped off to the reception area, where she ate a complimentary corn muffin and drank a glass of orange juice. Then she crossed the highway to Weeki Wachee. At the ticket counter, she told the woman with a nest of teased platinum hair that she was there for her tryout. "Oh, you must be the New York girl, Delores Taurus," the woman said, pulling a pencil from some cranny inside her hair. "Thelma is expecting you."

Delores walked behind the parking lot to a wooden bungalow that was the administration building. Thelma Foote, she thought, would be beautiful, like Pocahontas or Marlo Thomas. But the woman sitting at the desk in Thelma Foote's office was well into her fifties. Her skin wobbled like marshmallows, and she had short, mannish helmet-hair. She wore thick, black-framed eyeglasses, which made her eyes seem to protrude more than they already did, a white windbreaker, baggy khaki pants, and a pair of spotless white Keds. She looked to Delores like one of the old women who lugged their shopping carts behind them on the Grand Concourse; nothing like Marlo Thomas. This had to be Thelma Foote's secretary. The woman rose from her desk and extended her freckled unadorned hand. "Hey, sugar, I've already heard so much about you." She scrutinized Delores up and down. "You are a tall drink of water, aren't you? So far, I'd say the reports have not been exaggerated. How do you do? I'm Thelma Foote."

Delores shook her hand firmly. "So nice to meet you," she said. "I'm Delores."

Thelma Foote offered Delores a chair across from her desk. "So," she said, "tell me everything about yourself."

"I'm from New York City," she began. "My parents are entertainers, though my mother keeps her hand in the fashion business. They travel quite a bit. My mother is part French. We came here two years ago. I saw the mermaids and knew that, someday, I wanted to be one of them. We always take our vacations at the seashore; I practice my mermaid routines there. One time, the recreation director at the hotel we were staying at saw me. He asked me if I would be in a show they were putting on at the pool. I said yes, and every day for a week, I swam for the guests. At the end of the week he offered me a job for a lot of money. My parents said I should finish high school. High school was such a gas, you know, with all the parties and stuff." Delores giggled. "And I have a little brother. His name is West, but I call him Westie."

Delores could feel her face flush as the words poured out of her. This was the person she would have been had those two people in the bus been her parents: pretty, popular, well-dressed, slightly stuck-up Delores Taurus. She thought about the blond girl on the bus, and how snugly her bell-bottoms had fit her. That's how well the name Delores Taurus suited her. She wondered if Thelma Foote believed what she was saying. The whole time Delores was talking, Thelma Foote was running the zipper of her windbreaker up and down. One of the teeth was broken, and the zipper was jammed. She glowered at the impaired zipper as she gave it one final tug. Nothing happened. "Goddam piece of crap," she muttered under her breath. Then she looked up at Delores with a taut smile. "Well, sweetie cakes, you certainly have quite a story. Let's take a walk over to the bell, shall we?"

Thelma had been doing this job for enough years that she'd heard it all before. She could recognize the fakes, the liars, the girls who came from nowhere and would end up in the same place. It was something about the timbre in their voices, or how they never looked directly at her. She could winnow out the ones who wouldn't have the staying power to make it, and the ones who didn't take being a mermaid seriously. This one was nervy, thought Thelma, had the cut of determination. If she came from such a fancy family though, why hadn't they done anything about her teeth? Never mind. Even if her story was made up and she'd come from nowhere, somewhere would definitely be her next stop.

Thelma and Delores headed across the lawn toward the girls' dormitory. Thelma was short, and whatever else she was, was hidden behind the lopsided jacket and baggy pants. Delores was tall, close to six feet in the platforms. When Thelma put her arm around her, she practically had to leap in the air to do so.

"Did you ever dance ballet?" she asked Delores.

"Of course I've taken lessons," Delores lied. She remembered a story she once read in *Teen Girl* about Karen Carpenter, or someone like that. Karen had such a natural singing voice, the article said, that her parents worried how formal training might ruin its uniqueness. "But my parents always felt that I was a natural and that lessons would only mess up my personal style." She turned toward Thelma to see if she was buying it.

"We shall soon see if you look as good in the water as you do out of it." Thelma nodded, as if she were agreeing with herself. "Ah, here's the famous bell, where dreams are made and hearts are broken."

They stopped before a metal capsule that was indeed in the shape of a bell. It was open at the top and filled with water, and it had windows all around it. The bell stood about twelve feet tall and nine feet wide—just big enough for one swimmer. Thelma told Delores that the water temperature was 74.5 degrees, the same as it was in the Springs. Most pools are heated to between 80 and 83 degrees. This would be cold—"plenty cold"—she said.

Delores stripped down to her electric-green suit. She shook her long brown hair so it fell around her shoulders. "So what do you want me to do?" she asked.

"I want you to get into that tank and show me what you've got. Convince me you're a mermaid."

Delores arched her back and moved her head from side to side, loosening her neck muscles.

She stepped into the bell. At first, she just swam in circles. Then she did a couple of twirls and pinwheels and basic ballet movements. She smiled and pretended to lip-synch to a song, like the girls in the show. Molly had told her that the mermaids swam sixteen feet beneath the surface and that sometimes they needed to stand totally still. The way they controlled their buoyancy was by taking air in or letting it out at the right times. Delores was able to hold her breath for a little over a minute. Keeping her eyes open in the clear spring water was hard. Mermaids never wore masks, and the water made everything blurry. Everywhere she looked, all she could see were the thick, black frames of Thelma Foote's glasses pressed up against the glass windows. After about ten minutes, she hoisted herself half out of the water. She waited for Thelma to speak.

Thelma yanked her zipper one more time. "Crap," she whispered, looking momentarily distracted. Then she turned her attention to Delores. "Lord knows, you're photogenic enough, and you've got enough damn grace to make Esther Williams look like a frog. I want you to do one more thing. I want you to swim on your back, forward, underwater."

Molly had warned her about this part. If you swam forward on your back underwater, there was no way water wouldn't go up your nose. "If you're going to lose it, that's when it happens," she'd said. "Just keep your eyes straight ahead and don't panic." Delores plunged back into the tank. She arched her back and did the scissors kick to get herself underwater. The water burned as it went up her nose. The urge to come to the surface was so strong that she felt tears come to her eyes. She tried to concentrate on the water before her, just as Molly had said she should. She noticed that the sun reflected on it in such a way that all of the bubbles looked like tiny diamonds. She thought about what it must be like to be able to swim in this clear water every day and see the diamonds and the turtles and the manatees that would float by. She pretended that she was swimming in the real springs and that the audience inside the amphitheater was applauding and whispering to one another: "Do you think she's a real mermaid?" It gave her the courage to do a backflip and keep her legs perfectly straight. She came out of the flip and swam to the window where Thelma Foote was peering in on her. She put her face right up against the glass so that she and Thelma were nose to nose, but for the thin piece of Plexiglas between them. The move startled Thelma. Delores smiled a mysterious smile and swam away.

In all her life, Delores had never been as sure of herself as she was at that moment. She'd passed the tryout and would become a mermaid; that was for sure. It wasn't until she climbed out of the bell that she realized how cold she was. She was shivering and blue-lipped, like a kid who's stayed in the pool too long. Thelma Foote wrapped a thick white towel around her. "Way to go, doll face, you just earned yourself a tail. You are officially a mermaid. What do you think of that?"

"How much will I get paid?" asked Delores, cocking her head to the side so she could get the water out of her ear.

"You'll live here with the other girls." Thelma pointed at the A-frame dormitory behind them. "You'll flip burgers, you'll clean the pool area, you'll take tickets. And you'll get to swim in the show. You'll make fifty dollars a week plus whatever you pick up in tips. I'd say that was payment enough."

Delores turned her head upside down and shook her wet hair. Drops of water fell on Thelma Foote's Keds. Delores stood up and flipped her hair backward. "I'll talk to my parents," she said, still affecting her new coolness.

"You do that," said Thelma. "That is, if you can reach them while they're traveling."

Back at the motel, Delores took a hot bath. "Bath" was a fancy word for it, as the tub was so small her knees were practically touching her chin. She sat with her back to the faucet and let the hot water run over her. She'd never had good news before. It was the first time someone had ever chosen her for anything. Thelma Foote said she was photogenic, said she had earned her tail. It was odd, this feeling. Delores knew how to deal with disappointment. She was as used to that as milk in her cereal. But praise, and getting what you wished for? She wanted to cry for how happy she felt.

She thought about her friend Ellen, and how perfect Ellen's life had always seemed to her. In the light of what had just happened to her, Ellen's life now seemed ordinary, nothing to envy anymore. She thought about her mom and wondered what place she would have in her new life. And she thought about Westie, and the talcumy smell of the top of his head.

Delores got out of the tub and put on a pair of jeans and one of the slinky Halston jersey tops her mother had rescued from the magazine. She sat outside in the plastic chair in front of her room and let the sun fill her until the chill inside her was gone. Now was a good time to write to Westie. On a postcard that pictured the pink hotel with its orange tiled roof, she wrote:

Dear Westie, This is where I am staying now. Today I passed my tryouts to become a mermaid. Every day I'll get to swim in the beautiful clear springs. It's a dream come true. I will send you a mermaid doll so you can see what I look like. I miss you. Love, Delores

Then she went into her room, closed the shades, and pulled out the bathing cap filled with silver dollars. There were sixty-nine left. After she paid the five-dollar hotel bill, she'd have sixty-four dollars to her name. Delores brushed her hair and packed her bag. Just as she was about to close the lid on Otto, he said: "Hey, kiddo, don't forget about me." She tucked the bus ticket into the pocket of her suitcase, pleased with the thought that she wouldn't be needing it anytime soon.

It was after two by the time Delores knocked on Thelma Foote's door at the administration building.

"I've discussed it with my parents," she said. "They think this is a good opportunity for me, so yes, I'd be happy to be a mermaid. Can I put my stuff in the dorm now?"

Thelma Foote's wink was magnified a dozen times behind her thick lenses. "Child, someday I would like to meet those entertainer parents of yours," she said. "In the meantime, let them rest assured that we will take good care of you here. So c'mon now, let's get you fixed up."

Delores would never want for water again.

Three

THERE WAS NEVER enough water in New York City. Delores craved the water the way a boozer craves drink. Out of it, her large bony limbs were all edges and jerky movements. Under it, her arms made graceful arcs and her long legs rippled. For seven dollars a year, she got to swim in a small, crowded pool at the Bronx YMCA every day after school. Delores would make up stories in the water and act them out. Mostly they had to do with her being a beautiful princess who lived in a castle. She'd turn somersaults and invent little dances to show off to the fish and turtles who lived down there with her. One time, Henry, the cute older guy who taught swimming, even shouted: "Go, tiger!" after watching her wallop across the pool doing the butterfly stroke. He couldn't have known that, the whole time, she'd been pretending to ride on the back of a dolphin.

The lady from Baltimore had sent the Walkers two pictures of Roy holding Delores over his head in front of the obelisk, as she had promised. The pictures were folded into a note-card with a painting of a sunflower on the front of it. In a generous scrawl, the woman had written: *Splendid memories of your time in the sun. You make a beautiful mermaid.*

When Delores had shown the photograph to her friend
Ellen, they noticed how her father was staring into the
camera with his lopsided gap-toothed grin. "He looks like
Alfred E. Neuman," Delores said, and laughed. *MAD* was
her father's favorite. He kept back copies of it in the bathroom. In fact, *MAD* magazine was the only magazine she'd
ever seen in the house. "God, he *does* look like Alfred E.
Neuman," said Ellen. "I wonder if he knows it?"

"He must," said Delores.

Her mother had seemed to accept her father's disap-
pearance as another of life's inevitable disappointments.
For the first few weeks after he'd left, she'd say to Delores,
"He'll be back. He always comes back," as if she were talking about a runaway cat. Sometimes, she'd stare at the
phone, willing it to ring; it never rang. "There's probably
someone I should call," she said one night, "but I'll be
darned if I know who that is." As the weeks went by, her
husband's absence seemed to inhabit her. Dark circles, like
pits, formed under her eyes. She developed a nervous
cough. Some days she didn't even bother to put a comb
through her matted hair. She'd forget to buy food for dinner. If Delores didn't bathe Westie, he'd go to bed un-
washed. Then late one afternoon, about six weeks after her
father took off, her mother began to settle into an un-
steady peace. "The son of a bitch is really gone," she said
to Delores. "But the real pisser is, he took the car."

West didn't seem to notice his father's absence. The
house was quieter, that was for sure. His mom was distracted, but Delores played with him, fed him, and kept
him clean. Delores had assumed that her father would

send for her and West as soon as he got to wherever he was going. She felt a little guilty for imagining that life might be easier with him, that away from her mom he'd be more relaxed and kind of fun. She imagined he'd driven the old Pontiac somewhere out west. He'd settle down in a private house. The house would have a screened-in porch and a swing in the backyard. He would be tanned and happy, no more bad temper. He'd lose weight and grow honey-colored sideburns, and he'd still wear his Yankees cap everywhere. Behind the house would be a pool. Nothing fancy, just big enough for her to swim laps. There would be a barbecue in the backyard. He'd cook steak and baked potatoes. It would be sunny all the time.

To make ends meet, her mother took on a second job at night. During the day she worked at the checkout counter of a nearby Gristedes. After that, she'd go to her job cleaning fancy offices in a steel-and-glass office building on the West Side of Manhattan. Often she would bring home souvenirs. Once it was the suede jacket with fringes that she found at the fashion magazine in the building. "It was in the corner by the trash," she explained to Delores. "I'm sure they meant to throw it away." Another time she brought home a clock that had an airplane as a second hand and showed the time in places all over the world, like Halifax and the Azores. It had fallen off someone's desk at the insurance company, she said, though remarkably it hadn't broken. She kept the clock on top of the television and seemed to take some pride in always knowing what time it was in Zaire. Over the next few months, she brought home a leather briefcase, a pair of Biba suede boots, a man's Timex with a slightly bent catch, a Betsey Johnson dress, and two pairs of bell-bottom jeans. "God, those people at the magazine are such slobs," her mother would complain, pulling the scavenged items from a Macy's shopping bag. She'd try on all of the clothing first, and anything that didn't fit (which was most things), she'd hand off to Delores.

Every morning before school, Delores would bring Westie to the woman who lived three floors beneath them. She was pale and thin and slightly stooped. She had no kids and no husband. Delores only knew her as Helene. Helene wore her hair in braids pinned to the top of her head. She was of an indeterminate age and never wore makeup or perfume. The most distinguishing thing about her sparse and spotless apartment was the giant globe that sat in the middle of the living room. On one of those mornings, Delores spun the globe and arbitrarily stuck her finger on a spot somewhere outside of Guatemala. As she squinted to see where she was, she turned to Westie, and said, "Don't worry, no matter where I go, I'll always take care of you." Helene studied the globe while Westie wriggled in her translucent arms. "You've got moxie, dear," she said to Delores in a thin voice. "And moxie will get you a long ways." Delores didn't know what "moxie" meant, but liked the sound of it. It sounded foreign, and vaguely aquatic.

Just before school was to let out for the summer, and with no sign of her father, her mother said to Delores: "We can't go on like this, hon. I can't support the three of us on what I'm making. You need to get a job. Maybe you could

wait tables or bag groceries, something to cover some of
the bills we pay around here."

Delores considered her skills and came up blank. She
lay on her bed and looked at her feet. Size 10. Would she
always feel like this, she wondered, trapped in this small
house, with her sad mother, her baby brother, and these
big feet? Then she remembered what Helene had said to
her. She had moxie. She wondered what a girl with moxie
could do. She thought about the thing she loved the most.
Her body flushed with pleasure as she imagined diving
into the deep end of the pool. Just thinking about the
smell of chlorine made the back of her throat tingle.
Maybe she could get a job at Miramar pool. No, no, of
course she couldn't do that. She didn't even have her
Senior Lifesaving Certificate.

Under her bed in an old Miles shoebox, Delores stored
her "treasures." Aside from Otto, there was the picture of
her father and her at Weeki Wachee and a birthday card
with the face of a black bear that glowed in the dark with
the words: "Goodness gracious sakes alive, can it be that
you are five?" It was signed: "Your mother and father."
Delores had kept it these past eleven years because it was
the only birthday card they had ever given her.

And then there were the sacred pamphlets from Weeki
Wachee Springs. Printed on thick glossy paper with colored pictures of the mermaids in various costumes, the
pamphlets promised "crystal-clear blue waters," and "the
most beautiful women on land or sea." The paper was limp
now, and the creases were nearly slits from the many times
she had bent the brochures this way and that to study the

photographs. As she stared at them again, she noticed something she had never seen before. Down on the bottom, under the driving instructions, was a telephone number and address. Because Weeki Wachee occupied such a large part of Delores's imagination, it had never dawned on her that it would actually have an address and a phone number. It would be as if by calling information, you could actually dial up Oz.

A phone call to Florida was out of the question. Her mother talked about "long distance" as if it were an ermine coat. "Well, I'm glad *she* can afford long distance," she once said, after a neighbor bragged about calling her son in California. Delores would have to write a letter, which was another skill she most certainly did not have. She went through her back issues of *Teen Girl*, because she remembered that they'd once run an article on how to write a letter. The article had eight tips for good letter writing, including: "Be dignified." "Be courteous." "Be friendly." "Avoid sounding too self-centered." "Make your points quickly." She tore out a page from her loose-leaf notebook and began to compose.

How do you do, Sirs,

My name is Delores Walker. Ever since I visited Weeki Wachee nearly three years ago, I have wanted to become a mermaid at your park. I am a good swimmer. My coach says I am good enough to become a professional, no bragging intended. Please advise me about what I have to do to qualify for the position. I am nearly seventeen, which seems to me a perfect age for a mermaid. I look forward to hearing from you.

It occurred to her that maybe they'd want to see her picture. She rummaged through her box of treasures and came up with one taken two summers earlier at Orchard Beach. She had on her white bathing suit with the strawberry print. At the last minute, she'd put her father's Yankees hat askew on her head. The brim of the hat obscured her face enough so that you couldn't really see her teeth. She lay on a blanket, elbow propped in the sand, chin cupped in her hand. Her father was standing above her and his shadow lay by her side. Delores was just over five feet nine inches. She had breasts that jutted out like Dairy Queen ice-cream cones, and her high waist made her long slender legs look even longer than they were. When her father had seen a flamingo at Cypress Gardens, he'd turned to her mother and said, "Delores looks like one of them things." The way the camera caught her that day at Orchard Beach made her look taller and leaner than she was. Delores was pleased, and thought she looked as much like a mermaid as any civilian could.

P.S. Here is a picture of me that I hope will be useful. Before she sealed the envelope, she kissed her picture and crossed her fingers.

Two weeks later, a letter arrived addressed to her and postmarked Weeki Wachee Springs, Florida. Delores sat with the envelope in her lap and ran her fingers back and forth across it, as if by doing so she could divine its contents. It was four thirty in the afternoon. The days were longer now, and it was the time of year when the soft light and gentle air held promise. She closed her eyes and

thought about what her life would be like if they said no.
She pictured herself working alongside her mother, sweeping popcorn kernels off office floors and filching a cardigan
here, an umbrella there. "Please let them take me," she
whispered as she ripped open the envelope.

> *Dear Miss Walker,*
>
> *We appreciate your enthusiasm and your interest in Weeki
> Wachee. We are always interested in new applicants and would
> be happy to interview you and observe your swimming skills.
> Let us know when you will be able to visit us at the Springs, and
> we will set up an appointment.*
>
> *Sincerely,*
> *Thelma Foote*
> *Director*

As hard as she had wished for this, it had never occurred
to her that it would really happen. Now what was she supposed to do? She had no money, no way of getting to
Florida, and besides, how could she abandon West? Still,
she called up the Greyhound bus company just to find out
how much the fare would be to Weeki Wachee Springs.

"Wow, there's a first," said the man on the other end.
"Lemme see."

The man seemed to be talking to himself as he read the
names of cities on the map. "Orlando, St. Petersburg,
Gainesville. Ah, here we go, Tampa. Round-trip, New
York to Tampa, fifty dollars. One way, thirty bucks."

Delores barely had the composure to thank him. Thirty
dollars? Might as well be three hundred dollars. Three

thousand dollars. She could never lay her hands on that kind of money. She thought about her father and how he was wily that way, always having enough money to buy the clothes he wanted or take himself off to a Yankees game. It was odd, him being gone for so long and still not a word from him. She missed the familiarity of him.

She went into her mother's bedroom and opened the closet. His clothes were still hanging on the left side, same as if he were still there. She touched the sleeve of one of his white shirts, gone a little yellow with time. Maybe he had left some money in his pockets. Sticking her hand inside each of his trouser pockets, she came up empty, except for a half-full box of Sen-Sen. Suddenly, she could smell the sharp licorice candy. It was his smell. She pushed the pants to one side and started to go through his shirt pockets. Behind the pants were some shelves where her parents kept things like suitcases and hats. She'd often snooped into those shelves hoping to discover a secret, something in the house that she didn't know was there. She'd never found anything, and it had been years since the last time she'd looked.

She moved aside the suitcase and her mother's collection of hats. There was a box filled with old papers, official-looking envelopes with glassine oblongs where the address was meant to be. She found her mother's fox stole with the pointy face and beady eyes of an animal in flight. Tucked into the back corner of the shelf was something purple, something she never remembered having seen before. She pulled it from the shelf. It was a bag, a heavy purple bag with gold piping and the faded words SEAGRAM'S

CROWN ROYAL written across it. Delores took the bag from the shelf and wiped the dust from it. Then she sat on her mother's bed and pulled open the yellow string. The bag was filled with silver coins that were thick and heavy. She shook them out of the bag, and they made a jingly sound before rolling across the bed and falling on their faces. She studied them all: the bald eagles, a man who looked like President Eisenhower, a woman whom she took to be Lady Liberty. They were silver dollars from as far back as 1898 and there had to be close to two hundred of them. This had to be her father's sack. If her mother knew there was a bag of coins in her closet, she would have already spent every one of them.

For nearly sixteen years she'd seen her father every day and night and knew what little she knew of him. Now in his absence, she saw a whole other side of him. She imagined him holding one of the coins in his hands, maybe flipping it in the air a time or two and enjoying the weight of it, and how it felt smooth and cool as he closed his fist around it. It got her wondering why he hadn't taken the coins with him when he'd left. Had he forgotten they were there? Or maybe he'd left them, knowing that someday she'd find them and this would be his parting gift to her and her brother.

She'd take what she needed, plus a little more, and figure out how to leave the remainder of it for West. Delores went into her bedroom and found one of her old bathing caps. She brought it back into the bedroom and filled it with a hundred of the coins. She held the cap by the chin strap; it must have weighed as much as her own head. That reminded her of Otto and his empty head. That's where she'd hide the letter from Thelma Foote at Weeki Wachee. She put Otto and the bathing cap in the valise that she stored under her bed, then stuck the now half-filled Crown Royal bag behind her mother's fox stole and the hats and the boxes full of paper.

When her mother came home from the grocery store that night, Delores met her at the door. They would have two hours together before she had to report to her other job.

"I have a surprise for you," said Delores, smiling.

Her mother's eyes lit up. Surprises of a positive nature didn't often come her way.

"Why don't you relax and take a bubble bath? I'll run it for you, and keep you company. Then I'll make dinner."

"To what do I owe this honor?" her mother asked, slightly embarrassed by the attention.

"You'll see," said Delores, as she turned on the faucet. Her mother undressed in the bedroom, then tiptoed naked into the bathroom. As she slid into the warm bath, she sighed: "Ahh, my feet." It always came down to her feet, to standing all day in the grocery and at night in the office building. Delores could see how red and crusty they were at the heel. And her bunions, big as doorknobs. Her breasts floated to the surface as she lay back. Delores was always surprised by the sight of her mother's nipples. Her own were tiny and rosy; her mother's were cocoa-colored and the size of saucers. But she recognized how much she and her mother looked alike. They both had the same big hands, feet, breasts, and teeth. They were both tall with long faces like stretched rubber bands. Delores's eyes were big and nearly black, just like her mother's. Her mother closed her eyes and relaxed her head against the porcelain. Delores recognized that with the tension and exhaustion gone from her face, her mother might be a pretty woman.

"Thanks, hon," said her mother. "This is just what the doctor ordered."

Delores crouched next to the bathtub and put her face close to her mother's. "I got a job today."

"Oh yeah, that's great," said her mother, eyes still closed. "How much does it pay?"

"I don't know yet."

"When do you start?"

"As soon as I can get there."

"Get where?"

"To Florida. Weeki Wachee Springs."

Her mother sat up so quickly that bubbles flew overhead like snow.

"Weeki Wachee Springs? Where the mermaids are?" she asked.

"Yup," said Delores.

"How did that happen?"

"I wrote them a letter and they wrote back saying they would send me the money to come down and be a mermaid."

"You wrote them a letter?" It was inconceivable to her that her daughter was capable of writing a letter to as far away as Florida.

"Yes, and they're paying for my trip down there," she repeated. "Fifty dollars, round-trip, on the Greyhound bus."

"Do you have the money?"

Now that she'd told the first lie, every one that came after would be easier.

"No, they already bought me my ticket. All I have to do
is get on the bus."

Her mother lay back in the tub. She was bewildered, angry, proud, scared. Delores was just sixteen, not ready to
leave home. Who would look after West? So many emo-
tions, they were bumping into each other.

"What about school?" she asked. "You've got to finish
high school."

"School? All the mermaids live together, like in college,
and they all go to classes together. I'll still go to school."

Lying was fun. It came naturally to her. Delores wondered why she hadn't tried it sooner.

"If you go, why do West and I need to be here?" asked
her mother. "Maybe we'll go down to Weeki Wachee and
I'll become a mermaid, too." She folded her hands behind
her head and swished her legs back and forth in the tub the
way she thought a mermaid might.

"That's funny, Ma," said Delores.

But she didn't laugh. By now, the bubbles had thinned
out and her mother was a sad sight, lying in the bath wiggling her legs like that. She had a defeated air about her,
and Delores was afraid that if she stayed in this house long
enough, she would turn out the same way.

"Yeah, I'm nothing if not funny," said her mother, running some hot water. She got a distracted look in her eyes,
as if overtaken by a thought that displeased her. She became conscious of her nakedness, and wrapped her arms
around her knees. "What if I say you can't go?"

Delores was prepared for that question. "There's no job for me here," she said. "I'll make enough money down there that I'll be able to send some home each month."

"That's certainly a plus," said her mother. "When would you go?"

"Next Friday," said Delores. "It's the last day of school. I thought I'd leave on the four o'clock bus. That way, I get in around three on Saturday."

Her mother sank back underneath the bubbles. She knew she was supposed to want the best for her daughter and that she should recognize an opportunity when she saw it. Instead she felt angry, as if Delores had jumped the gun on fate, as if Delores had won and she was the loser being left behind. People came and went in her life with no consideration of what it would mean to her. She tried to hide her fear of being abandoned, of maybe disappearing altogether.

"This water's getting cold. Hand me a towel, hon." She stood before her daughter, wrapped in her towel and lost in thought. She looked down at Delores, who was sitting on the closed toilet seat. She looked so much the way she had at her age. Delores was only two years younger than she was when she'd had her.

"You do what you need to do. You got a whole big life in front of you. Just don't mess up." She was aware as she spoke them that these were the most difficult words she had ever said.

Delores smiled up at her. "I won't mess up, Ma. I promise."

That night, as Westie slept in his crib beside her,

Delores wrote him a note. It would be years before he was able to read it, but Delores felt like setting the record straight.

> *Dear Westie,*
>
> *It is not because I don't love you that I am leaving. I've never not loved you and I will always love you. My dream is to go to Florida and be a mermaid, and now that dream has come true. There are things I want to tell you, and when you get older and learn how to talk, we will talk on the phone once a week, I promise. I never thought that this could happen to me, and I hope when you grow up your dream will come true, whatever it is. Here is the best picture I have of myself, and I hope you will look at it often and remember that you have a big sister who loves you.*

She took the Miles shoebox from under her bed and found the picture of her father holding her aloft like a prize cup in front of the clamshell at Weeki Wachee. On the bottom of the note she scribbled: *P.S. The man in the picture is our father. He was very funny sometimes.*

Four

*F*OLDED UP IN A TEENSY KNOT of paper in her wallet was a quote Delores had ripped from *Teen Girl* years earlier. "If you have your self-esteem, you have everything," it said. It had seemed profound to her at the time.

In the three months that Delores had been at Weeki Wachee, she'd been giving her self-esteem the workout of its life. She'd been thrown in with six other girls who were different from anyone she'd ever met in the Bronx. There was Molly, of course. Then there was an impenetrable clique of three girls: Sheila, Sheila, and Helen. They were all from nearby Sebring and had been there the longest. Molly had a grudge against Helen and wanted Delores not to like her. Helen was the self-appointed class clown, the kind of girl who calls attention to herself by telling jokes in a shrill voice, then laughing wildly as if everyone were having as good a time as she was. Sometimes, when she'd bump into Molly at the park and there were other people present, Helen would stretch out her arms in a theatrical manner and announce for everyone to hear: "Good Gowee, it's Miss Mowee!" Then she'd laugh in a way that always started out sounding like a wail. Helen sang the same way she did

everything else: loud and showy. One evening, as all the
girls were in Thelma Foote's van driving into Tampa for
a movie, the radio was playing Barbra Streisand singing
"People." It became clear from the way Helen closed her
eyes and put both her hands to her mouth, as if she were
praying, that she felt a special connection to Barbra. By the
time Streisand got to the second verse of "People," Helen
was belting out the words with her, the two of them sounding for all the world like two cats in a rumble. Thelma Foote
pulled over to the side of the road and brought the van to a
jerky halt. "For heaven's sakes," she shouted, turning in her
seat to look at Helen, "if I wanted to go joyriding with Ethel
Merman, I would have invited her myself." Delores had
never heard of Ethel Merman, nor had Molly or any of the
other girls. Still, it made them laugh until they cried just to
know that Thelma felt the same way about Helen's singing
as they did.

The Sheilas were purportedly Helen's best friends, but it
didn't stop the one who was known as Scary Sheila from
saying to the others: "Ethel Merman, whoever she is,
would take a gun to her head and shoot herself if she ever
heard that." Scary Sheila had eyebrows that ran together
like a shoe brush. When she got angry, she'd raise one of
the eyebrows and say anything that came into her clever
brain. Everyone minded themselves around her, and of all
of them she was the only one who didn't think being a
mermaid was a dream come true. "I'm just here picking up
a little extra bread until I go back to the University of
Florida next semester," she'd say. But so far, six semesters
had come and gone, and Scary Sheila was still there.

Blonde Sheila, the third of the Sebring trio, had a bleached Farrah Fawcett hairdo and smoked nonstop. Whenever she'd talk about boys, she'd get loose and smirky and say things to try and shock the others. She called women she didn't like "backstreet whores." She loved to bring up the subject of virginity, always guessing who had hers and who didn't. She'd look down at her crotch and say, "Well, that cradle was robbed years ago," then explode into a raw combination of laughter and smoker's cough. Delores thought Blonde Sheila had a faded quality about her, as if she were already used up.

There weren't many boys at Weeki Wachee. There was one guy who would show up twice a week to play the Tin Man in "The Wizard of Oz" show. His name was Lester Pogoda. He lived with his family nearby and worked in their pharmacy on the days he wasn't swimming. Lester had red, lumpy skin that looked as if ants were crawling beneath it. He had the build of a swimmer, with a long slim waist and shoulders that fanned out like angels' wings. Out behind the mermaid amphitheater, there was a big rock next to where the Weeki Wachee River flowed. Often, Delores would see Lester on that rock wearing a polo shirt and a pair of shorts. He'd lie on his back with his chin jutting out and his face angled so that it was directly under the sun. He'd stay there for as long as forty minutes until his face looked as if it might explode and his shorts and polo shirt were soaked in sweat. Once, while Delores was serving as an usher for one of the shows, she came outside for a break. It was a cloudless ninety-two-degree day, and everyone who could manage it had ducked inside to an air-conditioned part of the park, everyone except Lester and his fiery face.

"Hey, Lester," she said.

"Oh, hey, Delores." He was sitting up on the rock, dabbing the sweat off his face.

"Pretty hot day for sunbathing."

"You're not kidding." He pulled his soaking-wet shirt away from his chest and waved it up and down like a fan.

"Aren't you sweltering?"

"I really am," he said, sounding anesthetized.

"Why don't you come in, out of the sun?" she asked.

"I can't," he said. "I have a medical condition."

"Oh, I'm sorry," said Delores, taken aback by this information.

"It's not life threatening or anything," he said. "It's just that I have this terrible acne. They say sun is the best cure for it. One time, a guest here, an older woman, saw me after the show. She told me that my face was unsightly. Can you imagine, she actually said the word 'unsightly'?" Lester's face got even redder. "She said the way to cure acne was to let the sun burn it away. She knew that because her son had had a bad case of it, and that's the only thing that worked for him. She said that her son's face got better and that he is now a famous linguist in Chapel Hill. I don't know," he said, running his fingers over his wet nubby skin, "maybe it's getting a little clearer."

Delores wasn't sure why Lester had told her all this. Maybe he would have told anyone who had come upon him at that moment. Seeing as she hadn't had a whole lot of experience with boys, she wasn't sure what to think.

The only other boy she ever knew was Henry from the Y. Sometimes he had complimented her on her hair and told her how he liked it when she wore it up. One time, he was swimming in the lane next to her. She was doing the breaststroke, he was doing the crawl. She could feel when he came near her by how the rhythm changed in the water. By accident, his hand brushed against her leg. She stopped swimming and merely floated. If she'd had to stand up at that moment, she couldn't have.

Later, when she'd gotten out of the pool, Henry had been waiting for her in the small corridor that led to the girls' locker room. He didn't say anything, just grabbed her close and kissed her. His tongue tasted like chlorine and she liked the way his nose bumped against hers. After that, they would kiss whenever they could find a private place. Neither of them ever spoke of it. Henry was the one who told her that she was good enough to become a professional swimmer, and Delores always wondered if he told her that so she would kiss him again.

Lester seemed different—less sure of himself than Henry. She knew how he felt. She felt that way about her teeth, her feet, her breasts. If someone had told her she could make herself smaller and more attractive by sitting under the scorching sun for forty minutes at a time, she'd have done it without question.

If she told Lester that she knew how alone and unattractive he felt, she would run the danger of cracking the facade of Delores Taurus. Instead, she tried to be encouraging. "You look good, Lester," she lied. "I can see an improvement just in the time that I've been here."

"Really?" he asked, his voice suddenly filled with life.

"Yeah," she said. "Really. Just don't go getting yourself a third-degree burn."

Delores got to know the shyest girl in the group, Adrienne, when they were both chosen to do a number with Molly and Scary Sheila in an upcoming show, "Carnival in Rio." Adrienne was tall and reedy and looked like a piccolo. When she spoke, her little, airy voice made her sound like one, too. Early each morning, they'd practice in the tank, then walk back to the dorm together to get ready for the next show. Scary Sheila kept calling Adrienne "Sparky," which seemed an aberrant gesture of affection coming from Sheila. Delores noticed how Adrienne flinched each time she heard the name "Sparky," as if a bug had just flown in her eye. On one of those mornings, when Delores and Adrienne were huddling in the tube, the heated hidden platform where they warmed up between scenes, Delores asked about the nickname.

Adrienne's voice got even flimsier. "It's a horrible story. Everyone else seems to know, so I might as well tell you. I'm from Zephyrhills, and I was the star majorette of the Zephyrhills High School marching band. Last year, for homecoming, I was chosen to do this trick where I light both balls of my baton on fire, throw the baton in the air, and catch it again. I'd done it perfectly millions of times in practice; it was no big deal."

Between deep breaths and long sighs, her story unfolded. On this particular evening, as Adrienne hurled the flaming baton into the air, she became distracted by some guy in the stands who was mooning the Zephyrhills Bulldogs as they were about to make their second-half entrance. The baton landed on the forty-yard line, igniting half the grass on the field. The Bulldogs were forced to forfeit the game, which they were winning by three touchdowns. After that, Adrienne was known around Zephyrhills High School as Sparky. "Even my teachers called me Sparky," she said. "It was so awful. Every time I hear that name, I think of that night and how humiliating it was. Finally, I got so depressed I dropped out of school and came here. Someone sent one of the Sheilas the story from the *Zephyrhills High Times* and she was quick to spread it around. I don't care, though. I'm still determined to become a majorette someday." She told Delores how since her arrival, nearly seven months earlier, she'd been attempting, without any success, to insinuate baton routines into the mermaid shows.

Twirling a baton underwater, thought Delores. *It can't be done.*

The Sebring trio figured Delores, with her fancy clothes and famous parents, for a snob, so they rejected her before she could them. During her second week there, Delores landed the role of one of the Lost Boys in "Peter Pan." Helen was playing Wendy. One afternoon, Helen got confused and couldn't find the air hose. Delores saw her panic. Without stepping out of her role, she swam over to her, took her hand, and pulled her over to the nearest hose as if she were introducing Wendy to some magic hideaway in Never Never Land.

After the show, she stood next to Helen under the hot

shower. "Thank you for helping me out down there," Helen said in almost a whisper.

"No big deal," said Delores.

"I suppose not," said Helen.

They didn't speak again for another three weeks. During that time, Delores got slightly larger roles, first as a fan dancer in "Carnival in Rio," and then as one of the von Trapp children in "The Sound of Music." Her skin had turned the color of chestnuts, and the sun was starting to bleach her hair. But her real beauty flourished in the Springs. There were no boundaries between Delores and the water. She embraced its swells and tempo and moved through it with airy grace. Even the girls who wished her the least well were charmed by her natural affinity with it. On the Friday night after Delores received a standing ovation for her solo performance of "Climb Every Mountain," Blonde Sheila came up to Delores as they were leaving the amphitheater.

"I like whiskers on kittens, too," she said in a strangely provocative manner.

"Uh, thanks," said Delores.

"So listen: me, Sheila, and Helen are hitchhiking into Port Richey tonight. There's this place, Hot Chick. You cannot believe how incredible their fried chicken is. We were thinking that maybe you'd want to come with us. What do you say?"

Molly, who was standing next to Delores, placed her hand over the scar on her neck, as if by hiding it, she might be chosen this time. She shot her a look that said, *If you go with them and leave me behind, I will put a knife through my heart.* So Delores told Blonde Sheila that she was expecting a phone call from her parents, who were on the road.

"You don't want to be hanging out with them," said Molly later. "Bad news, bad reputations. You know what I mean." So while the others went off to Hot Chick that night, she and Molly stayed behind with Adrienne and her best friend, sad Sharlene from Homestead. They listened to a Bee Gees album, and another one by Chicago. Sharlene had long, thick blond hair that she seemed to haul around. Since she never looked up, except when Adrienne spoke, the hair served as a shroud. She allowed as how, sometimes underwater, her hair would drape her face and she would get momentarily disoriented. "Why don't you try wearing a headband?" asked Delores. Sharlene and Adrienne exchanged startled looks. "That's a great idea," said Adrienne. Sharlene nodded. It was only eight thirty. Molly suggested that maybe they go watch some TV. Adrienne smiled and said, "I have a better idea. Let's twirl." Sharlene jumped up to retrieve the baton that Adrienne had given her. Adrienne ran to get hers. Delores whispered to Molly, "How much longer do we have to do this?"

When Delores landed the lead role of one of two sirens in "Song of the Sea," Scary Sheila rationalized it to the other two: "She's new meat. Thelma likes new meat." Still, the three of them decided to invite her to one of their "try-on" sessions. That's when they'd try on each other's clothes then borrow something from the others in order to make it look as if they had bigger wardrobes. Molly said it was because they wanted to wear all of Delores's fancy clothes that they'd invited her. Delores didn't care; she was pleased to be asked. But out of loyalty to Molly, she laughed and said, "I'm way bigger than you guys. Nothing will fit." By now, she and Molly were definitely best friends. In the dormitory, their beds were side by side. They even tried to work the same shifts.

Five

MOST DAYS, the mermaids performed two shows. Although they were twenty minutes each, it took them at least another twenty minutes to warm up and then another twenty to recover from the physical exhaustion of their performances. On the days they weren't performing, they would practice in the morning and serve as ushers in the afternoon shows. At lunch, they would man the refreshment stands, flipping hamburgers and cooking hot dogs. Every now and again they'd get to work in the gift shop, but that was a rare treat. Aside from the amphitheater, the gift shop was the only air-conditioned building at Weeki Wachee; because of their seniority, Scary Sheila, Blonde Sheila, or Helen worked there most days. On Sunday mornings, Thelma demanded that they all go to church nearby in Spring Hill. Blonde Sheila thought the preacher was cute, so she went happily, wearing her shortest baby-doll dress and strappiest sandals. Scary Sheila hated the services, rolling her eyes through most of the sermon. Helen loved the singing part and would join in, singing louder than anyone in the choir. The rest of them went as dutifully as they flipped hamburgers and cleaned the tank.

In her spare time, Delores would write postcards to Westie with pictures on them that she thought he would like. Once, she bought him a card with a picture of a sea turtle: *There's a turtle in the Springs that I've nicknamed Westie. Every time I swim he comes around. I think he knows me.*

Whenever she ushered, she would search the theater for a family that might be hers. Even when she swam, if she got really close to the glass, she could make out the figures in the first two rows of the audience. A couple of times, she saw a man with a navy blue cap and each time, she could have sworn it was her father. Then the man would stand up and she'd see that he was bent over or very tall, or she'd notice that he had a large dog at his feet. All men made her wary, even the ones who might have been her father.

In the Bronx, Delores had never been on a real date with a boy. She'd never played a kissing game at a party. Here, men—not even boys—said strange things to her. After the show, when she'd be available to pose for pictures in her mermaid outfit, they'd lean in and whisper things to her: "I sure would like a piece of that tail," or "Meet me for a beer when the park closes, eh?" They'd sometimes say these things within earshot of their wives and children.

Late one afternoon, she swam with Adrienne, Scary Sheila, and Molly in "Carnival in Rio." Her costume was a low-cut blouse with green and orange ruffles and the bottom half of a two-piece swimsuit. After they'd done a Ferris wheel, where they'd grip their feet onto each other's necks and spin around, she could see a man running toward the stage. He put his mouth on the glass and started licking it, right in front of her. One of the ushers tried to pull him away, but he shoved her away and kept doing it. Delores could see the slippery pinkness of his tongue pressed up against the glass. It was disgusting and it made her lose her concentration and forget to control her breathing. She started to rise to the surface, away from the others. Thelma Foote, who was directing the show, as always, from an underwater booth, got on her microphone and shouted urgently: "Delores Taurus, you need to equalize. Delores Taurus, you need to equalize."

She was still shaking a half hour later as she and Molly walked back to the dorm together. She told Molly about the man with the tongue. Molly just waved her hand. "That stuff happens all the time," she said. "Let's just put it this way. You're lucky it was his tongue and nothing else."

This was the kind of thing Delores would have usually told Otto, but Otto was packed away under her bed. She and Molly were the first to get back to the dorm, where they sat on their beds in silence. Delores longed to feel the reassurance of Otto in her hand, to see his cool ceramic head bobbing around like a fish that's been hooked.

"You still depressed about the guy with the tongue?"

"Not him," said Delores. She studied Molly's eager face, and Molly smiled one of her moonbeam smiles. "When you were a kid, did you ever have an imaginary friend, someone you talked to when you couldn't talk to anyone else?" Delores asked, without waiting for an answer. "I still do."

"You do?"

"Here, I'll show you," she said, reaching under her bed and pulling out her suitcase. As she unsnapped the latch,

Otto's sad, bejeweled head popped up. Molly started to laugh.

"What?" Delores asked, already regretting what she'd done.

"That's a funny-looking thing." Molly looked up at Delores. "Oh. Is that him?"

"I know. He looks like a hard-boiled egg. But he was the only one in my house I could talk to. Now I never get to see him. I mean, how would it look if anyone caught Delores Taurus talking to a puppet?"

"You're lucky you had him." Molly looked around the room. It was still empty. "Go on," she said. "Take him out. I'll guard."

She walked to the doorway where she stood with her arms folded, her eyes searching. Inside, Delores was whispering to Otto: "I miss him," she said. "I know it was a terrible thing he did, leaving us like that, but I miss him anyway."

Molly took her watch seriously, making sure no one would come upon Delores and Otto. From then on, any time Delores wanted to visit with Otto, Molly would stand guard. She told Delores that the moment she heard footsteps or voices, she'd whisper "lollapalooza" in time for Delores to put Otto back under her bed.

"Lollapalooza? Are you sure?" asked Delores.

The two of them doubled over laughing as Molly nodded her head yes and said it over and over again. "Lollapalooza, lollapalooza."

* * *

The night after the tongue incident, Delores called home.

"Hay-llo."

Her mother sounded like Lily Tomlin doing her telephone operator routine.

"Mom?"

"Oh yes, hello, Delores."

Her mother's voice seemed controlled, almost angry.

"Mom, it's me, Delores. Are you all right?"

"I'm perfectly all right. Why do you ask?"

"Mom, why are you talking like that?"

"Like what? I haven't the slightest idea what you're talking about."

"You sound a little, I don't know, mad or something."

"Why on earth would I have any reason to be mad? So how's it going in mermaid-land?"

"It's good. They like me. How's Westie?"

"He's with Helene at the moment."

"Yes, but how is he?"

"He's just fine, thank you."

"How's work?"

"Work is going real well, I'd have to say."

"Mom, have you heard anything from Daddy?"

"No. Why should I?"

The conversation continued this way, her mother's words floating over Delores's head like dandelion seeds. She finally gave up. "Gotta go, Mom, I'll try to call soon."

"Sure, call whenever you want."

Delores hung up. She considered that her mother might

have gone crazy or, even worse, that she hated her own daughter.

"How're your parents doing?" asked Molly, when Delores came back to the dorm.

"Um, they're really far away this time," she answered.

Six

IN FACT, Gail Walker was blossoming in her new life. Sometimes at night when she was cleaning the offices of *Cool*, the fashion magazine, she would sit at one of the gray metal desks in the maze of cubicles and stare out at the city below. The office was on the thirty-fifth floor and from some of the windows she could see the length of the Hudson River from the Statue of Liberty all the way up to the George Washington Bridge. When the bridge was lit at night, it looked as if angels had gathered around it.

Her favorite cubicle was the one with a desk that was covered with tiny ceramic figurines of dogs, as well as a plastic egg filled with Silly Putty, and a Pet Rock. All around were old photographs taken on sunny days in the country. In one of them, a young woman with tight blond curls was squinting into the sun. Next to her was a young man with dark features. In the crook of his arm he was holding a baby who was no larger than a cantaloupe. An older woman was walking toward them. She was smiling and carrying something in her hands, a basket of muffins maybe.

In another, more contemporary, photo, the young woman

with blond curls was standing barefoot on a beach. Behind her, the sky was streaked with the colors of sunset. There were pictures of a golden retriever and someone blowing out candles on a birthday cake. In another, the young woman with the curls was being smothered in the embrace of a middle-aged man wearing a safari jacket. There were pictures torn from magazines, shoes mainly, that were stuck on her bulletin board with pushpins. But the curly girl's personal pictures were much more to Gail's taste. She particularly liked the one of a little girl sitting on the beach. The little girl wore only a diaper, which stuck up in the rear like a duck's tail. She had tight blond curls and small dark eyes. In another, the same little girl was sitting on the woman's lap, their cheeks pressed together, their profiles obviously cut from the same template. Gail figured these were pictures of the curly girl and her mom. She couldn't imagine Delores putting up a picture of her anywhere. This Curly Girl, as Gail came to think of her, seemed to have a life that was filled with love and adventure, and sometimes when it was dark and empty outside, and chilly and airless inside, Gail would stare at those pictures so long and hard that, for a few moments at least, she could pour herself into them.

She'd let Delores go to Florida because she was broke and scared, and now her daughter was gone. Delores was on her own, and doing fine, it seemed. Gail knew she ought to be proud of that, but the only feelings she had were jagged, resentful ones. She stared again at the smiling woman in the photograph. *That woman would be repelled by me,* she thought.

One evening, as she wheeled her broom and trash can around the magazine's offices, she heard some shouting coming from Curly Girl's desk. She looked through a space in one of the partitions and saw a tall woman wearing leather pants and green glasses standing over the curly young blonde. The woman was screaming: "Do you have any idea what you are doing to our bottom line?" she yelled. "You fashionettes with your fancy degrees, what do you know about running a magazine? This isn't shopping. This is the real world, for chrissakes!"

The woman shook her head and walked away. Gail waited a few moments before she came toward Curly Girl's desk. "May I?" she asked, reaching down to pick up her garbage can.

"I'm so sorry, it's quite a horrid mess around here," said Curly Girl, bending down to scoop up a piece of paper that had missed the trash can.

Gail bent down at the same time. "It's okay, I can get it," she said, finding herself face-to-face with the girl under the desk.

"I might as well do something useful around here," said the girl, wiping tears from her cheeks. "Apparently I'm a failure at everything else."

They stood up again. Gail pointed to the pictures on Curly Girl's desk. "Judging from these," she said, "I'd say just the opposite is true." Curly Girl smiled a grateful smile, and Gail continued with her cleaning.

It gradually became a routine. On the evenings that Curly Girl worked late, which seemed to happen more and more, Gail would come by and they would say hello and exchange small talk about the weather or new stains on the carpet. "Red wine," said Curly Girl one night, pointing to a brownish-gray blob in the shape of an owl.

"I know a little something about food stains," said Gail, trying to sound professional. She bent down and began scrubbing.

On another night, as Gail dusted around Curly Girl's desk, she accidentally knocked over one of the framed photographs. "I'm so sorry," she said, righting it. At the same time, both of them stared at the photo of the little girl playing in the sand at the beach. "Is that you?" asked Gail, pointing to the baby in the diaper.

"Yup. That's me," said Curly Girl.

Gail studied the picture more closely and pointed to the woman. "She's really pretty. Is that your mom?"

"Mmmm. She was really beautiful," said Curly Girl, staring past the picture. "She died when I was six."

Gail let out an involuntary groan. "Oh God. That's terrible. I'm so sorry."

Curly Girl waved her hand in front of her face. "Anyway, I inherited her curly hair."

"And her good looks," added Gail.

After that, Gail had a feeling that Curly Girl looked forward to her visits. She always made sure to be friendly and reassuring. From time to time, she thought that Curly Girl recognized familiar items from fashion shoots dangling from the handle of her trash bin. They were little things: a tank top, a red suede belt, a tie-dyed scarf. One night, as

Curly Girl eyed a familiar-looking halter, she said to Gail, "You have good taste." There was no malice in her voice; she actually seemed pleased at Gail's choices.

Some nights, Gail would eavesdrop on the girl's phone conversation. She'd throw around words like "far out," "lovely," and "amazing," as if the world revealed itself to her in images and depths of feeling that Gail had never experienced. One night Gail came by just as Curly Girl was hanging up the phone.

"How are you doing tonight?" asked Curly Girl.

Gail reached for an answer that would convey the kind of purpose and enthusiasm she'd heard in Curly Girl's voice. "I'm just fine and dandy," she said. "And you?"

"We've got this photo shoot tomorrow. I have to be at Jones Beach by seven a.m. The insane photographer has got it in his head to do a shoot on sunken treasures. I've got less than twenty-four hours to come up with a mermaid's tail. A friggin' mermaid! Can you imagine?" For the first time since they'd met, she extended her hand. "By the way, we've never exchanged names. I'm Avalon," she said, in the same firm voice she'd used on the phone.

Unaccustomed to handshakes, Gail became aware of the girl's slender bones and squeezed her hand gingerly. "Oh, I'm Gail." She leaned her elbow on top of the partition. "This is some coincidence," said Gail, trying to sound dignified. "I have a daughter who's a mermaid. You know, not a real mermaid, but as close as it gets. She swims down in Florida, in Weeki Wachee."

"Super," said Curly Girl, wrapping a sprig of hair around

her finger. "If it's not too impertinent of me to ask, how do you come to have a daughter who's a mermaid?"

Gail laughed, unsure of how much to say. "It's a long story. She's a very talented swimmer."

"I'll bet she's that. What's her name?"

"Delores." Gail paused, and said, "I'm sorry, what did you say your name was again?"

Curly Girl let the piece of coiled hair drop to her shoulder. She put both of her hands on the seat of her chair as if she were about to rise.

"I'll tell you if you promise to keep it between us," she whispered, turning to see if anyone was nearby.

"Who would I tell?" asked Gail.

"It's really Evelyn. Evelyn Mandor. I changed it when I was at Vassar."

Gail smiled down at Evelyn. Avalon. "Can I make a long-distance call?"

Minutes later she put the phone down. "Lycra," she announced. "The secret of the tail is Lycra and flippers."

Gail Walker and Evelyn Mandor were improbable friends; the difference in their ages and their stations in life left too many spaces between them. But each recognized in the other something missing, something gone wrong. Both had lost mothers when they were very young, and both were striving for things that were still unarticulated. Avalon was thin and cultivated and had a job at an established magazine. Avalon, thought Gail, was everything

Delores wasn't, everything Gail wasn't. And though Gail knew it was an ugly thought, Avalon was sweet revenge against Delores. So it was important to her that Avalon trust and respect her as much as she feared that her daughter didn't. In trying to win the girl's affection, she found herself acting in ways that were, at times, unrecognizable. Gradually, her speech became peppered with words like "super" and "friggin'."

Avalon confided in Gail, and the older woman absorbed all of her minor triumphs or perceived slights as if they were her own. After some time, Gail started asking questions about *Cool* magazine. Avalon found she liked explaining fashion to her, enjoyed spinning out her version of office politics.

Shoes were Avalon's jurisdiction. Or, as she explained to Gail, "I do footwear." Six years out of college, she was stuck in the bowels of the fashion department, calling in boots for fall photo shoots, wrapping them up when the shoot was over, and making sure the messenger service delivered them back to the proper designer. She would point out scuff marks to Gail and complain to her about the haranguing phone call she was sure to get from the designer's rep. Maybe she'd send conciliatory flowers or, in the worst cases, she'd have *Cool* reimburse the company for the product. When she told Gail about the time the kleptomaniac stylist made off with a pair of three-hundred-dollar red Tony Lama cowboy boots, they exchanged looks, as if to acknowledge that Gail would never pinch something that expensive.

As she told Gail these stories, they would fall into a rou-

tine in which Gail would help catalog the merchandise
after Avalon called it in. Sometimes, she would come in a
little early to help Avalon pack up for photo shoots. More
and more, the job of unpacking fell strictly to Gail who
was becoming well versed in footwear.

Avalon said she knew how the editors at the magazine
called all the girls in her department the "fashionettes" behind their backs. It was a deprecating sobriquet they used
to distinguish themselves—the real journalists—from
those they considered to be the princesses. "I spent four
years at Vassar and graduated with an art history degree,"
she said. "Surely that's gotta count for something." Avalon's
father owned Mandor Farms, the largest dairy company in
New Jersey. That was the thing that everyone at the magazine knew about Avalon. It probably also explained why
Avalon was no longer Evelyn Mandor.

Lorraine, the managing editor with the crossed eyes and
chapped lips, and a man she referred to as *Le Misérable* figured in many of her anecdotes, which always came down to
this one thing: that no one recognized Avalon's true value.
Gail would always try to say something supportive and
sympathetic, though she had no idea who *Le Misérable* was.

Finally, she just asked Avalon about *Le Misérable*. Avalon
pointed to the photograph of the middle-aged man in the
safari jacket that was sitting on her desk. "That's him, Jean
Claude. He's the most famous fashion photographer in
America. He's the one who gives *Cool* its avant-garde look
and reputation. They pay him a fortune."

"Why do they call him *Le Misérable?*" asked Gail. Avalon
nodded toward the blowups on the wall: a woman wearing

little else than a studded dog collar; another of a girl lashed to the mast of a sailboat caught in a hurricane, her yellow sweater and pink hot pants nearly blowing off her body. "This was Jean Claude's idea of a resort-wear story," said Avalon. "Can you imagine? But the magazine is doing better than ever. The closer to death the models appear to be, the happier the advertisers."

If Jean Claude was a visionary, she said, he was also a bully who would throw tantrums on the set if the models were not just so. Avalon clutched her head, as though she were trying to keep her brains from spilling out, and in an imitation French accent started shouting: "She looks like *caca*. The bags under her eyes, I could pack *croque-monsieurs* in them. She is, what you call it, menopause? Get her out of my sight!"

An odd business, this fashion world, thought Gail, though she was grateful that the Sonia Rykiel body sweater, which ripped at the seams during the sailboat shoot, had been left balled up in the back of the fashion closet. With a little mending, it would be perfect for her or Delores.

During one of their evening chats, Avalon mentioned that she had to go to the annual CFAA meeting in early spring, and how she was already dreading it.

"What's CFAA?" Gail had asked.

"Council of Fashion Accessories of America," Avalon had said. "The only reason I have to go is because *Cool* is doing a trunk show down there, and I'm the slave who has to pack and unpack all the stuff. It's in Boca friggin' Raton."

Gail made a mental note to find out where Boca Raton was.

A few weeks before Christmas, Gail asked Avalon how the show was coming along.

"Oh great, just great," said Avalon with an edge of annoyance in her voice. "I was supposed to get an intern to come down and help me, and now they're telling me they don't have the budget for one. So it's me and twenty thousand pairs of shoes."

Later, when she thought about what happened next, Gail would think to herself how accurate the word "brainstorm" was. Like spontaneous combustion, need and desperation fused in her head and exploded into the question: "Why don't you let me be your intern?"

Avalon smiled slowly and politely. "Surely you're not serious."

Seven

AT THE END OF WORLD WAR II, a Navy frogman named Newton Perry came up with the idea of being able to stay underwater by breathing through an air hose supplied with air by a compressor. Perry, who had also been a onetime stunt double for movie Tarzan Johnny Weissmuller, was not ready to put his frogman years behind him. Drawn to Weeki Wachee by the abundance of its natural springs, Perry went there to perfect his hose-breathing technique. Maybe Perry was a showman at heart, or perhaps it was his time spent around the Tarzan set, but for whatever reason, he recognized that the indigenous marine life in the Springs would also be the perfect backdrop for an underwater show. He built a large glass wall alongside the spring, then added an eighteen-seat theater and hired a half-dozen women called Aquabelles to perform an underwater ballet while breathing through the air tubes hidden in the scenery. One of his most promising Aquabelles was a young woman named Thelma Foote, lithe and agile and rigorously athletic.

These were optimistic times in America. In Florida, real estate developers could barely keep up with the rush of promise-seekers flocking to the humid, syrupy sun. On land, dreams were being bought and sold like baseball cards; underwater, fantasies were still up for grabs. So when the industrious Mr. Perry opened the doors to Weeki Wachee Springs in October 1947, the show was an instant hit. The movie *Mr. Peabody and the Mermaid* was filmed in Weeki Wachee that same year. Ann Blyth had the starring role as Lenore, the mermaid, who couldn't speak but could only sing her ethereal siren song. Lenore, childlike and silent, captures the heart of an urbane married man, played by William Powell just days before his fiftieth birthday.

By the early 1950s, Weeki Wachee Springs was on the map and Newton Perry had become a local hero. The park was up there with Cypress Gardens as one of Florida's leading tourist attractions. And following in the steps of Ann Blyth and William Powell came Esther Williams and Don Knotts, who made movies there, as well as countless other celebrities who just wanted to see for themselves what all the fuss was about in the "City of Mermaids."

Every Monday morning, as she had for twenty years, Thelma Foote would gather "her girls," as she liked to call them, at the outdoor pavilion next to the tour boat rides. Thelma would stand with her arms behind her back and her legs spread apart. She always wore the same khakis, which bagged around her feet, and the white windbreaker, no matter how hot the temperature. "Good morning, my pretty ones," she'd begin. She'd give a rundown of the week's schedule: who would flip burgers, who would take in tickets, who would scrub the algae from the sheet of

Plexiglas that now stood between the audience and the Springs in the amphitheater.

The algae, always the algae. If algae was the enemy, Thelma Foote was its chief avenger. After each show, two girls wearing masks and flippers would scrub the Plexiglas windows with a nylon sponge and ammonia. When they finished, Thelma would take a flashlight and inspect every inch of the Plexiglas from one side to the other. If even a smudge of algae remained, Thelma would call them together again. "Have I not made it clear to you how quickly algae reproduces?" Her voice would have a slight tremor. "Left on its own, it could easily overrun the stage, the theater, the whole park. And then where would all of you pretty little girls go? The world isn't clamoring for mermaids, you know. Right here is the only place that'll have you. And if right here isn't right here anymore because you were too slovenly or lazy or selfish to protect yourself from this scourge, well then, pity us all."

The girls were always talking about Thelma Foote. They wondered how old she was. They wondered if she'd ever had a boyfriend. "Old Cow Eyes?" said Molly one night. "Not on your life, unless Elmer Fudd is single."

Sometimes, after the girls had already swum in the morning show and done at least one of their other chores, Thelma would make them stand at attention under the midday sun. They were tired and sweaty. Sharlene would bite the inside of her cheek and look up at Adrienne. One of the Sheilas would surreptitiously flip her a bird. Molly would scrunch her lips together as if to make moo sounds. She'd try to catch Delores's eye, but Delores would stare

straight ahead, afraid she'd laugh if Molly caught her looking. Lately, Thelma had been singling out Delores and
Molly, telling them to get back into the tank and not come
out until they'd used half a bottle of ammonia. Inside of
Delores there was a screechy voice insisting that none of
this was at all funny. It was Otto: "You want to spend the
rest of your life scrubbing the tank? You're Delores Taurus,
not some window washer."

When she was in the cool, clear water, all thoughts of
Thelma Foote and Otto and even her mother's icy behavior on the phone would vanish. Once, she got close
enough to a dolphin to touch it; its skin was smooth, like
Westie's tummy. Life was perfect when she was swimming
in the Springs. But on the days when she didn't swim, she
was always in the grip of the clammy heat. It enervated
her, in the same way Thelma Foote's constant demands and
magnified cow eyes did. Even the simplest tasks, like making her bed, made her drowsy. Cleaning the tank sapped
her of all the dreams and fantasies that had sustained her
for the past sixteen years. Lately, she'd even lost her desire
to talk with Otto, though his voice was beginning to inhabit her the way she used to occupy his shapeless cotton
body with her hand. And that voice was getting more rude
and bossy every day.

It was Lester Pogoda who finally opened Delores's eyes
about Thelma Foote.

Lester was out on his rock one afternoon when Thelma
had sent Delores and Molly back into the tank. After
Delores finished cleaning, she left the amphitheater with a
towel wrapped around her head and a sweatshirt over her

wet suit. She was tired and hungry, and the chill of the water wouldn't leave her.

"Hey," Lester called to her.

"Hey," she said back, wearily raising her arm.

"You must be exhausted."

"I'm pretty tired."

"It's nice out here."

Lester looked warm and shiny, like a sea lion basking in the sun. She noticed how his eyes turned green in the sunlight. Without the acne, he'd probably be cute.

"Mind if I join you?" she asked.

Lester sat up, took his towel, and wiped away the pool of sweat around him.

Delores crawled out next to him. Lester moved away, leaving her the good part, where it was concave. She took the towel from around her head, placed it over the spot, and lay down. Curled up in the open palm of the rock, blanketed by the unsparing sun, she fell to the bottom of a desperate sleep. Faces and images swirled past her: Westie, Henry, Otto's smooth white head, Lester's pitted red skin.

She slept like that for nearly a half hour. When she awoke, she found that Lester had draped his towel over her legs and shadowed her face with his baseball cap. He was still sitting up.

"You feel better?" he asked, looking down at her.

She was groggy and sweaty, and she kicked the towel from around her legs.

"I covered you up," he said shyly. "I didn't want you to look like a lobster, like me."

Delores sat up and rubbed her eyes. "This heat. How can you stand it?" she asked him.

"I grew up here. I've been coming to Weeki Wachee all my life," he said. "This is home."

"But still, the heat, the work, Old Cow Eyes. I don't know."

"Thelma Foote is from Floral City," said Lester. "That's where I live. She's all right."

"I don't think she's all right," said Delores. "I think she's weird and sadistic."

"She's had a tough time."

"Everyone's had a tough time," said Delores, instantly frightened that she might have given away too much.

"Yeah, but she had her troubles in public."

Delores slipped off her sweatshirt, folded it under her head, and lay back down. "What kind of troubles?" she asked.

"You gotta promise you won't tell anyone any of this," he said. "She'd kill me if she knew I told you."

"Don't worry. I'm great at keeping secrets."

"Okay, here goes. When Weeki Wachee opened back in the forties, every girl in town went over to audition. Thelma was one of the few they picked. Thelma's real smart. She could've gone to college, out of state even. But the day after she graduated from high school, she came here and did her tryout. They picked her to be an Aquabelle—that's what they called the mermaids back then—and it was a big deal for her. Let's face it, she was never great to look at." Lester covered his mouth as he laughed. "My father always said she looked like that actor Telly Savalas, you know, with the big lips and the eyes so far apart. And those glasses! But she was really good, and, believe it or not, she had a great body, so she got the job.

"There was even some talk about a movie, though nobody knows much about this." Lester told Delores a little-known fact, uncharted by film history. It was Thelma Foote—not Ann Blyth—who nearly starred opposite William Powell in *Mr. Peabody and the Mermaid*. Blyth had recently broken her back in a tobogganing accident, and the acrobatic underwater scenes were so painful for her to execute that director Irving Pichel considered replacing her with her stand-in, Thelma. At the last moment, Pichel decided to go ahead with Blyth, who was younger and prettier than Thelma and projected a sweeter disposition. At least that's what the papers said. "Thelma never talks about her close call with Hollywood," Lester continued. "But it had to have nearly killed her, don't you think? Anyway, everything went fine after that until her second Christmas here. They did this big Christmas spectacular called 'Jingle Shells.' Get it? As part of the plot, these two children get a bunch of presents. Inside each box, there's some big surprise. Thelma was supposed to come out of a big old hatbox. She was supposed to be a fairy who sprinkled this magic powder on the children that would take them away to Santa's secret place underwater. When it was time for Thelma to come out of the box, nothing happened. The people playing the children kept staring at the box and the narrator kept saying her line over and over again: 'I wonder what's inside this pretty hatbox? I wonder what's inside this pretty hatbox?' Of course, the audience couldn't hear anything that was going on underwater, but the other mermaids must have heard something because they all turned to look at the hatbox at the same time.

"It seems that Thelma was stuck. The lid wouldn't come open. She must've been pounding and scratching at it until finally someone realized what was going on. One of the girls pulled off the lid. Thelma was going crazy, flapping her arms and kicking trying to get to the surface. Her fairy wings were all bent and crushed. Maybe because she couldn't see without her glasses, she kept swimming in circles. Finally, the mermaid who was playing Mrs. Santa had to dive in and pull her out. After that, Thelma would never go into the water again. She was so embarrassed, I guess. They gave her this job because everyone felt sorry for her, and she's been doing it for about twenty years. She's pretty good at it, though she's rough on the mermaids, the prettiest ones anyway." Lester looked away.

Delores sat up and wrapped her sweatshirt around her waist. "There's still no reason for her to be so mean," she said, tugging the sleeves into a double knot. Before she climbed off the rock, she leaned over to Lester and whispered: "Don't worry, I won't tell anyone. And thanks."

When Delores got back to the dorm, Molly was wearing her bouffant bonnet hair-dryer. "Have a good time with Lester?" she shouted over the hot air.

Delores shrugged.

"That's not very enthusiastic. Lordy, everyone knows

Lester's got the world's biggest crush on you, Delores. He must have thought he was the luckiest duck in the world having you lie next to him on his rock."

Delores shrugged again. She never did tell Molly, or anyone else, the story about Thelma Foote getting caught in the box during "Jingle Shells." If there's one thing Delores Taurus understood about life, it was the importance of guarding secrets.

Eight

CHRISTMAS WAS A DIFFICULT TIME for Thelma Foote. Around the beginning of November she began making sneak visits, at odd hours, to the amphitheater. She'd bring a flashlight and a magnifying glass and search every inch of the Plexiglas lest some filament of algae had sprung up since her last visit. At four thirty one morning, she woke up Delores and Molly, screaming that the whole place was going to hell and that nobody cared but her. "Here," she said, shoving a bottle of ammonia and a couple of sponges into Molly's hand. "You and your little friend can make yourselves useful around here." So in the muted light of dawn, wearing their pajamas, masks, and flippers, Molly and Delores scrubbed the amphitheater wall and made the world a little safer for all future mermaids.

By the middle of November, rehearsals had begun on the Christmas extravaganza. This year, the owners of Weeki Wachee were insisting on bringing back an old favorite, "Frostie's Snowland." The costumes were frayed, and some had yellow age spots on them. Thelma argued at first, but it was no use. The owners didn't even live in Weeki Wachee and they barely paid attention to it other than to finance it. Even then, they were so cheap that there was always something that needed repairs. Thelma convinced herself that with proper mending and cleaning, they would be as good as new. But truly, the costumes looked as discouraged as she felt. What with the new Disney World doing booming business less than ninety miles away, attendance was dwindling. Even Dick Pope down in Cypress Gardens was feeling the pinch, and, rumor had it, he was spending thousands of dollars to beef up his show. She dreaded the small turnout for "Frostie's Snowland."

Dutifully, the girls and Lester ran through rehearsals every morning as Thelma watched in silence from the director's booth. The show was dated, she thought; it looked like some amateur high school production. She'd read about the Audio-Animatronics, or whatever they called it, over at Disney World. There were eighty-six automated figures in the Mickey Mouse Musical Revue alone. Mickey himself had thirty-three functions built into his forty-two-inch frame: he could tilt his head, wave his baton, turn around. There was a six-foot-four-inch replica of Abraham Lincoln, which could stand up and deliver one of his famous speeches, though it still had some kinks: occasionally, it would double over in a bow, or its knees would buckle. But compared with "Frostie's Snowland," Disney World was the future, its feet firmly planted in the Space Age. "Frostie's Snowland" was over, yesterday's news.

Thelma watched as Adrienne languidly negotiated an incomplete backflip and watched as Helen lip-synched three beats behind the "Frosty the Snowman" record. She could feel the life ebbing out of her. The air seemed thinner, she felt light-headed. *These people are eating up my life,* she thought, *nibbling away at it day after day. If I stay here any longer, I will be nothing, just the detritus of what used to be Thelma Foote.*

She rose to her feet and picked up her microphone. "Attention, attention," she shouted. "I want everyone to come to the surface immediately. Meet me inside the theater; I have an important announcement to make."

The shivering cast sat wrapped in towels waiting to hear what Thelma had to say.

"I'm not going to waste any words," she began. "This show is crap. It's stale and boring and not particularly attractive. Frankly, I'm not interested in doing a Christmas gala this year. If you all want to put your pretty little heads together and come up with a show, be my guest. But don't expect me to have anything to do with it. Good luck." She zipped up her windbreaker and headed straight out the door.

Lester shot Delores a look, as if to say, "See, I told you about the Christmas thing." And Lester, who rarely opened his mouth in a group, was the first to speak as they stared at one another in stunned silence.

"People come here just for the Christmas show," he said. "We've got to come up with something."

They sat down at one of the picnic tables and started talking about what they might do. Several weeks earlier, on a Friday night, they'd all piled into the Weeki Wachee van, and Thelma had driven them to Tampa, where they'd seen the movie everyone was talking about, *The Godfather*. On their way home, they couldn't stop talking about it: innocent Kay, fiery Sonny, spooky Michael, loyal Tom Hagen, and tragic Apollonia. They played back scenes to each other. The one in which Sonny nearly kills his sister's husband, Carlo, because Carlo beat up Sonny's sister, Connie, was a favorite. All of them had come from families where a Carlo and a Connie were real possibilities.

Of all people, it was Adrienne who came up with the idea first. "Maybe we should do a show in honor of *The Godfather*. Maybe we could do the opening wedding scene."

"Oh my God," said Sharlene, shoving a hunk of hair off her face. "That is the most brilliant idea I have ever heard."

"That's great, Einstein," said Helen, "but did it ever occur to you that we're all girls except, of course, for Lester? And guess what? *The Godfather* is all about men."

Everyone turned to Lester, who ran his fingers over his jawline. "I read the book," he said, trying to change the subject. "It's the best book I ever read."

"If mermaids can be astronauts," said Delores, "why can't they also be *family*?" She lowered her voice when she said *family*.

Despite an obvious answer, having to do with space suits versus business suits, the logic seemed irrefutable to them.

The people who worked at Weeki Wachee had never been cheerleaders. They had never been part of any cliques in high school. Like the people in *The Godfather*, they were outsiders with no one to turn to but each other. They took heart from how the characters in the movie had created their own world. That it was a world punctuated with loss and violence was overshadowed by the fact that the characters in it were self-made and powerful. The mermaids began talking to each other using a deep, lugubrious Italian accent. Even the Sheilas and Helen played along.

For the next three hours, they sat at the picnic table thinking the idea through. Lester would play Don Corleone; that was obvious. When Helen said it out loud, Lester demurred: "No, that's wrong. You need someone bigger than me to play Vito Corleone." Always behind the scenes, except when he was behind the counter at his father's pharmacy, lately he preferred not to be the center of attention. He hadn't always been that way. He had been four years old when his parents took him to see his first mermaid show. As the curtain rose, a mermaid with a green tail had swum by and blown a kiss to the audience. Ever since then, he'd wanted to become a merman. When he was six, he began to train seriously by swimming with his legs tied together with rope. A strong swimmer with a handsome face and the perfect body for a merman, Lester made it to Weeki Wachee by the time he was sixteen. By then, the acne had blossomed, and he began seeking out roles that allowed him to cover himself with masks and costumes. He was the Tin Man in "The Wizard of Oz," the Caterpillar in "Alice in Wonderland." When he thought about showing his real face, all he had to do was close his eyes and he could see how it would go. People would take one look at him, then turn away. They'd pretend not to have noticed his erupting skin, but, of course, that was all they could see.

"I really think one of you should play the Don," he argued. "You know, someone powerful and nice to look at." His eyes darted toward Delores.

Delores remembered the time that Henry had called her "Tiger," and how just the fact that he'd said it made her feel that her boundaries were not as narrow as she'd always assumed they were. "Lester," she said, "you'd be perfect as the Godfather. The strong, silent type."

Blonde Sheila stood up. "Go on, Lester, it'll be good for you to play a real guy for a change instead of that faggot Tin Man. I'm gonna play a guy, too. Johnny Fontane." She stabbed her chest with both thumbs. "A real ladies' man. I know something about being attracted to the opposite sex," she said in a leering voice.

"You know something about being attracted to a lamp," snickered Helen.

Molly suggested that Delores be Connie Corleone. She had the same big, dark eyes as Talia Shire, who'd played Connie in the movie. "You'd get to dance with Don Corleone," she said, smiling at Lester who was jabbing at a cuticle and not meeting the eyes of the others.

They planned how he and Delores would dance to the opening number until Johnny Fontane came onstage. Then Delores would swim to him, throw her arms around him and kiss him. ("Don't forget," Blonde Sheila had teased Delores, "no tongues.") The other mermaids would form a circle around the Don. They would move in closer until they were at the Don's shoulders, lightly patting his hair. As they plotted out the scene, Lester decided that maybe he could play Don Corleone.

For the next four weeks, they practiced every day for two hours before the morning show and again at night after the park had closed. Although Thelma Foote feigned indifference, occasionally she'd peek down into the tank during rehearsals. One evening, she cornered Delores just as she was closing down the grill in the refreshment stand. "You're holding back a little," she said. "This is Connie Corleone's moment to shine, to come out from behind the shadows of her brothers and her father. Be showy. Your moves should be aggressive, exaggerated, have a real snap to them."

A few days later, she pulled Blonde Sheila aside in the gift shop. "You're putting too much swagger into Johnny Fontane. Don't forget: he's broke, his career's in the toilet, and he's come begging. He's a lady-killer, but he's also so scared, he's about to pee in his pants." Another day, she told Lester how to hold his head just so, in order to convey the Don's polar qualities of tenderness and cruelty.

Eventually, Thelma started showing up at rehearsals, sitting in the director's booth with her microphone, interrupting them every few minutes with her maddening instructions: "Bow deeper. Humility. Remember humility," she shouted to Sharlene, who was playing Bonasera, the undertaker. "Thrust your chest forward, Delores. This is your wedding day."

For years, Thelma had been putting money away in a savings account. The money didn't add up to much, ten thousand dollars maybe. She called it her rainy-day fund, available should the day ever come that she was no longer employed at Weeki Wachee. Thelma sat at her desk one

night long after the park had closed and stared at the figures in her bankbook. The money was hers to use freely:
there was no one in her life to inherit it or lay claim to it.
The steady row of deposits told the story of a solitary life
with no excess, no surprises. She ran her fingers down the
numbers in the book, then wrote some numbers on a pad.
A couple of thousand dollars could lend some real class to
this "Godfather" thing. All the nagging and cajoling, all of
the emotional toll she had extracted from these girls and
countless others before them—maybe this was her chance
to pay them all back. Maybe this would help put Weeki
Wachee back on the map again, despite all the Disney
ruckus in Orlando. Back on the map, as the brochure
promised, as "one of Florida's premier tourist attractions."
She closed her bankbook and slipped it into the breast
pocket of her windbreaker.

Over the next few weeks, press releases about the new
show started showing up at newspapers in the area. Maybe
because *The Godfather* was such a big hit that year, papers as
far north as Tallahassee and as far south as Miami ran every
crumb that fell their way. There was an item about Connie
Corleone's wedding gown and its three-foot tail; Sylvia,
the comptroller, was quoted as telling someone that the
fake flowers were going to cost nearly five hundred dollars;
somebody with no name and a muffled voice phoned the
Tampa–St. Petersburg News to say that businessman Meyer
Lansky, who would be returning to Miami from Israel, had
purchased ten tickets for the Christmas premiere.

Christmas came on a Monday in 1972. Tuesday was the premiere. The show was scheduled to start at one p.m. By eleven thirty, the parking lot was overflowing; there were cars on the grass lining Route 19. Outside, it was sixty-three degrees, cool for December. People carried sweat-shirts or wore cardigan sweaters. Not since the time Elvis had shown up, unannounced, had there been such a com-motion at the park. People waited in line, trying to figure out whether or not they'd gotten a prime seat. Most every-one brought a camera.

By 12:55, the auditorium was filled. People stood in the back; little kids crouched in the aisles. The heavy black curtain was drawn across the stage when the seven mourn-ful trumpet notes of "The Godfather Waltz" began to play. As the lights came up, they revealed the words "The Merfather," painted in the same typeface as the movie logo—only instead of the handle controlling marionettes, there was a hand holding a fishing pole. Slowly, the curtain opened. At first, all you could see were those five-hundred-dollar flowers. As "The Godfather Waltz" swelled to its melancholy crescendo, out flowed Delores in her skin-tight, pearl-colored gown. The gown was cut low at the bust with a scalloped border. The long sleeves tapered to a V that ended on her knuckles. The tips of the Vs had giant pearls on them. There were sequins sewn all over the bod-ice and tail so that, no matter where she was, Delores would be as luminescent as a fish in the sun.

Lester played Don Corleone like someone who knows he's been given a short-term gift. Loath to squander a sec-ond of it, he calibrated his movements so that his Don was dignified, regal even. When Bonasera (Sharlene in a navy form-fitting vest and navy trousers that flowed into a tail) did a triple somersault and then kissed his hand, Lester held his head just as Thelma had instructed. He moved his arms in graceful sweeps; when he took Delores/Connie in his arms to dance, she became a little girl in the strength of his grip. When, along with Blonde Sheila/Johnny Fontane, he lip-synched "I Have but One Heart," a song that lasts nearly three minutes, he only had to suck air from the hose one time. Such was the power of his performance that he even forgot about his face.

Years earlier, Delores had saved a clip from *Teen Girl* called "You Can Be Anyone You Want to Be." The article said that if you could feel inside what it was like to be, say, Goldie Hawn, you wouldn't necessarily become Goldie Hawn, but you would be able to project all the things about Goldie Hawn that you admired, such as her good personality and her ability to look at the sunny side of life. The concept always stayed with Delores, although she could never figure out why anyone would want to be Goldie Hawn. And now as Blonde Sheila/Johnny Fontane sang to her, every flip that she did, every plié she executed, belonged to Connie Corleone, not Delores Walker.

Thelma Foote sat in the back of the auditorium, her elbows resting on her knees. If she felt proud of Lester and her girls, there was no telling from the expression on her face. Her mouth sagged and her eyes were flat. Only twenty minutes later, when the show was over, when the lights went down and the mermaids disappeared and the spotlight went to the surface of the water, where there was

a man in a rowboat smoking a cigar, wearing a fedora and a
wide-pin-striped suit and holding a fishing pole with a line
that reached down into the tank, did Thelma rise to her
feet with the rest of the crowd as the full notes and rueful
minor chords of the finale filled the wooden amphitheater.
No one was paying attention to Thelma, but if they had
been they would have noticed that Old Cow Eyes was imperceptibly waving her arms and folding at the waist, the
way that she would have if she was in the tank taking a
bow with the rest of her girls.

Nine

"THE MERFATHER" was a hit beyond anyone's expectations. The *Tampa Tribune* ran a story in its weekend "Getaway" section headlined: "Glorious Delores Taurus a Splash Hit in Weeki Wachee's 'Merfather'" and the *St. Petersburg Times* had a banner on its arts pages: "Weeki Wachee's Delores Taurus Swims with the Fishes and Steals the Show." Over the next two days, radio stations and newspapers from around the country called, wanting interviews with Delores and Lester. But the most intriguing call came from an Alan Sommers, an executive producer at WGUP, the ABC affiliate in Tampa. He was hoping to meet with a representative of the mermaids.

The latitude and longitude of Thelma Foote's life was the twenty-seven miles between Floral City and Weeki Wachee Springs. A drive to Tampa meant leaving her world, being judged by a stranger who had no reason to fear or even like her. It also meant she'd have to get dressed up. The morning that she was to meet Sommers, she ironed one of the few blouses in her closet, a light blue cotton Indian shirt with purple smocking, which she put on over a pair of new khaki pants. She'd leave the white windbreaker in the car, just in case.

The ABC offices were in one of the new beige office buildings in downtown Tampa. Thelma parked in the lot and went inside. As she waited in front of the brushed-metal doors of the elevator, she could hear the humming of the air-conditioning. They were powerful, these new systems. Best not to take a chance. Before the elevator came, she ran back outside to the car, grabbed the windbreaker, and zipped it up to her neck. When Mr. Sommers greeted her in the eighth-floor reception area, he said, "Nice to meet you, Miss Foote. May I take your jacket?"

"Oh no, thank you," she said, crossing her arms in front of her chest. "I'll just keep it on for now." Mr. Sommers brought her into an office with floor-to-ceiling windows that looked over Tampa Bay. "I'll have my girl get you some coffee," he said. "Some view, huh? I'm so close to the water, I could almost be a mermaid myself." He laughed and shook his head. "Sometimes I slay me," he said. Then he sat on the chair across from Thelma, laced his fingers together, and stared straight at her. "Look, I'm not going to beat around the bush, Miss Foote. I saw the show last week, and those girls are sensational."

Mr. Sommers articulated every syllable as if he were speaking into a microphone.

"Sennn-saaational! And not bad on the eyes, I might say." He smiled a quarter smile, then tried to sneak a glimpse of his own reflection in Thelma's eyeglasses. But as Thelma clutched the mug of coffee, the steam from it clouded her glasses. She tried to make eye contact with Sommers, but she might as well have been looking at dough rising, for all she could see.

"They are very special girls," she said, placing her cup on the table and staring at nothing. "I handpicked each one of them, and each one of them is a star in her own right."

"That's exactly what I was thinking," said Sommers, running his hands through his black curly hair. "You and I, Thelma, are obviously cut from the same cloth."

As the fog cleared, Thelma studied Sommers the same way she would a new girl auditioning in the bell. He moved with the jerkiness of someone who had memorized the motions of grace but had no understanding of what they meant: the handshake, more like a quick pinch; the smile, more of a wince; the discursive small talk. A short and trim man with a perfectly tailored double-breasted suit and gleaming shoes, he had the look of one of those fish she'd seen darting around the reefs at Weeki Wachee. Thelma knew her fish. This one, with his pointed features and sharp, small white teeth was a "Slippery Dick" if ever there was one.

Sommers continued, drumming his fingers on the arm of his chair. "As you are well aware from your business, Thelma—you don't mind if I call you Thelma, do you?— complacency is death. For us at WGUP to remain new and vital, we are constantly reinventing ourselves, upping the ante if you will. When I read about 'The Merfather,' I said to myself, 'Sommers, there's your ticket. Get your ass over to Weeki Wachee and see that show.' It was almost—and I say this with all due modesty—like divine intervention. After I saw those girls in action, I told my station manager: 'If we don't sign up those mermaids right now'" (Thelma flinched as he snapped his fingers for emphasis), " 'then you can bet your bottom dollar that those louses at WTAM will be nipping at their heels before they even have a chance to dry their hair.' Every now and then, the perfect moment and the perfect idea come together, and the result is, like . . . wow!"

Sommers threw his arms up into the air like a conductor winding up a symphony.

"So what I was thinking, Thelma, is this. How about if, every night, we use one of your girls in full mermaid regalia to deliver the weather report? I know what you're thinking—believe me, we've covered the bases on this— mermaids can't stand up in their tails, right? No *problema*. Who says you have to be standing to do the weather? First we talked about having them suspended by wires from the ceiling so they'd look as if they were floating. But the lawyers quickly nixed that idea: back problems, injuries, all that crap. But then I had this great idea." Sommers leaned forward in his chair, and Thelma recoiled in anticipation of more finger snapping.

"Why don't we have them reclining in a bathtub? They'd be in water, you know, it would be a little sexy. Well, I can tell you this, everyone loved this idea. Just *llllovvedd* it. It'll do wonders for the station, and frankly, I'm sure you people are feeling the squeeze from that new Disney World in Orlando. With the free publicity you'd get from us, it couldn't hurt you either. Whaddya say, Thelma?" He aimed his pointy-toothed smile at her.

Alan Sommers was the kind of fellow who would normally hunch his shoulders when he got near a woman like

Thelma, and push past her. Never a smile, a nod of the head, an acknowledgment that she existed. Men like him made her feel apologetic about her looks, her clothes, her age. And yet, there he was, sitting across from her, baring his little teeth with something akin to pleading in his eyes. Thelma rarely allowed herself to think about her close call with Hollywood, or the "Jingle Shells" fiasco, but now the memories hit her like a migraine. The smell of mildew filled her head as she thought of more years spent sitting in that amphitheater watching another performance of "The Mermaid Follies" or "The Little Prince." She'd spent her whole life at Weeki Wachee; everyone there regarded her as a has-been. She had to get out of there. She'd never kidded herself about that. Now her own words came back to her, the words she spoke to her girls before each show: "Finally, the only thing you have to fall back on is intuition," she'd say. "There's an inner voice inside all of us that knows when to breathe, how to move our heads just so, so that the hair flows around the head like a cape, the right moment to flash a smile. Pay attention to that little voice—it's what separates the stars from the hacks."

For once in her life, Thelma followed her own advice. "Sommers—you don't mind if I call you Sommers, do you?" she said. "The girls, the costumes, the bathtub, I'm all for it. Just one thing: they are still my girls, my young beauties. That means all negotiations go through me. What they're paid, what they say, what they wear—it all goes through me. Whatever you pay them, and I'm sure you'll want to be generous, I get a fifteen percent commission."

Sommers rubbed the shiny spot on his forehead where

his hair was beginning to recede. He raised his pen in the air as if to make a point, then put his pen down and smiled. "We are cut from the same cloth, aren't we, Foote?"

Thelma thought she had artistic integrity, that she appreciated beauty for beauty's sake. Slippery Dick clearly couldn't tell the difference between art and artichokes. He was so clearly what he was: a man about money, and how to make a bundle of it. No, they were not cut from the same cloth, but she knew how to play his game.

"I'm not finished, Sommers," she said. "Plus, I want a finder's fee of one thousand dollars. And I want the girls to be treated like ladies. As I am the only person who can give you the right to use these girls, my offer is nonnegotiable."

Sommers clicked his pen a few times, then bit down on his Rutgers University ring.

"Okay, how soon can they start?"

When Thelma Foote returned to Weeki Wachee the following morning, she called a special meeting of the girls.

It wasn't in her nature to be funny or ironic, and the few times she was, she would broadcast it with a wide, gummy smile that made her eyes seem even farther apart.

"I've just come back from a meeting with the folks at WGUP, the ABC affiliate in Tampa." She grinned. "And they've made me an offer I can't refuse." She waited for the laughter, but none came. *Oh hell,* she fumed to herself, *do I have to explain the damn joke?* But her dyspepsia subsided when she visualized how beholden the girls would feel to her for furthering their careers.

She told them about Mr. Sommers and his idea of having a mermaid do the weather each night. "Our friends at WGUP even came up with the clever idea of having you sit in a bathtub. You couldn't stand, of course, and if you sat behind a desk, the audience wouldn't get the full effect of the tail. Our friends came up with a pretty smart idea, if you ask me. So there you have it, my lovelies: the big time, the high life. And mark my words, this is just the beginning."

No one knew what to say. Wanting to be a mermaid was one thing; wanting to be a television weathergirl was quite another. After Thelma left, Blonde Sheila was the first to speak. "Cool. I'm up for sitting in a bathtub on TV." Sharlene worried how they would get back and forth from Tampa. "All this publicity," said Molly. "Who told everyone about us?"

"Who do you think?" said Scary Sheila. Helen did that thing with her hands, putting her fingers under her chin, and turning her thumb and forefinger into a pair of glasses.

But nobody laughed. They understood that it was Thelma Foote who had gotten them the fancy costumes, had phoned the papers, had urged them to make their characters believable. These girls, her girls, would be hard-pressed to find someone else who would do them favors unbidden and bring the kind of order and justice into their lives that she had. If they were *family*, then she was their Don. Although none of them would acknowledge her role outright, this would be the last time any of them would make reference to cow eyes when talking about Thelma Foote.

✦ ✦ ✦

Exhilarated by all that had happened, Delores called her mother to wish her a Merry Christmas. Just as she had for the past couple of months, her mother answered the phone with that lilting bend in her voice.

"Hay-llo," she said.

"Hi, Mom, it's me. You all right?"

"Oh, hello." Her voice flattened. "How are you?"

"I'm fine, really fine. We had our Christmas extravaganza, and I played Connie Corleone from *The Godfather.* People seemed to like it a lot. Merry Christmas, by the way. How's Westie?"

"Westie's fine. He's talking already."

"I miss him. I miss you, too."

"I'm sure he misses you, too. He likes all the postcards you send."

"Are you having a good day?"

"It's all right. No work today, that's good. But some bad news. Helene has breast cancer." She whispered the words "breast cancer."

"That's terrible, will she be all right?" asked Delores.

"Not sure—it doesn't look good. Poor woman. Oh, one more thing. Are you near Boca Raton?"

"Sure, I guess. Why?"

"Well, we might be coming down there somewhere in the middle of April."

"You and Westie?"

"Me, Westie, and Avalon."

"Who's Avalon?"

"Come on. Surely you know who Avalon is."

Thelma Foote had a rule about long distance: no calls before nine p.m., because that's when the rates changed. Any charges beyond the first three minutes were deducted from the girl's paycheck. Delores's three minutes were up.

"Honest, Mom, I have no idea who Avalon is. But I've gotta go."

"Okay then, good-bye."

Ten

THE NIGHT BEFORE Delores made her debut as a weathergirl on WGUP, she wrote a postcard to Westie with a picture of a flamingo on it. *Our father used to think I looked like one of these birds. Tomorrow I am going to be on television as a weathergirl in a bathtub. I will explain it more when you get older. Things happen that you can never have imagined in your whole life. You'll see.*

Delores had spent twelve dollars on postcards and toys for Westie, money that she took from the silver coins that were still in the bathing cap she kept in her suitcase underneath her bed. By now, she was making fifty dollars a week plus as much as twenty dollars a week in tips. Each week, she'd send twenty dollars to her mother, keep thirty dollars to spend on movies and what few clothes she bought, and put twenty dollars in a plastic Weeki Wachee shopping bag that she also kept under her bed. The shopping bag was filled with money she was saving for Westie. She would add to it each week, hoping that when he grew up, he'd never have to do anything just for the money. It was a comforting ritual because it implied that she would be part of Westie's future. The role of being somebody's big sister was her lifeline to the real world, which was seeming further away than ever.

Late the next afternoon, Thelma and Delores got into the van to drive to Tampa. It had been wet and humid all that March, and Thelma made sure that each of her girls had a plastic fold-up rain bonnet. Her thinking was puzzling, since the girls spent most of their time underwater, but once Thelma got a notion like that, there was no talking her out of it. Before she started the car, Thelma shook out her bonnet, folded it up, and put it into its plastic case. Delores did the same. Thelma then opened the glove compartment and drew out a pair of leather camel-colored gloves with brown sweat stains on the palms. "I am many things around here, but chauffeur is not one of them," she said, pulling the gloves onto each hand and snapping them closed at the wrist. "You can bet your sweet ass that Dick Pope doesn't spend his days driving water-skiers hither and yon." Thelma shifted to reverse and released the clutch. The car hiccuped before stalling, causing both of them to bounce off their seats. "Just this once," said Thelma, starting the engine again. "I'll make the introduction and then the ball's in Sommers's court." Delores wondered if Thelma even knew she was there. "What does he think, that my girls will swim to Tampa every day?" The car lurched forward now. "He wants my girls, he provides car and driver. End of story, that's all she wrote."

Then, as if she'd just noticed Delores, Thelma turned to her with one of her waxy smiles. "So, my pet, you're it," she said. "You're our first TV star. I chose you because you're the only one among them who's got more sense than a mackerel. Now's the time to put Mommy and Daddy's showbiz genes to the test." She winked. "Don't mess up, you hear?"

Delores wondered why everyone was always telling her not to mess up. That's what her mother had said when she told her she was going to Florida, and now Thelma said it, too. It seemed to Delores that, of all of them, she was the only one who *hadn't* messed up.

When they arrived at the studio in Tampa, they took the elevator up to the eighth floor. Delores was impressed that the receptionist seemed to recognize Thelma. "Hey, Miss F. I'll call him and let him know you're here." Delores couldn't imagine anyone calling Thelma "Miss F.," but noted that Thelma seemed pleased and nodded demurely in her direction. Delores heard the receptionist say into the phone, "She's here," then whisper something that sounded like "Oh, you." She told them that Sommers was expecting them and they should go right into his office.

Thelma had talked about Alan Sommers in a way that made Delores expect he would be as handsome and polite as Dick Clark. Nothing could have been further from the truth. He was short and skinny and didn't have that neat pompadour that made Dick Clark look so suave. He had tight knots of ringlets, the kind of hair that *Teen Girl* declared could be easily tamed by ironing. His brow was deeply lined, but his skin was soft and pink. He was a jumpy fellow who talked in rapid jabs of words.

"Mr. Sommers, I'd like you to meet Delores Taurus, our number one mermaid," said Thelma.

Sommers grabbed Delores's hand and blinked his gray fisheyes at her.

"So you're our new weather gal," he said, pumping her hand. "How do you do? Mmmm, you look a little hot and humid to me." He pelted her with his laugh, then turned to Thelma. "Faan-tasstic bones! We'll need to play down the teeth and do something about the tits. Big is super. Too big is cheap." No one had ever said these kinds of things in front of Delores, and she didn't know where to look.

Thelma took off her glasses and blew into them before wiping them on her jacket. "Delores is from a family of entertainers," she said, glaring in Sommers's direction. "She understands how to play to a camera."

"Excellent, excellent," said Sommers. "We sure could use some professionals around here." He looked her up and down. "You're perfection. We'll just do a touch of hair and makeup, and then we'll be ready for our run-through. Be back to you in a jiffy, Miss F." Sommers took Delores by the arm and led her to a small white room, bare except for a large mirror rimmed by blazing lightbulbs, something that looked like a dentist's chair, and a makeup artist named Brandy.

"Our first sea goddess," said Sommers, gently shoving Delores into the chair. "Make her beautiful, dewy, as if she's just been washed ashore. Inspire me." He gave Brandy the thumbs-up.

Brandy wore a pink smock and had a silk scarf tied bandana-style around her straight black hair. She spilled some foundation onto a small piece of foam rubber and began dabbing at Delores's face. She used her pinky to rub in a little blush. She kept pulling bottles and tubes from what looked like a giant tool kit, only its sliding trays were filled with brushes and lipsticks and tiny pots and tubes in colors that were shadows and whispers of other colors. She didn't say much, just kept cupping Delores's chin in her hand and turning her from side to side as if she were a piece of sculpture. "Tawny works your cheekbones," she said at one point; and "Burgundy is flattering to your natural skin tone," at another. Delores watched her own face in the mirror as the blotches of color blended into one. She thought about Ellen and how many times they'd sat together in her room, trying to follow the makeup tips from *Teen Girl.* Now she was sitting before a professional makeup artist who was telling her how to maximize the fullness of her lips and matte the shiny parts of her nose.

For a moment, Delores looked beyond the reflection of her own face in the mirror. Through the open door, down the hall, she could make out Thelma Foote's profile. Thelma was backing away, the way she might have if a German shepherd had come lunging toward her. She could make out Sommers's bristly head of hair and saw him leaning in toward Thelma, his face up close to hers. He said something. Then Thelma stood up straight and tugged at the tips of the collar on her windbreaker. Whatever she said back, she punctuated by wagging a scolding finger at him. Sommers's shoulders slumped, as if her words had leveled him. He reached in his pocket. He pulled out something, a cookie maybe. Yes, it was a Fig Newton. He popped it into his mouth. Delores had no idea what she was seeing or what they were saying, only that some kind of a showdown had occurred, and it looked as if Thelma had won.

The makeup artist was poofing the final touches of powder to Delores's face when Sommers stuck his head inside
the door. "Hi, gorgeous," he said, as sweet and sour as
lemon candy. "Brandy, you are beyond belief. A-maazing.
We still need to work out the bathtub logistics." He tapped
on the face of his watch. "Time's a-tickin'."

Brandy ran her tongue over her teeth. She took Delores's
thick brown hair into her hands and let it fall through her
fingers like mud. "Manageable, just needs a trim." She
snipped Delores's bangs until they were about an inch
long—"Let's open up that pretty face of yours"—then rummaged through her tool kit until she came upon a tube of
VO5. She squeezed a quarter-sized dollop into her hands
and rubbed it into Delores's hair. "That's it; now every part
of you glows. Break a leg . . . uhh . . . Snap a tail." She helped
Delores into her costume—a green bustier made to look as
if it were covered with fish scales, and a thick black wetsuit
bottom, which the TV audience would never see but was
meant to keep Delores warm as she sat in the bathtub.
When she was dressed, Sommers put his hand on the small
of her back and nudged her onto the set.

The set was very cold. There were no windows. The
walls were insulated so that no noise would bounce off
them, which made everyone sound as if they were talking
in a jar. The anchorman sat at a desk that was a streamlined
console made of Formica, which had been grained in order
to make it look like wood. The background, which looked
on the screen as if it were a live shot of Tampa's historic
Ybor City, was actually a blown-up photograph. Even the
plants were made of some artificial material.

Next to the console was an antique claw-foot bathtub. It was deep and round, with a roll trim and shiny brass fixtures. Unlike everything else on the set, it was real. The old bathtub, filled with water, was an anachronism in the midst of the sleek newsroom, and it gave the whole set the feel of a garage sale. Sommers cupped his hand around Delores's elbow. Two cameramen were poised behind their lenses, waiting to see how the new weather segment would play out on the screen. The anchorman, Chuck Varne, a legend around Tampa, was seated at his desk going over his script. Delores recognized his face from the billboards that were all over Tampa: "WGUP'S CHUCK VARNE TELLS IT AS IT IS," the signs said.

When Chuck Varne looked up at Delores, he bit his lower lip and narrowed his eyes. "So you're the new weather gal," he said in a rotund voice. "At least our viewers won't just have to look at us old guys anymore." But privately, he was thinking: *Good God, it's come to this. Now we're putting young hookers on the show.* The guy who did sports, Lloyd Graf, was also on the set. He was a big man with a wide head and a low forehead. Like most sports reporters, he came off as affable and eager and not particularly brainy. "Welcome aboard," he said, eyeing Delores's costume. "Well, this is something different." With mock courtesy, Sommers held out his hand and said to Delores, "Let me help you onto your throne, Miss Taurus."

Everything about this felt wrong. The bustier was too tight, making it hard for her to breathe. She felt as if someone were trying to laminate her breasts. With all that makeup caked on her face, she worried that if she opened

her mouth too wide, it would all slide off. And the bathtub!
It had seemed like a funny idea from afar—delivering the
weather from a bathtub. But now that she saw it standing
there like a clown with a fat stomach and floppy feet,
Delores realized that it was all part of a big joke. The joke
was that she was young and half-naked, and the bathtub
implied something less innocent than bubbles and rubber
ducks.

The cameramen smirked at each other and raked their
eyes across her body in a way that made her want to cover
up. Sommers was being cloying and overly solicitous. She
knew she could walk out now, before she placed a single
toe in the tub. But *not* quitting had become a habit with
Delores: the bus to Tampa, her tryout in the bell, cleaning
the tank again and again. Now she had the chance to be on
local television. Something would come of this, take her to
the next place, wherever that was. She was not about to let
two leering cameramen and some frizzy-haired clod stand
in her way.

Delores put one foot into the water. It was tepid. Since
there was no plumbing in the studio, two interns had spent
the afternoon dumping buckets of water into the tub, both
of them wondering, no doubt, why they had decided to
major in communications. She stepped in with the other
foot, acting as if what she was doing was the most natural
thing in the world.

"Okay, doll, you can sit," said Sommers. Delores held on
to both sides and lowered herself into the water until only
her head was visible over the rim. She knew right away it

wasn't working, that from the camera's point of view she must have looked like a bobbing tennis ball.

One of the cameramen called Sommers to come look through his lens. "You can't even see her tits," he whispered. "What the hell's the point if you can't see her tits?" Sommers bit down on his college ring. Then his quacky voice filled up the airtight studio. "This is not a barnyard, this is a local television station," he shouted. "There will be no smart talk or foul language around Miss Taurus. She is a part of our team now, and you will treat her with respect. End of story. That's all she wrote."

It was his last words that gave Delores the clue. Thelma.

Sometimes when she least expected it, something like this would happen to remind Delores that she wasn't as alone as she thought she was: a talk with Molly, a letter from Ellen, and now this assurance that Thelma had taken her side. She remembered how once, when she was a little girl, she'd fallen asleep while sitting on the couch between her parents watching TV. She became vaguely aware of her father's rough hands stroking her hair out of her face and the warm, safe feeling that settled over her. That's how this felt.

Delores could have told Sommers how to resolve the bathtub dilemma, but she had no desire to make his job any easier. So she waited until he came up with the brilliant idea himself. "I've got it!" He shook his fist in the air as if he'd just won the heavyweight title. "She'll sit on the side of the tub with her tail in the water. That's it. Now all we need is the tail. I need a tail!" he hollered. The interns were called into the studio. Sommers explained the situation, then sank his teeth into his college ring. "We're not in London. This is fucking Florida. Excuse my French, doll," he glanced at Delores. "Find me a mermaid's tail. Now! You have exactly sixty minutes, sixty *minutos*. We go on the air in two hours. Don't stand there staring at me. I don't even know how to swim." He reached into his pocket for another of those fig cookies.

No one paid attention to Delores, who was still sitting in the tub. The interns looked beleaguered; one had his shirt hanging out of the back of his pants. They reminded Delores of how put-upon she and Molly felt each time Thelma Foote sent them in to clean the tank. The water in the tub had turned cold. She got out and stood by the anchor desk, a curious sight in her black tights and green scaly halter, and with her big, wet feet. One of the interns turned to her. He had shoulder-length hair, skinny arms, and soft baby hands. "You must be freezing," he said. She nodded, hugging herself and trying to conceal her trembling. "Here," he said, taking off his blue blazer. "Put it around you."

"I'm soaked," she said.

"I'm Armando." He smiled.

She slipped the jacket around her. "Wait a minute," she called after him. He turned around. "I can help you." She gave him the number at Weeki Wachee and told him to ask for Molly Pouncey. "Make sure you tell her I said to call, and tell her the tail is for me."

* * *

Whenever Sommers talked about the mermaid weather-girl, he would include the story of the last-minute tail hunt. "It came to me out of the blue," he would say. "Suddenly, I have a vision of our gorgeous girl sitting on the edge of the tub swishing her tail. Only problem, there is no tail. I go crazy. We have less than a half hour. There's got to be a tail somewhere around here. We got ducks and mice in Orlando, for chrissakes, someone in this crazy state has to have a tail. So I tell my people, I say, 'I don't care what you do or how much you have to spend, just get me a damn tail.' Miraculously, we find one. I send one of the boys way the hell out to the other side of the state, practically, to get it. Ever try to get anywhere fast during rush hour? I radio our guy in the traffic helicopter to help navigate our boy through shortcuts. I'm like Westmoreland over here, radio-ing our helicopter, then calling our boy on his CB with di-rections. He finally gets here with the tail—a fine piece it is, nearly three feet long—and with three minutes to spare, the genius security guard says, 'Wait a minute, what's that? You can't take that thing into the studio.' They call me and I run downstairs like the place is on fire. 'Just gimme that,' I say, grabbing the tail from the kid's hand. The security guy's busting a gut. I tell him if he wants to hold on to his job, to move over and let the tail through. I make it back upstairs with less than a minute to go. And the rest is his-tory."

Sommers would tell the story with the self-aggrandizing bravado of a man in the midst of creating his own legend. He would relish saying that, had a tail not miraculously appeared at the last moment, he'd be back in Middletown,

New York, selling light switches and ant traps in his father's hardware store. In his telling, Armando, the intern who found the tail, went nameless. So did Molly and Helen, who were the ones who drove like the blazes to get the thing to the studio on time while Armando was sitting next to them, taking calls from Sommers on his CB and trying to sound as if he wasn't going to throw up at any moment.

People in the business who followed WGUP's news ratings or read the trades would ultimately call Sommers a wizard. His detractors, offended by his sudden and public success, would snicker while calling him the Albert Einstein of local television. Although he would try to affect an air of modesty and self-deprecation by making himself the butt of the jokes when he told these stories, it was clear from his relish in telling them that he judged the enormous success of the show to be his alone.

But anyone with a discerning eye who witnessed Delores's debut that first night saw immediately that the girl had the kind of grace upon which infatuations are built and fortunes are made. The moment the camera turned on her, Delores swelled like a gorged bee. She stared out at the audience, her eyes wide and looking skyward, in a way that made it seem as if she had just emerged from the bottom of the sea. The short bangs gave a round innocence to her face, which she accentuated by modulating her voice to just above a whisper.

Gripping the side of the tub with one hand, and holding the wooden pointer with the other, she extended her chest forward, cocked her head, and sent the right amount of quiver through her tail to make the water in the tub ripple just so. With her pointer, she made a swirling motion around the magnetic clouds hovering over Orlando to indicate the path of an oncoming cold front. She learned to write backward from the rear side of a Plexiglas map and talk about barometric pressure and wind currents with the ease of someone who had been speaking that language her entire life. Within weeks, Delores Taurus became a phenomenon in the Tampa area. Sommers decided to use only Delores as a weathergirl and not rotate her with the others. Women found her adorable; men thought she was sexy. Even little children sat through the first twenty minutes of the news, waiting for the mermaid lady to come on with the weather.

Eleven

*T*HE RAIN CONTINUED through March into early April, yet attendance was up at Weeki Wachee. At first, the other girls were excited by Delores's success, thinking somehow it would rub off on them. But it quickly became clear that the increase in attendance was all about Delores. People would whistle and stomp their feet at the mere mention of her name, and when she was in one of the routines, all eyes were on her; the others might as well have been in the chorus. Even the marquee outside the park featured her name in big red letters: DELORES TAURUS LIVE! One afternoon, as she stood in front of the park waiting for the WGUP car to pick her up, Lester Pogoda came by. It wasn't as if he'd casually wandered by; he'd been planning all day how he'd bump into her.

"How you doing, Lester?" said Delores.

"This weather, it's killing my skin," said Lester. "No sun for days, but I don't have to tell you that, I guess."

People always talked to Delores about the weather now. She'd never understood how important it was in people's lives. "Can't you do something about this rain?" they'd ask her, as if by sticking a magnetic sun or thunderbolt on the

screen, she could create a balmy day or swamp the place
with thunder and rain. Was it her imagination, or was
everyone at Weeki Wachee a little snippy to her right now
because of the bad weather?

"Yeah," she said to Lester, "it's starting to get me down,
too. This weather job, I mean."

Lester looked surprised. "You're not really having a hard
time? I mean, with all this fame and everybody wanting to
see you, you must feel like a million bucks."

"Oh, I feel okay. It's just a lot, between working here and
doing the news every night..."

"Why don't you rotate with some of the other girls
here?" he asked.

"Thelma. She won't let me."

"I don't want to add to your worries," said Lester, choosing his words carefully. "But some of the girls are having a
hard time with your fame. I can't name names, but one of
them is telling people that you've got something going on
with that station-manager guy, Sommers or Winters or
whatever."

Normally, Delores would have guessed that it was
Blonde Sheila who was spreading that rumor, but ever since
Blonde Sheila started dating the preacher at the Spring Hill
Church, she'd been going to Bible school and finding reli-
gion. Blonde Sheila, who saw sex in everything and could
cuss as well as any man, was trying awfully hard to become
righteous in the hands of God and not half as much fun.
"Who's saying that?" she asked Lester.

"Doesn't matter," he said, shaking his head and closing

his eyes. "The point is, it's probably just jealousy, but they're gossiping about you, and I thought you should know."

"And you? Are you gossiping about me, too?" she asked.

"No," he said, not meeting her stare. "Why would I do that?"

"I don't know," she said. "Just wondered."

That night, when Delores came back from the station, she noticed that someone had rearranged the letters on the marquee: DELORES TAURUS LIVE! now. read DIVE U LOSER SLUT!

The rain bonnets had become an ongoing joke, with the girls showing up to practice with them on their heads. Thelma even wore hers in the director's booth one afternoon, that's how buoyed her spirits were. One night, shortly after her conversation with Lester, Delores had a brainstorm of her own. After the camera was already on her, and the anchorman had introduced the weather segment, she whipped out a plastic bonnet that she had tucked into her halter. She tied it around her head and began her segment by saying, "Is it ever going to stop raining in the Tampa Bay area?" Later that night, she found herself seated next to Sharlene at dinner. Sharlene stared at her food as she talked, her face obliterated by a veil of hair. "That was a funny thing you did tonight on the news," she said. "Thanks," said Delores. "I didn't know that anyone here was watching."

"Yeah, we all watch. We thought you were real cool tonight. For what it's worth, Adrienne and I don't believe what they're saying about you and that TV producer."

"What're they saying about me and that TV producer?" asked Delores.

"Oh, nothing," said Sharlene, lowering her veil of hair around her.

Every night, after the lights went out, the conversation would inevitably take a turn toward sex. On this particular night, Blonde Sheila was talking about guys whose ding-dongs were so small you couldn't even tell if they were inside you or not. Then Helen turned to Delores and said, "Speaking of small, what's with you and that little TV guy? Is he going to make you a star, or is he just going to make you?"

"There's nothing going on between me and him," said Delores. "He's a real pig."

"Well, with you half-naked in that bathtub every night, the guy must have the worst case of blue balls in the state of Florida," said Helen. In the darkness, she could hear the girls choking on their laughter. The next morning, Delores asked Molly whether blue balls were some kind of flower, and why was that so funny?

Molly told her she thought it was a thing that guys got before they had sex, but the way she said it made Delores think that Molly had as little idea what it was as she did.

After that night when she called Sommers a pig, it seemed as if the girls were less chilly toward her.

A few evenings later, Delores confided to Otto, "I think things are going pretty well for me." Although she didn't say it directly, there was a slight flip in her tone that implied she felt hope for the future. Little Otto, who'd been stuck in an airless suitcase for way too long, was not feeling as sanguine as she was. For one thing, his white skirt was starting to yellow with age. In the past, Delores had hand-washed him, making sure to keep him pristine. Now he was relegated to under the bed, a secret too mortifying to be shared with anyone except Molly. Ordinarily, his voice was shrill. But lately, it had taken on a piteous tone of hurt and indignation. She'd barely gotten him situated on her hand before he started in: "Why are you letting them use you like this?" he demanded. "You're a television star. How much money are you making? Not enough. Who's getting all the credit? Mr. Brillo Head. Do you think they like you for your good personality and brains? Think again, doll. That's what he calls you, isn't it? Doll. But then I guess I'm not one to talk."

He started to laugh, making a loony, billowing sound. Molly was standing guard and, as promised, whispered their code word when the others were coming. "Lollapalooza," she said. Then again, more urgently, "Lollapalooza!" Otto was shaking with laughter now and Delores worried his rhinestones might come loose. What was she to do but to put him back in the suitcase? Besides, she really didn't want to hear what he was saying. Otto used to be an escape for Delores and the bleakness she felt about her life. With him came a world where there was quiet and order and beauty, and all of the things that she desired. When she played with him, that world became present to her. If anyone had seen them together, they'd have been charmed by the young girl inventing skits for her morose-looking puppet. It was her secret that, while she was acting them out, the skits were her life and the puppet her alchemist. Now Thelma Foote and Alan Sommers were the puppet masters, and she was in their hands. Otto was becoming irrelevant.

She stared down at the sad little figure with his yellowing cotton skirt and made a mental note to wash him as soon as she could. She folded him carefully and placed him back in the suitcase. After she snapped the latch, she turned around to make sure that no one was coming. Then she patted the top of the suitcase as if it were the head of a bunny. "I'm sorry," she whispered. "I'm really sorry."

Had she given it a second thought, Delores might have remembered that the middle of April held meaning for her. But the way things were, she barely had time to attend to her own schedule. Since his success, Sommers had become feverish with ideas: he added goldfish to the bathtub and backup music appropriate to the day's forecast ("Raindrops Keep Fallin' on My Head" during most of March, then "Here Comes the Sun" when the skies finally cleared), and he devised a rating scale for the weather ranging from one to five tails (really bad weather, one mermaid tail; perfect weather, five).

All of these additions were a headache for the crew, but had little consequence for Delores—until Sommers had his latest epiphany. The viewers would phone in the details of their upcoming special occasions, and Delores would work them into her forecast. So every night, instead of just talking about scattered clouds and northeast winds, she'd have to recite all kinds of names and numbers: "Bartow's Enid and Larry Swigert can expect isolated showers and eighty-nine percent humidity for their twenty-fifth anniversary barbecue tomorrow night. But the skies will brighten early

Saturday morning, when the thermometer will hit sixty-
eight degrees with light humidity, just in time for Ronnie
Frankel's bar mitzvah at Beth David Synagogue."

"Scriptwriting isn't in our contract," Thelma announced
to Sommers. "We need to renegotiate our fees."

"You don't understand, do you? We are making television history," he shot back. "We are reaching out to our audience. We're saying, 'Hey, you out there in the butt-hole
of nowhere, you are just as important as we are. Your lives
are our lives and we are one big, happy family.' They hear
Delores Taurus mention their names on television, or
maybe their friends' names or their first cousins'. Then
they tune in again the next night to see if she names someone else they know. It's personal. Personal, that's the name
of the game! They all feel as if she knows them." He
nipped at his college ring. "It's genius. Pure genius, if I do
say so myself. So tell me, Miss F., do you have a big birthday or special anniversary coming up? I could get your
name on the air. I have some pull, you know." He closed
his eyes, shrugged his shoulders, and gave a little laugh, as
if once again his keen wit had snuck up on him.

Thelma put her hands on her sacrum and stuck out her
stomach the way women who are late in their pregnancy
do. "Let me make myself clear," she said. "I honestly don't
care if you're reaching out to the moon. A deal is a deal,
and our deal didn't call for my girl to have to memorize
half the Tampa phone book. And yes, I do have a special
day coming up. Tomorrow marks the three-month anniversary of the first time I shook your bony little hand and

found myself knee-high in all your horse manure. You play your cards wrong, Mr. S., and tomorrow could also be the day we celebrate the last time Delores Taurus sits her pretty little fanny down in your precious little studio."

Thelma waited for Sommers to go back at her. In truth, she loved sparring with him. It was the closest she'd ever come to opening up to a man. Her jousts with him felt physical: a jab, a punch in the gut, a split lip. Often when they were finished, she felt spent and faintly satisfied. Mostly, men didn't interest her one way or the other. All that strutting and preening and cock-a-doodle-dooing didn't amount to a hill of beans when it came down to it. She'd never understood what all the fuss was about. But this shouting at a man, saying the crudest, meanest things she could think of, this had heat and fire and juice and all those semidisgusting words that women used when they talked about men.

Few people had laid claim to Thelma's loyalty. Sure, her girls felt an obligation to her while they were in her service, but it was such a tenuous connection that she could count on one hand how many even remembered to send her a Christmas card after they were gone. But not since Newton Perry handpicked her to be one of the Aquabelles had the line ever extended the other way. Oh, she would have gladly given Mr. Perry all the loyalty in China but for the fact that he chose Ann Blyth and not her for the role of the mermaid in *Mr. Peabody and the Mermaid*. He cast his vote for the "prettier girl with the slimmer, more pleasing physique, and the sweeter aspect."

Words like that can scorch a young girl's heart forever and reconfigure her frame of mind. From then on, Thelma covered up, never exposing her body to anyone's judgment again. And if she wasn't sweet enough, well, there were things other than a sultry pout and pretty doe eyes that a girl could use to her advantage. Thelma was organized and could get things done. Maybe people didn't take to her naturally, but once they understood that she knew what was what and could bring out the best in their theatrical and aquatic skills, they usually came around. For all these years she'd managed Weeki Wachee, reporting to no one except for a man named Don McKeene, the accountant employed by the owners. But he was strictly a bean counter, a flabby man with a curious bluish tongue. As far as Thelma knew, he never even watched a performance; he cared only about the bottom line. Thelma was the one who gave Weeki Wachee its pizzazz—as Sommers would say, its sizzle.

Thelma hoarded her sense of loyalty and obligation to others, as if giving it would weaken her. Besides, no one had ever asked for it. So there it sat like an earthworm cut in half, groping and reaching blindly for the piece that would make it whole again. She saw in Sommers the other half of that worm, not that he'd given any indication that he felt the same way. Through some concoction of indebtedness for dragging her into the real world and a sense that her success was bound up with his, she took all those years of unspent gratitude and dumped it at his pointed, little tasseled shoes. It didn't change the intensity with which she and Sommers fought their battles. It was just that

Thelma liked being a part of the WGUP local news team, and she liked making the girl one of them, too. Delores Taurus reminded Thelma of her younger self, before Ann Blyth had come along, when she had thought that everything was possible and nothing could keep her from becoming the most famous mermaid in the world.

Twelve

ONE EVENING, just after the WGUP driver dropped Delores off at Weeki Wachee, Thelma called her from her office. Adrienne answered and mouthed to Delores, "It's Thelma." Exhausted from having performed two shows and doing the weather that night, Delores made shushing motions with her hands. "I'm not here," she whispered, certain that Thelma was calling her to clean the tank. "You don't know where I am."

Adrienne said she hadn't seen Delores all day.

"Should she reappear anytime soon," said Thelma, "I have some news that might interest her. Enrich her, actually."

Ten minutes later, Delores was seated across from Thelma Foote in her office. Thelma had hiked herself up so that she was sitting on her desk with her hands folded and her feet swaying back and forth. Her Keds thumping against the desk sounded like a bouncing rubber ball. The more she talked, the faster they bounced.

"The bangs are really working for you. The kewpie doll thing you do with your eyes, it's fetching, but you've got to remember to blink. Otherwise you run the risk of looking terrified. Also, when you say someone's name, stare into the camera and pretend that you're talking just to them. A little smile would make it even more personal. Personal, that's the word they like to use. The station thinks you're doing good work. Mr. Sommers—an effective man, don't you think?—would like to give you an increase in salary now that you're having to do all that yakking about people's birthdays and christenings and whatnot. So in addition to what you're making here, you're going to clear another eighty-five dollars a week from WGUP. A nice hunk of change, I'd say. This could be big."

Delores knew that there was more money at stake than eighty-five dollars a week. She knew that Thelma Foote was getting some of it, and that because she was a girl— well, barely a girl, a cartoon figure was more like it—she was probably making a whole lot less than everyone else on the show, just as Otto had said. She was beginning to realize how much Thelma Foote depended on her, how much Weeki Wachee depended on her. Even WGUP had gotten better ratings since she'd been on the air. Maybe this was a good time to ask for more money, make some demands. Hers was the only name on the marquee outside. That's why ticket sales were up.

Thelma was still kicking the desk and talking about how if Delores played her cards right, there was no telling what could be next. She didn't seem to hear the phone ring, even though it was right next to her thigh. After about eight rings, Delores stared at it as if she might pick it up herself.

"Oh, all right already," said Thelma, annoyed by the interruption. "Yes," she said, shouting abruptly into the receiver. Delores was close enough to Thelma and the phone so that she could hear the person on the other end: not so much the words as the cadence. It was a woman, and she had a voice that slid up and down like a kazoo. Something about it was familiar.

A smile sprawled across Thelma's face. "Well, how are you? Good. I'm fine and dandy, too. Oh yes, a fashion convention. Sounds very interesting. Son of a gun, she's sitting right here! Yes, life sure is full of surprises."

Of course. It was her mother. She was on her way to Boca Raton for that fashion accessories meeting and she was coming through Weeki Wachee to see her.

"Vice versa, Mrs. Walker," said Thelma rising to her feet. "No, no. The pleasure is all *mine.* Hold on, please."

Thelma passed the phone down to Delores.

"Hi, Mom."

There it was again: "Hay-llo."

She and Westie would get to the Best Western late that night. They agreed to meet at the motel for breakfast at eight the next morning. "Right, it is hunky-dory. See you tomorrow." Delores put down the phone, then looked up at Thelma wide-eyed. "She's on the road, some fashion show. She'll stop by here tomorrow. She's looking forward to meeting you."

"Oh brother," said Thelma, "can I not wait to meet her."

The next morning, at eight a.m. sharp, as planned, Delores sat in the lobby of the Best Western, waiting for her mother and Westie.

After not seeing one another for almost a year, Delores and Gail Walker stared at one another for what must have been a full sixty seconds before one of them uttered the other's name. Only Westie, a real toddler now with plump cheeks, sandy hair, and a gap between his two front teeth, looked familiar. Mother and daughter were glamorized makeovers of themselves. Delores was tan and resplendent with success, and her mother, once sallow with disappointment, looked as if she'd been given a fresh coat of paint. She'd colored and cut her hair. The pockets under her eyes were gone, and her eyes were bright with expectation and a little mascara. Delores could see from her red bell-bottoms and red patent-leather high-heeled boots that she still had her hand in the fashion closet.

And, of course, there was the way she talked.

"Well, here we all are again." She turned to little Westie who hadn't said a word yet. "Westie, this is where you were conceptualized."

"Mom, don't you mean conceived?" asked Delores.

"Whatever. The point is, Westie, this is where you started, where your life began. And now look, here we all are." Her voice went flat again. "Well, not all exactly, but you and me and your sister. That's close enough."

At two and a half, Westie wasn't a baby anymore. Delores recognized the stuffed dolphin she'd sent him nearly six months earlier. It was gray and nubby and had clearly been put through the washing machine many times. He held it to his chest and stared at Delores reproachfully, as if she might try to take it away from him.

Delores knelt before him; he leaned into his mother's

legs. He didn't recognize her. He had no idea she was his sister, the one who sent him all those postcards and who kept a plastic bag stuffed with cash just for him.

"Hey, Westie, hey, little man," she said, taking his hand between her thumb and forefinger. "Do you want to come and see some mermaids? And some turtles and maybe even a dolphin?" She wagged the tail on his raggedy stuffed animal and he pulled it away from her.

"He calls it Dorph," said her mother. "I tried to tell him that it was a dolphin, but he insists on calling it Dorph."

Delores continued in a tiny voice. "I have an idea. Maybe Dorph has a sister. How about you, me, Dorph, and Mommy go to the park and see if we can find her?"

"Westie, that's a fun idea, isn't it?" said her mother. "Dorph would like that, too. C'mon, let's go." They each took his hand to walk across the highway, but he pushed Delores away. When they got to the park, the first thing they saw was the sign with her name on it. She wished Westie could read. Her mother walked past the sign without noticing, until Delores nodded toward it. Her mother stared at the chunky black metal letters advertising her daughter's name.

"Oh, there you are," she said, running her fingers over the *D* and *E*. "How nice."

That's when her mother understood: people don't go putting people's names on signs unless they're a real somebody. Her daughter had become a somebody. She thought about Avalon and how she and Delores, young as they were, had already surpassed her with their accomplishments. She was thirty-five years old, nearly thirty-six. That was old enough to have polluted her life with failure, but maybe young enough to become somebody, too.

Westie cuddled Dorph and stared at the sculpture of the two mermaids just beyond them. Delores looked over where Westie was staring; it was the same obelisk that her father had tried to duplicate when he thrust her up in the air for that famous picture more than two years before. She thought back to the odd trio that was her family then. She would have never believed that she would actually miss her mother's self-pity and whininess. She forgot about her father's bad temper and remembered the strength in his arms and his loopy Alfred E. Neuman smile. She wondered if he knew of her success. If he did, would it even matter?

Everything about this morning made Delores want to cry: her mother, all dolled up, barely noticing her, much less acknowledging her success; Westie not even recognizing her. This was her family: three pieces on a chessboard, each going its own way. And the fourth piece, her father, was gone, spilled over into a corner somewhere with no one even looking for him.

She welled up with dread: the beginning of an awful day. In less than an hour, she would introduce her mother to Thelma Foote. Then she'd meet the other girls and see the show and come with her to WGUP and meet Sommers. All that she had created in the persona of Delores Taurus could come undone today with just one word from her mother— about their dingy apartment in the Bronx, about her jobs cleaning office buildings and working in a supermarket, about Delores's missing father—about almost anything that she was likely to mention.

Delores rapped on Thelma's door at precisely nine a.m. Thelma jumped up and greeted the three of them as effusively as if the Disney family had come to visit. She'd even dressed for the occasion. Her Keds were spotless and Delores thought she could still see the crease marks on what was clearly a brand-new windbreaker. Sometimes, right before the show, Thelma would whip out a tube of Sugar Blush natural lipstick and give it to one of the girls. "It will enhance your natural color," she'd say. Now, it appeared, Thelma had put on a little Sugar Blush of her own. It was the only color on her unmade-up pale face and made her look as if she'd just eaten a wild cherry Life Saver.

Thelma took Gail Walker's hand in both of her own and shook it heartily. "Mrs. Walker—or should I call you Mrs. Taurus?—we are so honored to have you here." Then, looking down at Westie and speaking a wee bit louder: "And you must be the little brother we hear so much about. How do you do, Westie? I'm Thelma Foote."

Westie glared up at Thelma as if he thought she might try to kiss him or kidnap him.

"Please," said Thelma. "Have a seat. Welcome to our funny little family. You must be so proud of your daughter's success. She's really turned things around here at Weeki Wachee."

Gail smiled a new kind of smile. She stretched her lips, lowered her eyes, and, no, it couldn't be possible, she was sucking in her cheeks just a little so that there'd be two little apples of cheekbones where there never were before. "My daughter has always had an attitude for the water."

Oh God, she means "aptitude," thought Delores, hoping that Thelma missed it.

"You should have seen her in the Christmas show," Thelma continued. "That's when it became clear that Miss Taurus here was star material, the real McCoy."

Her mother's expression stayed fixed. "I think a flair for drama runs in our family. I'd have liked to be here at Christmas, but things just got so hectic back home."

Delores could see that her mother was trying. She looked pretty good. Maybe she had really lifted herself out of the gummy drudgery of her life. With her new vibrant voice and her crispy dialect, who could tell? She'd reshaped her New York accent. "Wawkah" was now "Wahker," and her vowels had acquired arches: "Westie doesn't feel *abahndoned* by his older sister. He knows she *adohrs* him." Her consonants had become rolling hills: "I'll be meeting the woman I work for, Avalon *Mandhorr*, in Boca *Ratone*. We'll be doing the accessories show there."

Delores understood that if you behaved a certain way long enough and told the same story over and over, the act of repetition was all you needed to fog the truth. Was her own act as transparent as her mother's? By now, she believed that she really was Delores Taurus, and she didn't need to prop herself up with as many lies and inventions. Did her mother still allow herself old private pleasures like watching *Glen Campbell,* or was that too common for the woman she was trying to become? And what of her father? Had her mother rubbed him out of this version of her life altogether?

If Thelma wanted to know where the singing Mr. Walker was, or exactly what Gail Walker did in the fashion business, she held her tongue, just as she had done when Delores first came to audition in the bell. She let Delores's mother talk in that way she did, never betraying by so much as a fumble with her zipper whether or not she bought it. As the two women talked, Delores looked over at Westie. He had thrown Dorph to the floor and was leaning against his mother's shoulder, looking as if he might cry. Delores felt badly for him.

"What if Westie and I go off on a little adventure?" she suddenly said. "We'll meet the two of you at the amphitheater at ten thirty. That'll give me plenty of time to get ready for the eleven o'clock show."

Westie looked to his mother, who nodded at him. "Well now, doesn't that sound like a treat? Go on. Go with your sister and have an adventure." The boy seemed dubious, but when Delores smiled down at him and took his hand, he gave it to her. Maybe he did remember her.

"C'mon, Westie," said Delores. "There's someone who wants to meet you."

Sometimes Delores would catch tree frogs by the side of the Springs. They were tiny creatures with thin, moist skin, and she'd cup them in her hands for just a moment or two. After she let them go, she could feel the sticky residue from the tips of their toes. Westie's warm hand in hers felt like one of those frogs, and she was careful not to hold it too tight.

They walked past the amphitheater down to the bank of the Weeki Wachee River. The sun shone high in the sky, and the river was still and shimmery. Delores crouched by the water; Westie crouched next to her. "If you look closely, maybe we'll see Dorph's sister. Or remember the sea turtle I told you about? He lives near here, and I call him Westie, after you. If we sit real quiet, maybe he'll come by."

Westie took in a gulp of air and held his breath for as long as he could. A few skinny carp floated past, but no dolphins or sea turtles. Westie had on a pair of shorts and a short-sleeved striped polo shirt. Delores wore her bathing suit under her shorts and sleeveless blouse. She stared at him. His chubby little legs had muscle in them now. He would have his daddy's build, that was for sure. Then she remembered that she had been only a few months older than he was now the first time her mother had thrown her into the lake.

"Westie," she whispered. "Wanna go out and find the turtle?"

Westie nodded his head yes.

"Okay, here's what we'll do. You'll climb on my back and hold on as tight as you can. And together we'll swim out and find him. Okay?" Westie looked at her, his eyes filled with wonder and worry. Delores stripped down to her bathing suit and took off her sandals. She helped him take off his shirt and shoes, then bent down. "Hop on," she said, as if she were giving him a piggyback ride. He straddled her back like a little monkey. Slowly, she walked into the river, the muddy bottom of it oozing between her toes. When she was waist-deep, she told Westie again to hold on tight. She let her body fall forward in the warm water and used the wide-arcing breaststroke and frog kick to propel her forward. They swam this way for a while, the water making slurping sounds against their bodies. Then Delores saw the creature wandering through the murky water beneath them as if he were window-shopping. She could tell by his pale olive coloring and heart-shaped carapace that it was the same turtle that had swum by her many times during the show, the one she had named Westie. She whispered to her brother: "I see him. Hold your breath and keep your eyes open and hold on as tight as you can. Don't be scared."

Reassured by his sister's ease in the water, Westie did as he was told. Delores dove underneath the water. She swam up close to the old sea turtle and he studied her through his heavy-lidded eyes. Then a curious thing happened. The turtle floated up to Westie and just slightly bumped his round head against the boy's cheek before swimming away. Delores swam to the surface again. "Did you see him?" Delores asked. Behind her head, she could hear Westie giggling. "The turtle touched me," he said. "The turtle touched me."

These kinds of things happened here.

"See, he knows you," said Delores. "Next time we'll go looking for Dorph's sister."

She stopped worrying about what would happen the rest of the day; Westie had seen the magic of the place, and she knew he would never forget.

Later that morning, Delores swam in the "Cinderella" show. When it was over, she floated up to the Plexiglas window, as she always did, and scoured the audience. She could make out her mother and the little boy at her side.

They were both on their feet, and she thought that the little boy was pointing and jumping up and down, but the eyes play funny tricks sixteen feet underwater, so she couldn't be sure.

After the show, Thelma came down from the booth and caught up with Westie and Gail. "Talented little gal you've got there," she said, arching her eyebrows. "A real fish in the water, don't you think?"

"Delores has flair in the water," Gail said. "It runs in her family."

Thelma nodded, trying to coax more enthusiasm out of this woman. "Combine that with her father's creative talents, and I'd say she's got it made."

Gail wondered what Thelma could possibly know about Roy Walker's talents, which, other than throwing food around the house, were pretty minimal. "Yes, well, her father is a piece of work, I will say that." The two women nodded the way women do when they talk about difficult men. "And what about you, young man?" said Thelma, spacing her words carefully. "Do you want to be a merman when you grow up?"

Westie fidgeted with his tattered dolphin and ignored her. Thelma remembered why she disliked children so much. They were self-absorbed, sulky little creatures and frankly, not very interesting, this one even less so than most. But then again, look at his mother. Thelma's judgment about Gail Walker hadn't veered an inch from the moment she met her that morning. She was a scared person, who seemed to resent her own daughter's success; sad, really. She would hate it if her own sadness were that palpable to other people. But, of course, it wasn't. Anyway, if she were honest, she'd have to say she wasn't sad, exactly: discouraged sometimes, but not sad. "Sad" was too complete. Whatever it was she felt, she kept it under wraps—unlike Gail Walker. It was funny how Gail and Delores looked so much alike, both tall and big-boned, yet one was brimming with life while the other seemed to bleed it out. But the thing that really got to Thelma was how Gail treated Delores. Not that Thelma knew a whole lot about maternal feelings, but she knew enough to know that any mother in the world would consider herself lucky to have a daughter like Delores Taurus. Any mother, that is, except this one.

She was really trying with Gail Walker, and it wasn't often that Thelma put out this kind of an effort, making small talk, being nice to a child. But all she was getting back was a person with a fake, fancy accent and outrageous clothes. The worst part was that Gail hadn't asked Thelma a single question about herself or about running an enterprise like Weeki Wachee. Even at her hoity-toity fashion magazine, it wasn't every day she was going to meet someone who supervised mermaids for a living. Thelma was hardly one of those women's libbers, God forbid, but it always surprised her when one of her own sex was curt or dismissive. She understood that maybe she was threatening, being an independent businesswoman and all, but still, if other women weren't going to be generous to her, who would be?

"So, should we go find Delores?" Thelma continued,

with gristle in her voice. Delores had gone back to the dorm to change. She had told them she had a quick errand to run and said she would meet them in front of the theater by the river. Westie was the first to notice Delores coming across the lawn. He broke loose from his mother and ran to her. "Hey, Westie," she called out. He could see she had a white package with a blue ribbon in one hand. "Hi," he said.

"Did you like the show?" she asked. He reached for her empty hand. "I have an idea," she whispered. "Come with me. We'll tell Mom and Thelma that we'll meet them later."

Gail put a tentative arm around Delores's shoulder. "That was a very interesting show. I can't believe that someone with so much talent would come from my gene pool."

Delores was tempted to say, "You mean your gene puddle," but for the fact that her mother insisted on keeping her arm around her. She recognized the faint odor of Mum.

When she finally wriggled free, she said, "Listen, Mom, Thelma, I'm going to take Westie back to the dorm for a few minutes. I'll introduce him to the other girls, and then we can all get some lunch at the refreshment stand."

Her mother looked at her watch and tapped its face with her nail. "Oh, sweetie," she said. "I'm sorry, but I'm afraid Westie and I are going to have to run along. I spoke to Avalon earlier, and she wants me in Boca ASAP. Apparently the merchandise arrived sooner than expected, and we really need to get prepared for the show." That was the truth, sort of. She had spoken to Avalon earlier in the day, and Avalon had been close to tears. "Everything arrived late," she had said. "So I'm sitting here in my room, drowning in shoes and watches and who knows what. I'll never get this stuff opened and tagged in time."

"Would it help if I came a little earlier?" Gail had asked.

"Would it help?" Avalon cried. "It would be ... it would be a godsend."

"Okeydokey then. I'll be there as soon as I can."

Gail had assumed that Delores would be happy if she left early. *She certainly doesn't need me here,* she rationalized. *She's got all those girls around her, not to mention that Thelma Foote. What a weirdo, that one.* She hated the way Thelma Foote hovered around Delores and kept whispering her praises as if she wasn't aware enough of her own daughter's accomplishments. How could a woman like that—was she even a woman at all?—understand what it was like to be a mother, to have to make the kinds of choices she'd made, to bring up a little boy on her own? People like her tried to put Gail in her place. But uh-uh, she was working too hard to let someone like Thelma Foote make her feel inferior.

Delores and Thelma exchanged looks. "I just need a few minutes because I want to take Westie back to the dorm with me," said Delores. "We'll be right back." She held Westie's hand a little tighter, turned around, and headed toward the dorm.

For the first time since she had left the Bronx, Delores had that hollow feeling inside her. It stuck to the back of ⸰

her throat like liver and made it hard for her to speak. How she'd worried about her mother. What if she'd shown up with her hair uncombed or wearing some awful outfit she'd gotten on sale at Alexander's? It would have been humiliating. Delores hadn't bargained for the makeup and the boots and the new way of speaking. It had never occurred to her that her mother's fantasy of who she could become might equal, or maybe even supersede, her own. She was starting to realize that becoming a mermaid and living underwater wasn't the only way to separate from the Walkers of the Grand Concourse. Her mother had made the escape without ever leaving home.

A couple of times her mother had mentioned to Westie that they needed to buy a present for Helene—Helene with the big globe in her room and the thin wax-papery arms. Helene was doing poorly with her breast cancer, her mother had told her earlier. "She's probably not going to make it," she had whispered. She had already started looking for someone else to take care of Westie. No father, no mother, and now his babysitter was about to be gone. Westie might as well be an orphan.

An idea took form. Maybe it was crazy, but in the scheme of things, it seemed crazy in a good way. "C'mon, Westie." She was nearly running now. When they got to the dorm, she found Molly and pulled her aside. "This is my brother," she said, looking around the room. "Westie, this is my friend Molly."

Molly couldn't take her eyes off of Westie. "He's a real cute one," she said.

Delores looked down at her little brother, then whispered to Molly, "I want him to talk to Otto. Do you think you could stand watch for a few minutes?"

"Little brothers. They're the best," said Molly. "Go on. I'm here."

Delores took Westie over to her bed. She picked him up and put him on the bed. The woolen blanket was itchy under his bare thighs and he kept squirming until he nearly slid off. "Just a minute, Westie," said Delores. "I have something to show you." She knelt down, pulled her suitcase from under the bed, and unwrapped Otto. Placing the puppet on her lap and straightening out his stained skirt, she sat down next to Westie. "This is my friend Otto. You met him when you were very little," she said. "No one else knows him but you. Not Mommy, not Helene. Other than you, he's the best friend I have."

"Hi, Westie," said Otto, in his sweet, croaky voice. "I've heard so much about you."

Westie started and looked up at Otto's soap-white head.

Otto continued: "I used to live where you live, but now I live here. I spend most of my time in the suitcase under Delores's bed. I don't see her as often as I used to."

Delores whispered in Westie's ear: "Otto's very lonely here. I think he'd be happier at home, with you. Do you think you could take care of him for me?"

Westie blinked hard, then touched Otto's head. "He's soft, isn't he?" said Delores. Westie nodded his head yes. Otto continued: "I'd love to come live with you, Westie. And one day soon, we'll all live together again, won't we, Delores?"

"We will, I promise."

Delores put Otto in Westie's lap, next to Dorph. "Will you take him?" Westie nodded his head yes again. "Now, every time you talk to Otto, you'll also be talking to me." She took his hand. "Look, I'll show you how to make him come alive."

Westie was captivated by the puppet, his rhinestone tears and the way he could make him dance and twist around and clap his hands. "I like Otto," said Westie. "I'll take care of him."

"You've made Otto very happy," she said, scratching Dorph. "I'll bet you that Otto and Dorph become great buddies."

Delores heard Molly's whisper behind the closed door, and her floating "lollapalooza" jarred her back into place. It was time for them to go. Delores put Dorph in Westie's free hand and kissed Otto on the head. "See you soon," she said to him. And to Westie she said, "Okay, little man, we have a deal. We'll all be together some day. Remember that."

Thelma and her mother were waiting for them outside the dorm. Thelma was wearing sunglasses and a baseball cap pulled down over her forehead. She hadn't bothered reapplying the Sugar Blush from earlier that morning, so her lips were pale and stern. Her hands were folded behind her back and her feet were planted a couple of inches apart. If Delores hadn't known who these two people were, she would have thought that the woman in the wind-breaker and the white Keds was standing guard over the woman with the heavy makeup and the red patent-leather boots.

"Time to get this show on the road," said her mother, as soon as she saw Delores and Westie. "I'll call from Boca. It was wonderful to see you doing so great." She leaned close to Delores and whispered under her breath: "We've come a long way, baby. Don'tcha think?" It was the first time in a long time that Delores had heard her round her vowels and drop her consonants.

Delores kissed Westie good-bye and patted Otto. "Don't forget what I told you," she said, then turned and ran back into the dorm.

There was a large bathroom in the dorm. On one side were three separate showers, each with its own white plastic shower curtain. Opposite the showers were three bathroom stalls separated by the standard gray metal walls. Delores locked herself in one of the stalls and sat on the toilet crying. She held her hands over her mouth so she wouldn't cry out loud. Every now and then, she'd flush the toilet in order to drown out the sounds of her blowing her nose. She had no idea how long she'd been sitting there when she became aware of someone in the next stall. Judging by the white, frosted nail polish on the short, stubby toes, they had to be Molly's feet. Delores tried to breathe normally and not make any gulping noise.

"Delores, is that you?" Molly said.

She cleared her throat. "Yup. Oh, hi, Molly."

"Hey. Your brother's adorable. He looks like you."

"Nah, more like my father," said Delores, tears welling up again.

"Brothers, they are out of sight," said Molly.

"That's the truth," whispered Delores.

"Did I ever tell you how I got that scar on my neck?"

"Uh-uh."

"My brother Larry. One day, when I was ten and he was four, we were sitting at the kitchen table cutting out pictures from a magazine. We must have been making a card for my parents, or something, I can't remember. All of a sudden, out of nowhere, Larry reached across the table and cut my neck with the scissors. It didn't hurt as much as it shocked me. I guess he just wanted to see what would happen. There was blood everywhere; it was really a mess. I got up and went and found my mother. She took me to the hospital and I had twenty-seven stitches. I never cried, not one time. Isn't that funny? Anyway, Larry's almost eleven and I miss him like crazy. No one in my family ever talked about what happened until just now."

Neither of them spoke for a few minutes. Finally, Delores said: "Does everyone in your family have names with Ls in them?"

Molly started to laugh. Then Delores laughed. Soon they were laughing so hard that they could see each other's feet swaying underneath the partition.

They both flushed and met at the sink; Delores splashed some water on her face. Molly told her what had just happened. Thelma had called, and Sharlene had answered the phone. "Thelma yelled at Sharlene, poor thing, and told her that she was a lazy slob, and if she kept up the way she was going, she might as well get herself a waitressing job at Howard Johnson's right now. She said the tank was disgusting, and it was embarrassing to have strangers see it. Sharlene started crying and Thelma told her to buck up and not be such a candy ass. So guess who's cleaning the tank at this moment? Sharlene and Adrienne. Can you imagine?"

At that moment, Delores felt sympathetic toward Thelma. She thought about what it might feel like to live in this penned-in, artificial world for twenty-five years and to put up with the people who passed through: dropouts, runaways, girls in desperate situations with nowhere else to go, liars like herself. Just last week, Blonde Sheila disappeared for two days. No one knew where she was, and Thelma ended up calling the police. It was quite a to-do until Blonde Sheila came back beaming.

"Where the hell were you?" Thelma asked her. It turned out, she and the preacher from the Spring Hill Church had gone to Ocala for a two-day Bible study retreat. "God summoned me there," Blonde Sheila said, with more than a little sanctimony. Hives the size of quarters erupted on Thelma's neck. "I don't give a fart if God summons you to Bethlehem," she screamed in front of everyone. "The next time you pull a disappearing act like that, you and your cute little born-again tail are out of here! You get that?"

Thelma couldn't be enjoying her job. She deserved better.

Suddenly an idea fixed itself in Delores's mind, and all that mattered was getting to Thelma Foote's office as fast as she could. She hoped she was still there, she thought, as she ran across the park. She hoped she hadn't yet gone to lunch.

Thelma's door was slightly ajar. Delores knocked.

"What?" Thelma's voice was tight.

"Can I come in?" Delores said softly.

"Oh, it's you. Don't tell me she's still here."

"Who?"

"Your mother, who else?"

Delores had to smile. "She was that bad, huh?"

"No, of course not," said Thelma, taking off her glasses. Without her glasses, Thelma's eyes looked tired and naked.

"It's just been a long couple of weeks. Your mother's a perfectly nice woman."

"You don't really think she's all that nice." Delores raised her voice. "You think she's obnoxious and boring and a big phony."

Delores sat on the metal foldout chair across from Thelma. "And you know what else? I'm a big phony, too. I come from the Bronx and live in a really small, dark apartment with food stains everywhere. My father walked out on us a year ago, and no one knows where he is. He isn't in the entertainment business, or at least wasn't the last time I saw him. He worked in a wholesale grocery store. My mother bags groceries at Gristedes. At night, she works as a maid cleaning office buildings. One of the offices happens to be that stupid fashion magazine she goes on about. Most of my clothes are things that she stole that didn't fit her. She's completely made up the way she talks, the words she uses, the hair and makeup. It's all a lie. The only real person in my family is Westie, who, as far as I can tell, is being raised by an old-maid lady who lives in our apartment building and will probably die soon. When I lived in the Bronx, I was ugly and unpopular. I've never been on a date and if I hadn't gotten the job here, I'd probably be working at some grocery store in the Bronx, too. So there, now you know everything there is to know about me."

Delores slumped into the metal backrest of the chair and waited.

Thelma put on her glasses and her eyes came to life again.

She cupped her chin in her hand and stared at Delores without blinking. When she finally spoke, her words were filled with affection. "Oh my dear," she said. "You must be starving. Let's go get some lunch."

Part Two

Thirteen

ROY WALKER SAT on the edge of his bed wearing a sleeveless undershirt and a pair of pale blue boxer shorts. As he did every morning when he awoke, he got up, walked around his bed fifteen times, then fell to the floor for his fifty sit-ups and twenty push-ups.

Since he'd left home, he'd formed many habits like this. He got into the shower, cold water only, and soaped up his whole body. Then he took the bar of soap and ran it through his hair, kneading his fingers into his scalp to ensure a thorough massage. Somewhere he'd heard that the secret to keeping your hair was to make sure the blood circulated vigorously on the top of the head. Roy had always prided himself on his thick, wavy hair, which was down to his shoulders by now, and he was certain that the patch of baldness on the crown of his head, tiny as a teacup, would prove to be just an aberration.

Because the windows inside his trailer were no larger than tissue boxes, he could never gauge the weather for sure until he stepped outside. Looked like rain. A sheet of low, gray clouds floated overhead. At any moment, there'd be a steady, hard rain on his metal roof, soaking the laundry hanging on the clothesline, filling the buckets with water, and turning the ground into a muck of silt. Then it would only be a matter of minutes before the sun would bear down and all that had been soaked was baked dry again.

Roy stepped back into his trailer and made his bed, careful to fold the hospital corners at precise angles. He had virtually no possessions: a few changes of clothing, including two Hawaiian shirts; two sets of sheets; a blanket; a pillow; a sturdy pair of shoes; a toothbrush; a razor; a hairbrush; his New York Yankees cap; his wraparound sunglasses. He took extra care of what he had. He'd sold the car to a fellow from Bradenton who gave him six hundred dollars in cash. That was a year ago, and he still hadn't spent it all. In the business he was in, there wasn't a whole lot to need.

Roy sat on his bed and looked around his trailer. He didn't often let his mind wander to the past, but somehow the sound of the rain and the smell of the soaking earth brought his thoughts back to what it had been like to be in that apartment in the Bronx on a stormy day. It had smelled like wet towels, and he'd felt as if they were suffocating him. Sometimes he had screamed just to be heard, to feel the sound of his own voice. Sometimes he'd left and gone anywhere, just to assure himself that he was alive and that there was something else beyond those walls. And then he had done the thing he was most ashamed of. He had walked out on his family and run away from home.

Here he was living in a place that was a quarter the size of that cramped apartment; he was as alone as it was possible for a man to be. While he tried not to think about the

family he'd left behind, the knowledge of what he had
done scarred his every moment. He never dreamed of re-
demption; the ascetic life he was now leading seemed to
be the closest he would get.

When he first left, he had no idea where he was going.
He had never been anywhere, except for Florida. He got
onto I-95 south and thought he'd just keep driving until
something occurred to him. The first night, he drove until
eight in the morning and got as far as the border between
North and South Carolina. Barely able to keep his eyes
open, he had been led by a succession of green and orange
billboards into a place called the South of the Border
Motel. After ten hours of a dreamless, uncomplicated
sleep, he had driven for another twelve hours until he
found himself outside of Sarasota. He hadn't had a real
meal in days, and his belly was aching to be filled. Maybe
that's why he had been drawn to a modest-looking diner
with the words GIANT CAFÉ written in a playful script across
a pink awning. A giant steak, a giant plate of French fries.
It had made his mouth water to just think about it.

Inside the café, a man so tall that he had to stoop slightly
to avoid bumping his head on the ceiling greeted Roy. Roy
had never seen anyone this tall. He had to be nearly eight
feet. His shoes looked to be the size of planters, and his
hands easily spanned the width of an air conditioner. His
smile was shy and almost plaintive, and his sad beagle eyes
made him less menacing than he might have been—that
and the way he hunkered down and spoke kindly to the two

midgets who were sitting at the soda fountain. Roy sat at an empty table and looked through the menu. He became engrossed reading about the "succulent steak smothered in onions" and might not have noticed anyone standing over him, except for the dark shadow that suddenly dimmed his view of the menu. "What can I get for you today?" The voice, deep and hollow, sounded as if it were rising up out of a drainpipe.

Roy ordered his steak and a glass of beer to go with it. As he ate, he stared into the distance, aware of nothing in particular except how the sweet smell of onions lingered. At some point, his eyes settled on a wall filled with framed newspaper clippings. In each, the tall man at the front door was pictured with his tree-sized arm around some famous person who, in comparison, looked as if they had fallen out of his pocket. Roy recognized Elizabeth Taylor and Tony Perkins and Steve Lawrence; Lawrence was about Roy's height, so seemed short enough even when not posing next to an eight-foot man. Roy gathered from the captions that the tall man was famous, that the place he was in was famous. Venice, Florida. He'd never heard of it, but according to the newspaper clippings, it was the winter home of Hanratty's Circus, one of the largest in the world. That explained everything: the midgets, the giant, the Giant Café.

The only time Roy had ever been to the circus had been with Delores, when she was still a little girl. He remembered the colors and how the acrobats had seemed to fly. He pictured the faces of the aerialists, first rigid with concentration, then flashing triumphant smiles after they had danced across the high wire and made the audience cry out in delight. Some people had even turned away, frightened at the prospect of witnessing the consequences of a turned foot or a missed step. Roy remembered that time at the mermaid park when, for just a few seconds, all eyes had been on him and the crowd had held its breath as he'd hauled Delores above his head and struck the pose of a nearby statue. People like him didn't draw crowds. Yet the one time he had, he'd felt a rush of pleasure and possibility that he often thought about but had never found a way to duplicate.

The midgets broke his daydreams. They were being held spellbound by a man with a perfectly waxed six-inch flattop and baggy gray pants. He must have said something funny because they all started to laugh, a tinkling laugh. Roy wondered if the man was a clown in the circus. Roy tried not to stare but he gradually became aware that by being ordinary-looking, he was the odd man out in this little place.

He tried to put his mind to productive thoughts, like getting a job. But thoughts of his family wouldn't leave him. What sort of man up and leaves a wife and two children, for God's sake, for no reason? For a moment, he even considered whether he should go back. Then he remembered the night of the liver scene and what had happened next. He could never go back. He had reasons, all right, most of them having to do with the way he'd lived and breathed misery for so long, he'd almost stopped caring.

He had left, he told himself, because if he didn't, the rage inside of him would eat him up or kill them all. Maybe Gail brought out the rage in him. They were so young when they got married and had a baby. When it came down to it, Gail was a survivor. She was also a looker in her better days. She'd do fine. Delores was a clever girl and would find her way. And the little one: well, he really didn't know much about the little one, only that he was a mama's boy. Mama's boys always find someone to protect them.

At least he'd left some money behind: those silver dollars he'd been squirreling away all those years. He'd loved staring at the old scratched-up profiles, wondering whose hands they had passed through and what they had bought. Gail would probably rummage through his things and find them soon enough.

Roy's mind circled back to where he was. This place felt comfortable. The people seemed friendly. Nice weather. He liked the hoopla around him. When the giant came back to take his dishes, he leaned down and asked Roy: "Will there be anything else?"

Roy said, "Yes, sir. Do you mind if I ask you a question?"

The giant grimaced as if anticipating the question of how tall he was.

"Sure," he said.

Roy thought for a moment. "I was wondering if you knew how a man could go about getting work around here."

The giant smiled. "Well, you know there's only one show in town. How are you on the high wire?"

Roy smiled. "I've never been on the high wire, but I've got a swell set of biceps on me. Check these out." Roy rolled up his sleeves and flexed his muscles, the way he imagined the strong man in the circus might.

The giant poked Roy's bulging arm with one of his fingers.

"Not bad," he said. "Been eating your spinach, have you? Are you a wrestler or something?"

"No," said Roy. "I lift cartons of canned food and detergent for a living. Or at least I did."

The giant had the vulnerable look of a person used to tolerating indignities, and Roy felt instinctively as if he understood. "There's always room for one more roustabout," he said.

"Roustabout. What's that?"

"They're the guys who do the heavy lifting," he said. "They help with the rigging, they set up the tents, load and unload. Whatever needs doing."

"My kind of work," said Roy. "I could do that. Do you mind if I ask you one more question?"

"Shoot."

"What is your name?"

"Rex," he said. "T. Rex, but Rex for short. And you are?"

"Roy Walker. Roy for short." He grinned. "You from around here, Rex?"

"No. None of us are from anywhere, really. My mother is from Saginaw, Michigan, and my father is from Toronto, which is how I got my name, I suppose."

"Oh, so T. Rex is a Canadian name, then?"

His laugh was more of a rumble. "Rex is my professional name. My Christian name is Albert Tillingham. Doesn't quite have the same ring to it, does it?"

Rex tore a sheet of paper from his order book and scribbled something on it. "This is the name of the fellow you want to see about work. You here by foot or car?" he asked.

"Car."

"You won't need a car if you stick around. Just go straight down Tamiami Trail and make a left on Venice Boulevard. Go about half a block and, on your left, you'll come to a park filled with trailers. There's a banner over the entrance that says Hanratty's Circus. That's us. Ask anyone there where Finn is, and they'll direct you right to him. Finn's the guy who runs it, the gaffer we call him. He's always looking for another hand. Make sure to tell him you got his name from Rex, not T. Rex. Only outsiders call me that."

Rex handed the sheet of paper to Roy.

"Thank you, sir," he said, reaching into his pants pocket. "Now, what's the damage?" Roy had the habit of holding his wallet with two hands, one hand on top and one on the bottom. To anyone watching, it would have seemed that the hand on top was trying to get the hand on the bottom to close the wallet and put it away. Money was always tight and he never spent it without thinking. He'd already planned to leave Rex more than the 10 percent tip he usually gave.

"Nah, put that away," said Rex. "Your money's no good in this place. Go get a couple of weeks of work under your belt, then come back and we'll talk about you treating me to the biggest lobster we can find around here."

Roy looked at his wallet and up at Rex. "You sure?"

"Yup, sure as can be," he said.

Roy slipped his wallet back into his pocket and held out his hand.

"Well, Mr. Rex, you've got yourself a deal. I'll do everything in my power to make good on that lobster dinner."

"Deal," said Rex, aware of how tightly Roy was gripping his hand.

Finn had signed him up right away.

He became an able roustabout: setting up the tents, feeding and cleaning up after the animals, washing Nehru and all the other elephants. Each week, he'd fill a pail with soap and water and take a large broom, the kind they use to clean hospital floors, and scrub the elephants. Had Roy viewed his life with irony, he might have seen this as retribution for all of the stains he'd left on the walls in the Bronx. But he didn't. Washing them, particularly Nehru, had become one of his most pleasurable chores.

Lately, he'd also been one of the catchers who stood under the net during the show's main attraction: the American Arroyo Brothers. The Arroyos, Leonard and Ernesto, had recently returned from a tour of duty in Vietnam. Before their act, they would climb their thirty-foot rigs to their platforms, where Ernesto would pull out an American flag from under his spandex shirt. He would unfurl it for all to see, while, across the way, Leonard would stand on his platform and salute it. The audience would go wild. It added a touch of danger and patriotism to what was already a flying trapeze act of unsurpassed daring, made beautiful by its precise timing.

The brothers would hang from their feet on facing fly bars. Leonard would grip his bar, swing forward, and then let go, as he launched forward into a somersault or two before falling, cannonball-like, but with his arms outstretched, toward Ernesto. Ernesto, his feet still wound around the catch bar, would swing forward just in time to catch Leonard in midair, where they grasped each other's elbows, slid their hands down to their wrists, and swung together in perfect synchrony, ready for another flight.

A split second could make the difference between the catch and death. Even the net beneath them was no guarantee of safety. Landing in it improperly could mean a broken neck, or worse. Should one of them topple, Roy was there to break the fall. The American Arroyo Brothers entrusted their lives to him; once, after Roy was a few minutes late for a rehearsal, Leonard grabbed him by the shoulder and said, "Hey, man, I didn't make it out of Nam alive so I could bite the big one here. You get what I'm saying?" Roy clenched his fists. Had he been holding something in his hand, he would have certainly flung it at Leonard. His face got taut and his heart pounded but he swallowed hard and said nothing. He knew enough to keep his temper in check at this place.

By now, the rain had stopped. When Roy came out of his trailer, the fourteen Pomeranians were already out practicing in their ruffled tutus, front paws waving in the air, hind legs dancing to some soundless cha-cha. Lucy, the bicycle-riding chimp, was tooling around the campgrounds on her Schwinn tricycle. The tumblers were practicing a seven-person pyramid, the one created by German high-wire-walker Karl Wallenda. This particular act, which Wallenda had created with a woman standing on a chair at the top, had a sad history. Nearly ten years earlier, while the pyramid was being performed in Detroit, one of the members faltered and three men fell to the ground. Two died of their injuries and the third, Karl Wallenda's son, was paralyzed from the waist down. The seven-person pyramid had rarely been performed since, but Dave Hanratty, the owner of the circus, wanted to include the act in the next show as a symbol that life goes on. He thought it wouldn't much hurt ticket sales, either.

Mr. Hanratty had asked Roy personally whether he would act as the catcher for that act, and that was a big deal. As Roy wandered through the campgrounds, people waved or nodded at him: the clowns, the little people, the calliope player, the elephant trainer. And of course Carmen, the aerialist, who made even the simplest sentence sound like a seduction, greeted him with a creamy, "Hey there, Mr. Catch Me If You Can."

The thought flashed through his mind: if only Gail could see him now, a well-respected man, a tan and muscular man with long hair and important responsibilities. What would she say to that?

Fourteen

"WHAT WAS THE name again?"
"Walker. Gail Walker."

The hotel clerk ran his finger down a list of names as he tapped a pencil against his forehead.

"I'm sorry, but we don't seem to have any Walkers. Is it possible it could be under another name?"

"I'm here with the CFAA Convention. Maybe it's under Mandor. Avalon Mandor," Gail said, trying to sound pleasant.

"Avalon. Interesting name," he said, twirling the eraser into the side of his cheek.

"Ahh, yes, here we go. Avalon Mandor: one assistant, plus child. Assistant—?" He looked up. "Could that be you?"

Gail hadn't quite thought of herself as an assistant. She had certainly made it sound to Thelma and Delores as if she were equal to Avalon, if not running the CFAA. But the truth was, ever since the cab pulled up to this hotel, pink as Westie's Play-Doh, with its turrets, pointed arches, and swaggering palm trees, Gail had felt overwhelmed by the size and ritziness of it all. The one time she had gone into New York City to shop at Saks Fifth Avenue, she'd felt as if she were trespassing—that Alexander's was where she really belonged. This hotel, with the men in their starchy blue uniforms reaching for her bags, calling her ma'am, and wishing her a good stay made her feel the same way— as if everyone was wondering what exactly a woman of her station thought she was doing here. So she allowed that, yes, she could very well be Avalon Mandor's assistant.

"We have a room for you and the little guy," he said, looking down at Westie. "This, uh, time of year, particularly with this, uh, convention, we get booked so far in advance. It's a little, uh, modest, but cozy. And you'll be only minutes from the beach. Room 101."

Gail took the key. "Sounds fine," she said, surprised by the sharpness in her voice. She picked up Westie in one arm, their bags in the other, and said she would make her own way to the room, thank you. The room was half in the basement and half aboveground, so that there was a band of light across the top of the window. It was dark and small, and the constant revving sound of the generator made the walls vibrate slightly. A narrow bed was covered with a pale yellow blanket, full of those little nubs of wool that indicate the blanket has been well used. Next to the bed was a fold-up canvas cot. There were no pictures on the wall, just the purple stain of something spilled or thrown. Wine perhaps. And there was a folding metal luggage rack and a scratched wooden bed stand with a gooseneck lamp.

"They've certainly put me in my place," Gail said to Westie, as she searched the wall for a switch that would turn on the gooseneck. Westie sat at the foot of the bed, hugging his stuffed turtle. Tired and hungry, he'd only

talked to Otto and Dorph since they'd left Weeki Wachee
six hours earlier.

Weeki Wachee, she thought. *I have a daughter who's a mermaid
at Weeki Wachee. And she's good. Darn good. That strange Thelma
woman with those goggle eyes kept telling me how talented my own
daughter was, as if I couldn't see for myself. Delores is growing up,
when she's not being an awful teenager. But she sure was sweet with
Westie. I was a mother at her age. Now, here I am, in Boca Raton with
a fashion magazine. Strange world.*

According to Avalon, fashion was serious business,
maybe the number one business in America. It was about
how people looked. No, about how people wanted to
look. That's what counted. *Cool* magazine told women who
they could be. If they just worked a little harder at it, had
more whatchamacallit? Oh, you know, self-esteem. Avalon
said that the models in the magazines looked the way the
readers wished could look. Ha, fat chance that would
ever happen. Of course they never told the readers that.
They made it seem as if anyone who wanted could go
out and spend one hundred dollars for a pair of sandals or
wear those zillion-dollar see-through dresses. They called
everything "a real pick-me-up": cucumber facial masks,
skin-tight blue jeans, eyebrow plucking. A real pick-me-
up. Big business, this one, and here she was, plunked down
right in the middle of it. Gail Walker has self-esteem, yes
siree, that's for sure. Otherwise, what would she be doing
in a Boca Raton resort on the eve of one of the biggest
CFAA conferences in the history of accessories?

She opened her suitcase and started to spread her

clothes out on the bed next to Westie. She was admiring her new green velvet bell-bottoms when the phone rang. She let it ring twice, so it didn't sound as if she was eager for someone to call.

"Hay-llo," she sang, eyeing her reflection in the mirror on the bathroom door. "Ah, Avalon. How's it going?" She stood up straight and sucked in her stomach.

"Terrible," said Avalon, her voice exhausted. Gail's eyes widened with concern as Avalon continued: "Can you meet me in the lobby in a half hour? We're having dinner with some advertisers. It was supposed to be the publisher and me, but her plane got delayed. The buyer is expecting more than just me. The editor will kill me if I screw this up. I know it's asking a lot, but can you come? Are you up for that?" There was silence at both ends of the phone. Both were thinking different versions of the same thing. Gail had never met an advertiser. The only person Gail had ever spoken to at the magazine was Avalon. What would she say? Would she act appropriately? Would anyone believe that she worked there or would it quickly become obvious that she was the cleaning woman?

"What about my son? What will I do with Westie?" asked Gail, trying to tamp down the anxiety in her voice.

"Oh, don't worry about him," said Avalon. "The hotel has a babysitting service. I've already arranged for them to come pick him up in fifteen minutes. They'll feed him dinner, hamburgers most likely. There'll be some other kids."

Gail wasn't sure about leaving Westie. "I don't know about that," she said. "Having him go off with strangers."

"Oh, silly," said Avalon. "All the big hotels have babysitting services. They're used to dealing with new kids. He'll be fine, honest."

Avalon could be so thoughtful sometimes.

"The people we're having dinner with are from Timex," Avalon continued. "They've been in the magazine for years. We're seeing the account executive from the Atlanta agency and two of her creatives. So we need to work the conversation around timepieces as an essential accessory. Don't worry. I hear this woman's a real hoot. Just relax and have a good time. You're a saint to do this. Okay, gotta get ready. See you in the lobby in a half hour."

Gail hung up the phone, pushed over her folded clothes, and sat down on the bed next to Westie. "I can't do this," she said aloud. At times like this, when she felt so utterly frightened and alone, she had to reach back into her history and remember other instances in her life when loneliness had echoed inside of her. After her mother died. After Roy left. After Delores left. The feeling that she couldn't go on so overwhelmed her at those times, even thinking about it set bats loose in her stomach. She pulled her hair out of her face and studied the pretty clothes laid out on the bed. She would wear the green velvet pants that were left over from a New Year's Eve fashion story. Nothing too gaudy—a white silk blouse from the same shoot and a pair of gold hoop earrings that one of the editors must have dropped under her desk.

Getting dressed up always buoyed Gail's mood. It made her feel more firmly in place. Westie would have fun playing with kids his age. He'd been around adults too much lately. She'd get through the dinner tonight. All she had to do was be natural. As Avalon said, all she had to do was relax and have a good time and not forget to mention timepieces. Everything would be fine. It made her smile to think that here she was, living proof of what a pick-me-up fashion could be. She hugged Westie, careful not to muss her hair. "Guess what, honey?" she said in as perky a voice as she could muster. "In a few minutes a nice lady from the hotel is going to pick you up and take you to play. It'll be like being with Helene, only there will be other kids there. You'll get to eat hamburgers and maybe even watch a movie. Doesn't that sound like fun?"

A ribbon of patchouli perfume floated under Westie's nose. He tried to wave it away but patchouli stays put. He hugged Dorph and stuck his thumb in his mouth, something he did only when he needed to comfort himself.

A half hour later, Gail walked into the hotel lobby, her brown platform heels clacking against the marble floor. There was Avalon, with her curly hair swept up on top of her head like a bushel of apples. She was wearing a pink-and-white-checked strapless sheath. Gail had never seen Avalon outside the office. She looked entirely different: more beautiful, more confident, and taller. She was standing with a plump woman who looked to be in her late twenties. No one had teased hair in 1973, yet here was this young woman with a voluminous flip set in place by hairspray. She wore a magenta-colored miniskirt and a plunging, pink silk blouse and apparently gave no thought to how the outfit exposed her heavy thighs and pale bosom. She was already a hoot, and she hadn't even said anything yet.

Avalon put her hand on the woman's arm. "Crystal Landy, I'd like you to meet my colleague, Gail Walker."

Crystal Landy stuck out her hand. "It is a real pleasure to meet you. I am such a fan of your magazine. Obviously, I am not one of your couture readers, but I get a kick out of what you folks in New York call style." Her wire-thin bangles made the sound of loose change as she shook Gail's hand.

Having never come upon the word "couture," Gail forced a smile as she shook Crystal's hand and searched for the right thing to say. "Style is as style does," she said, pleased to have passed that juncture.

At dinner, Gail sat between Crystal and one of the young creatives named Jeremy. Jeremy seemed to have his mind and gaze fixed on something other than the three of them, so mostly, at first, Crystal talked. She said she'd grown up in Florida, up north in Gainesville. Her family was still there, but she rarely went home. "Gainesville isn't big enough for both me and my mother." She then turned to Gail and asked about her family.

"Well, I have a daughter who's seventeen and a little boy, nearly three," Gail said. So far, so good. She asked Crystal: "And you. Are you married? Do you have kids?" Crystal's cheeks flushed and her expression turned somber. "I was engaged to be married. My fiancé got killed in Vietnam."

The table fell silent and Gail saw that Crystal didn't know where to settle her eyes. Gail said the first thing that came into mind. "Your fiancé died a hero. My husband took off in the car nearly three years ago and I haven't seen or heard from him since. Not the most courageous man I've ever met." Crystal recognized Gail's generosity, and though she found her manner odd, she made it her business to include her in the conversation for the rest of the evening. "So," she said, turning to Gail, "what accessory are you in?"

Gail was prepared for this question. "Mostly I work in footwear, you know, shoes, boots, sandals. But I also work with timepieces as they are an essential accessory." Gail glimpsed the hunk of watch on Crystal's left wrist. "I see that you are wearing a Rolodex. Now that's a statement in itself, isn't it?" she asked, pleased with herself, despite having confused the expensive watch with an address file.

"I'll say it is," Crystal said, with a little laugh. "It certainly saves wear and tear on the phone book."

Gail laughed along, although she had no idea why.

"And what's your statement?" Crystal asked. "What are you wearing that most says who you are?"

Gail did a mental inventory running from the platform shoes up to the hoop earrings. "I'd have to say that my biggest statement is about what I'm not wearing." She thought about the wedding band that she'd long ago stashed away in her dresser drawer behind her underwear. She thought about the light blue cleaning-company uniform, its white collar and dark blue insignia over the right breast; her white lace-up shoes with their thick crepe soles; the garbage pail she dragged behind her like the scent of cheap perfume. She could feel herself disappearing.

"Now my daughter, there's a girl with a statement," she said, brightening. "Every day she wears a mermaid's tail. Honestly, I think by now she's actually become a mermaid."

"That's weird. Why does she wear a mermaid tail?" asked Crystal.

Everyone at the table turned toward Gail.

"She's works at that place with the mermaid shows, Weeki Wachee."

"Holy cow, I saw them on TV," said young Jeremy, as if someone had just shaken him awake. "Didn't they do some spoof of *The Godfather*?"

"Yes, it was last Christmas," Avalon piped in. "They did a show called 'The Merfather,' and it was written about all over the place."

"My daughter had the starring role. She was Connie, Don Corleone's daughter."

"Wait, I read about her," said Crystal. "What's her name again?"

"Delores. Delores Taurus."

"Right," said Crystal. "And the papers said something about how Delores Taurus swims with the fishes."

"Mermaids—wow!" said Jeremy. "They're supposed to cause shipwrecks and floods, and cool stuff like that. They're real seductresses."

"Can you imagine that?" said Crystal, raising one eyebrow and smiling at Gail.

Avalon watched the two women talk. She saw how hard Gail was trying and that there was something about her that drew people out and made them comfortable around her. *Maybe I could help her get a real job at the magazine,* she thought. *Crazier things have happened.* After dinner, Avalon walked Gail back to her room. "You were great tonight," she said. "Thank you so much. I owe you a big one."

Gail turned red and started to laugh. "Are you kidding? I got to see my daughter, I got to see Boca Raton. You don't owe me a thing."

"I really do," said Avalon. "You're the only person at that place who's ever been kind to me, much less helped me out. I owe you a lot."

Fifteen

"THERE'S A STORM CLOUD system moving up the Gulf of Mexico. Expect torrential downpours and hurricane-force winds tomorrow. It's going to be a wet one for President Nixon's buddy Bebe Rebozo, who'll be in town for a business meeting. Rebozo was born right here in Tampa on November 17, 1912." Delores tilted her head and widened her eyes, staring directly into the camera as she spoke of Bebe Rebozo's birthday.

It was August, and she'd been on the air for four months. The show had been number one in the ratings, and, as a result, Alan Sommers had been asked to address the National Association of Broadcasters Convention in the spring. Soon after, local news programs around the country fell all over themselves to add gimmicks to their presentations and turn their reporters into personalities.

For the past week, Delores had been on the phone with Wally, the meteorologist from Miami, more than usual. He'd been teaching her about weather systems and helping her identify cold fronts and other patterns. Today Delores and Wally were watching the satellite images of white storm clouds forming over the Gulf. The clouds spun in a circle like a swirl of white angels. The photos were irresistibly beautiful, and Sommers put them on every night. With each shot, the clouds came closer and the dance got more frenetic until the sky turned the color of a sweat stain and the waves got higher and more turbulent, spitting out large puddles of foam at the shore.

Wally had explained to her that there was no accurate way to predict when and where a storm might hit. After bullying its way through the Bahamas, less than one hundred miles from the U.S. mainland, the one they were calling Hurricane Claudia whooshed up the Gulf of Mexico at forty miles per hour. By the time she made landfall on the St. Petersburg coastline, the oomph had gone out of her gusts; tides were just five feet above normal and the winds were expected to get up to only thirty to forty miles per hour by morning.

Delores was a quick study, and although someone else would write up her reports, they would use the information that she would receive from Wally. During the six o'clock news, reports started coming over the wire downgrading the storm from a Category 1 hurricane to just a rainstorm. Still, people by the coastline were advised to consider evacuating their homes should the winds pick up and the storm reverse itself.

Sommers stood in front of the AP machine as updates about Claudia clicked across the page. If only this storm would reach its potential and actually become a hurricane, this would be the kind of story that could put him on the map for good. The bigwigs in New York, the network guys, would be watching. They knew him as the guy who'd put a mermaid in a bathtub and watched his ratings go sky-high. Big deal—so he was a novelty act. This was the kind of story where you had to go with your gut, make split-second decisions in the heat of the moment, even when they flew in the face of logic.

Words raced inside Sommers's head, picking up the tempo of the newswire. Now or never. Now or never. Now or never. We need something with traction. Sizzle. Okay, we've got raging sea. Palm trees stooped by the wind. Good. Good. Work with that. Reporter's hair whipping around in wind. Nice touch. Sea spray in the face. Right. Whose face? Pretty face. Good body wouldn't hurt. A soaking wet, nice body. Brilliant. All my reporters are guys. Holy shit. I've got it. We send the water gal. Our mermaid. Jeee-zuss. Hello, Walter Cronkite! Now all we need is a hurricane.

Delores was still sitting on the edge of the bathtub, having just finished her segment, when she noticed Sommers lurking behind the cameraman. He stared at her hungrily. Not the way the other men stared at her—she'd gotten used to that. As she prepared to step out of the water and wrap herself in her robe, Sommers came forward. "Allow me," he said, holding it for her. "You were fabuloso tonight, as always."

"Thanks."

"That's some storm brewing out there. They say it could turn into a full-blown hurricane." He crossed his fingers and held them up in front of her. "Look, I won't beat around the bush. This could be a big story for me. For all of us. I need a top-notch talent to go out to Belleair Beach and cover that thing. I think you're the ticket, Miss—or do you prefer Ms.?—Taurus. I mean it's right up your alley: weather, water. Lots of water. What do you think? Big story, big chance. You get this one right, and you're playing ball with the big boys. Everyone will be watching. This could be your ticket out of the fish-tank and into the fire. Catch my drift? Or should I say, catch my draft, as it were?"

"What if I don't catch either?" Delores immediately covered her mouth with her hand. It was the first time she had talked back to him. He threw back his head and went har-har-har, baring all of his ferrety teeth. "She's beautiful and brainy, and on top of all that, she has a sense of humor. Fantastic."

Just as quickly, he stopped laughing. "So what do you say? You with me or not?"

"Yeah. Okay, I'll do it."

"Attagirl," he said. "You've got real *cojones*. Here's what you're going to do..." He laid it out: the hair, the outfit, the windy setting. "Right now, we're not exactly dealing with hurricane conditions, which is not to say that the situation can't change just like that." He snapped his fingers. "So you're going to have to goose this one a little, if you know what I mean." He called over the cameraman and the producer who would go with Delores, and Chuck Varne, the anchorman. "Use your imaginations out there. I want wind and rain and the works. Okay, guys? Let's go get us a hurricane!"

Delores changed her clothes and stepped out into the street with the others. She opened up her umbrella, expecting that the wind would eventually blow it inside out, but it didn't. She got into the front of the van next to Armando, the intern, who was driving. Doug Perry, the young up-and-coming producer, and Bo Quince, the cameraman who had been at the station longer than anyone, sat behind them. Armando turned the windshield wipers on to the highest speed and they made a scraping noise against the glass. "It's not so bad," he said. "Yeah, maybe it'll get worse," said Delores. Bo gave one of those "I've seen it all before" shrugs.

Through the crackle and static of the two-way radio on the dashboard, Sommers's voice became another presence in the car. "Where are you now?" he said. "We're just coming up onto the Watergate complex," Doug cracked. "Need anything, boss?"

"Very funny," Sommers shot back. "I need your ETA so we know when to schedule your spot."

Old Bo got on the radio and spoke clearly. "Hey, Al, Bo here. It's raining real hard, but I'd be hard-pressed to call this a hurricane. You sure you want to go live with this?"

Sommers came back: "I don't care if it's drizzling. We're looking at extreme storm conditions; that's our story. Do you read me?"

Doug again: "We read every page of you."

When Sommers answered again, it was through a mouthful of food. He chewed and swallowed his words so that no one could understand him. "Fig Newtons," said Bo and Doug simultaneously.

"Can someone explode from eating too many Fig Newtons?" asked Delores.

"If Sommers exploded, all that would be left of him

would be his pointy little shoes," said Doug. "Do you think his toes come to a point, too?"

"Has anyone ever seen his feet?" asked Delores.

"I have," said Bo. "But I really can't speak about them in mixed company."

They kept up the patter, all except Armando, who was driving at about twenty miles per hour, hugging the steering wheel so close that his chin nearly touched it. From time to time, Delores would lean over and whisper, "You're doing great," or "I think we're almost there."

As they got closer to Belleair Beach, they came upon a policeman who held up his hand in front of the car and made them stop. He poked his head into the window and said to Armando, "We're suggesting that people along this coastline evacuate, just in case." Doug flashed their press credentials. "Sure thing, be my guest," said the cop, waving them ahead. When they arrived at Belleair, the wind was blowing and the sand was shifting, and the beach was lined with curious onlookers eager to watch the storm make landfall. Bo wasted no time setting up his camera. Armando stood behind him with a strobe light, and Doug stood off to the side listening to instructions from Sommers. "Make sure you keep the camera on the girl," he ordered. "Get her close up. I want to see hair blowing, palm trees swaying. I wanna feel a hurricane. Is that too much to ask?"

Delores miked up, then looked to Doug for further cues. "Snap up your jacket," he told her. "Toss your hair a little, mess it up." Delores held her head upside down and shook it. It looked much more disheveled when she stood up.

"Nice," said Doug, who then shouted into his headphone to Sommers: "THE HAIR IS GOOD!" Next, he ordered Bo to keep the camera on Delores. "Make it seem as if she's the only one here. Get the best weather shots you can." Then he repeated to Sommers, "NICE FOAM OFF THE OCEAN, TREES ARE SWAYING. WE'RE GOOD TO GO." As he listened to Sommers, he glanced at Bo and Delores and with his free index finger made a circling motion around the side of his head and tapped his temple. It was a relief to Delores that she wasn't the only person who thought Sommers was nuts.

Doug had told her to say just what she saw. "Try to sound a little tense," he said. "Make it as dramatic as you can. If you're at a loss for words, look at me and I'll give you some cues." So this was real reporting, she thought. It was fun. Not that hard really; you just said what people told you to say. There were plenty of whitecaps, and the feverish water was beautiful, but it seemed to her like just another rainy day. But because Sommers decided it was a story, suddenly it was a story. Neat.

"Doug," she whispered, not wanting Sommers to hear. She shrugged her shoulders and held out her hands as if to say, "Now what?"

"Tell them where you are and that all of West Florida is watching with bated breath to see the course that Hurricane Claudia will take," whispered Doug. "Talk about the menacing winds and the raging sea. No, the *gusting* winds and the *roiling* sea, there you go. Don't forget the possible shoreline evacuation. The cops are out in droves. Well, at least one cop is out, but I'm sure there are others. Go ahead. You'll be great."

Back in the studio, Chuck Varne was seated at his anchor desk waiting to be cued up for the live report from Belleair Beach. Varne had been an anchorman since the early sixties and revered the masters of his craft: Edward R. Murrow, Eric Sevareid, Charles Collingwood. Grudgingly, he gave in to the antics of his contemporaries, but in small ways—the perfectly creased white linen pocket handkerchief he wore in his breast pocket each day, his wire-rimmed glasses (he drew the line at contact lenses)—he tried to carry the integrity of Murrow and his colleagues to the WGUP news desk. As he introduced Delores's live feed, he said the following: "We are about to hear our own mermaid singing, live from Belleair Beach with an update on Hurricane Claudia." The allusion to a mermaid singing came from T. S. Eliot's poem "The Love Song of J. Alfred Prufrock." Nobody would get this, nor would they care, thought Varne. But it was his little joke on all of them and having the last laugh was often what got him through the day.

Everyone in the studio grew silent as they watched Delores begin her report: "We're out here at Belleair Beach. All of West Florida is watching with bated breath to see the course that Hurricane Claudia will take." She sounded a little like a kid in a school play, but with some urging from Doug, she was able to inject more life into her voice. "Right now, the winds are gusting and the sea is roiling." She did the thing she did with her eyes, and Doug winked at her. Of course she had no idea Sommers had just said into his ear: "The girl's doing good. She's not as dumb as she looks."

Delores continued with animation: "The cops are out in

droves and are urging folks along shoreline communities
to evacuate. The water is a beautiful greenish black..."

Just then, she glimpsed something out of the corner of
her eye. It was a little boy playing in the surf. Doug started
making swirling motions with his hands urging her to
quicken the pace. She picked up again. "The waves are
slamming into the shore, and all around me you can see..."
Again, she noticed something out of the corner of her eye.
The boy was gone, and in his place was a grown man waving his arms, shouting, and running into the water. Others
were running behind him. She knew immediately that the
boy had been swept away by a wave. Without thinking,
Delores threw off her slicker and mike and ran into the water. She swam against the tide and ducked under the waves.

No one in the studio had any idea what was going on.
For a few moments they stared dumbly at the blank screen,
then Sommers began repeating, "Ohmygod, ohmygod."
Only Chuck had the presence of mind to say, *"Something has
happened at Belleair Beach. Stay with us as this drama unfolds."*

Doug shouted into Chuck's earpiece: "She's in the water.
She's gone after some kid who's drowning. She's in the water. We'll keep the camera on her."

Chuck stiffened perceptibly. *"Ladies and gentlemen, we have
an extraordinary situation on our hands. Our reporter has gone in the
ocean to rescue a young child who's been swept out to sea..."*

The air roared into the empty mike. A lurching camera
stayed on Delores as she swam toward what might have
been the speck of a boy.

"She appears to be swimming against the tide..." Chuck continued.

The riptide tore at her, but she knew enough not to fight it and stayed beneath the waves where it was less chaotic. Despite the stinging salt, she was able to keep her eyes open. "Swim, Westie, swim." The words rushed through her and filled her with calm. She'd swum out far enough to where the waves were quiet. In the distance, she could make out the head of the little boy. He had red hair, thatches of which would appear, then disappear, in the course of the currents.

"She is swimming toward something. I can't quite make it out, but it could be the young child..."

The water was almost tranquil out here. She swam until she could grab the boy under his chin with her right hand. Then she reached across his chest with her left hand and secured her hold under his right armpit. She hadn't done this cross-chest carry since she learned it in the Bronx, yet she felt as if she'd been practicing every day. The boy's shirt rode up on him, and she could feel his tiny ribs in the palm of her hand. "Swim, Westie," she said in his ear. "Stay with me and keep swimming." She could hear the boy crying, so she knew that he was conscious. She did the scissors kick and followed the pull of the tide, knowing that at some point it would carry her close to shore.

"She appears to have reached the child..."

She stayed above the water, the boy firmly in her grasp.

"...and now she is pulling him back to shore..."

She hadn't realized how tired she was until they finally reached the shore. When she tried to stand, her legs went wobbly underneath her.

"She's collapsed on the sand..."

People who'd been watching from the shore rushed forward to help her.

"*. . . people are coming from everywhere to try and help her. She still has the child in her grasp. Incredible.*"

Armando remembered that they kept an old gray blanket in the back of the van, which they used to wrap the lighting equipment. He ran and got it and made a bundle of the two of them.

"*She must be freezing and in shock. Someone has just wrapped her and the child in a blanket . . .*"

Water streaked across everyone's face. Tears, saltwater—who could tell the difference? The boy's father squatted beside Delores and hugged her. From the way his lips tightened as he spoke, it was clear how shaken and grateful he was, but, with the waves and wind, it was hard to hear him.

"*. . . the man crouching next to the two of them appears to be the little boy's father. We can't make out what he's saying, but clearly he is overcome with emotion at what has just transpired here.*"

The boy reached out to the man, and he lifted him into his arms. With the child nuzzled into his chest, the father rushed off away from the crowd before Doug could get his name and age.

"*We don't know the name of the child or his father, and we may never know who they are. But they will certainly never forget the name Delores Taurus.*"

For a man who prided himself on his unflappability, Chuck was visibly moved. Anyone with a color TV would notice the flush in his cheeks. The tightness in his throat was there for all to hear.

"*This is one of those moments in live television when even those of us who've seen it all are rendered speechless. I am . . . well, I am overwhelmed. We'll be back to you in a minute with more about Hurricane Claudia.*"

When the red light on the camera was off, Armando helped Delores to her feet, draping the blanket around her shoulders. He put his hand on the small of her back and helped her to the van. She lay on the floor in the back of the van, and he sat down next to her. "You need to get into something dry," he said, pulling off the blue Disney World sweatshirt he was wearing underneath his rain jacket. "Here, put this on, and wear the blanket around your waist."

His gesture brought her back to where she was, and even made her smile. "You're always giving me your clothes," she said.

"Don't you think it's better that way than the other way around? I'll wait outside while you change."

"Holy shit," cried Doug. "That was unbelievable. And we got it all on tape." Then the weight of it all sank in.

On the way back to the studio, no one spoke for a long while. Then Doug started: "Can you imagine Sommers hopping up and down in those little shoes the whole time?" he said. "He must have been going out of his mind. I'll bet you any amount of money that I know what he'll say to Delores when we get back." He mimicked Sommers's rat-a-tat delivery: "Delores, sweetie, that was magnificent. MAGNIFICENT! They'll love this in New York. It was an inspired idea, genius really, me sending you out there. You must admit."

They all laughed except for Bo. He stared out the

window as if he hadn't heard a thing. "I thought you were a goner. You and that poor little boy, I swear to God, I really didn't think you'd make it." The van got quiet again, but for the constant thud of the rain. Delores was next to Armando in the front seat. He studied her face and noticed her flinch at the mention of the boy. He reached over and squeezed her hand, a gentle, quick squeeze. His hand was warm and she found his touch comforting. She was filled with a longing to curl herself around him. She crossed her arms and hugged her shoulders, determined to resist the urge.

When they finally made it back to the studio, Delores held the blanket tightly around her, aware of what a sight she was with her tangled wet hair, bare feet, and oversized Mickey Mouse sweatshirt. They rode the elevator to the eighth floor, and when the doors opened, Sommers and Chuck were standing there, waiting for them. Chuck was still in his suit because he was always in his suit. He reached out his hand to shake Delores's hand, but she was holding on to her blanket with both hands. So he put his hands in his pockets and spoke in his perfectly modulated tones. "You certainly put on quite a show out there, young lady," he said. "Your courage and determination are startling."

Sommers was dwarfed behind him, wearing a T-shirt and a pair of blue jeans. Delores could see the tension in his face from the way his eyebrows bounced up and down. He reached out and awkwardly squeezed Delores's arm. In her bare feet, she was the same height as he was. "I'm so sorry to have put you through that," he said, without his normal ebullience. "You had me going, Miss Taurus. I was scared, I gotta tell you. Really scared." His voice filled with emotion, and he turned away from her. Through his cotton T-shirt, Delores could see how small and close together his shoulder blades were, like folded butterfly wings. It didn't make her like him any better, but she saw how vulnerable he was. He continued: "But you were tremendous out there." Doug rolled his eyes as if to say, "Here we go!" Sommers went on: "I know that I can be a bit . . . well, you know how I can be. But you really were tremendous. And to say that you'll wow New York is an understatement. This is just the beginning for you."

Delores was too tired to think about beginnings. All she could think about was Westie and Thelma and the silky quiet waters of the Springs. The storm wasn't due to hit hard until morning, plenty of time for her to get home. She turned to Armando. "Do you think you could drive me back to Weeki Wachee?" she asked. Sommers nodded and gave them a thumbs-up.

As soon as they got into the van, Delores leaned against Armando and fell asleep. He thought about what he'd have done had he been in her place earlier that evening, and about how much the inside of the van smelled like the sea.

Lifeguards at beaches everywhere perform acts like this one all the time, rescuing the lost and reckless, mostly in total anonymity. But live TV reporting was still a new phenomenon, and local stations would cover supermarket openings and greased-pig-catching contests just to show off their new equipment. So the story of the little boy saved by the TV weathergirl instantly became a big one, partly because of the inherent drama playing out on the screen, but mostly because the hero was a girl, and not just any girl, but Florida's favorite mermaid.

Later, the story would take on its own mythology. Doug would tell the story with an emphasis on his own coolness under fire and claim that Sommers had squealed to Delores: "That was magnificent. Magnificent!" Chuck Varne would liken it to Murrow's reporting at Trafalgar Square, with the bombs dropping and the sirens wailing. And Sommers would tell it as if he had directed an epic: the winds had been raging at seventy-five miles an hour; the tides had been ten feet high; the boy had been half dead.

But what really happened was true enough to make its way into living rooms across the country.

Sixteen

AVE HANRATTY WAS NO STRANGER to hurricanes, having lived through the big one in '35. He understood that hurricanes were bad news for anyone in their way and that circuses were particularly vulnerable. There are animals to shelter and equipment to tether. Circuses are also filled with people for whom danger is commonplace. Try telling the sword-swallower or the guy who gets shot out of a cannon that a storm has the power to uproot a tree or whisk the roof off a house. They'll take it as a dare. Watch me ride the wind, they'll say, or roll over it in a barrel. Then there were the trailers. He never liked to be inside a trailer when the winds came up. It made the Tilt-A-Whirl feel like a ride in a kiddie car. And the racket—the creaking, banging, and rattling of it all.

Hanratty was also a man who understood how to protect his investment and minimize his losses, and, to that end, he'd made an arrangement with Rex three years earlier. He would pay for installing awnings on all the windows and would cover his insurance bills if Rex would let the troupe take shelter in the Giant Café whenever the wind or rain threatened to get out of hand. That way, everyone would be under one roof and he could keep an eye on them. The café also had a telephone and a small television set, which was more than anyone in the circus other than Hanratty had.

A somber, heavyset man with jowls that almost fell off his face, he always wore a hat and a jacket, even on the hottest days, because he had come of age at a time when that's how gentlemen of distinction dressed. The irony that he was in a profession requiring everyone around him to be half nude most of the time didn't escape him. If anything, it added to the aura of power and respect that he cultivated. He'd made a bundle in the circus business, starting up in the Florida Panhandle with only a cart and some unfortunate freaks—the latter a fact now obliterated from his biography and, almost as successfully, from his memory.

He had a knack for knowing what would entertain people and hold their attention and a talent for hiring people whose nerve and prowess knew no bounds. From the beginning, he never mingled with his workers. They knew nothing about him other than that he was enormously wealthy, and that, while they were in his employ, he virtually owned them. That was enough so that on the afternoon before Hurricane Claudia was scheduled to blow into town, they packed up what valuables they had and shut down their trailers and, with Lucy the chimp in hand, headed to the Giant Café, just as Hanratty had ordered them to do.

With the jalousies closed and the awnings snapped into place, the café was stifling. The trainers had, only hours earlier, led their elephants and lions into the animal houses,

and their pungent odors mixed with the others: the cam-
phor smell of the liniment that the jugglers smoothed into
their joints; the cloying fragrance of the French cologne
that Carmen, the aerialist, doused on herself each morning; the tang of freshly brewing coffee and the bubbling of
stale vegetable fat. It was a concoction potent enough to
make your eyes water and your stomach seize up.

Hanratty removed his hat but kept his jacket buttoned.
He waited until the troupe settled down, then stood up in
front of the café and clinked a water glass with a teaspoon.
"Ladies and gentlemen, I am sorry for the disruption," he
said, "but according to the bulletins from the National
Weather Service, we've got one doozy of a storm headed
our way, and I have deemed it wiser for us to stick it out for
the time being inside these walls of concrete. Mr. Rex has
been kind enough to offer up some free pie and coffee for
everyone, so let's all settle in and pray for the best."
Hanratty bowed his head as if to lead the group in a moment of silence, but before anyone could say, "In the name
of . . . ," Sichey the clown was balancing a spoon on his
nose and Leonard Arroyo had sprung into a handstand on
one of the tables.

Roy sat quietly in the back of the café, scraping the
meringue off the top of his pie and forking the sweet
lemon filling into his mouth. He never understood putting
things on top of food. Food was food; why try to fancy it
up with whipped cream or some ridiculous French gravy?
Gail had been forever slapping a scoop of Breyers vanilla
on a slice of apple pie and calling it pie à la mode. It didn't
make anything different. The apple pie was still apple pie;

they were still who they were. That whole French bit
drove him nuts back then. He started to get angry even
thinking about it. So he quickly turned his mind to the free
pie and had a second helping.

As the afternoon drew on, the troupe grew quieter, sated
by pie, heat, and the narrow confines of the place. From
time to time, one of them would put his head down on the
table and nod off for a while. Rex sat off in a corner with
the midgets, and they passed the time by telling each
other jokes. Even Lucy, who had been running up and
down the café, throwing her arms around people and grin-
ning her mocking smiley faces, had settled down in the lap
of her trainer. It left them with little to do other than listen
to the reports from the radio or watch the quivering black-
and-white pictures on the television.

Roy was walking around, stretching his legs, when he
chanced to look up and see what was happening on the
screen. It seemed as if some reporter had just run into
the ocean. This was more interesting than anything he'd
seen all afternoon, and he moved closer to the television.
The sound of nothing but the microphone soaking up the
wind seemed to catch everyone's attention. Then the anchorman, Chuck Varne, said something about the reporter
jumping into the water to save a little boy. The camera
seemed to be careening. This wasn't the kind of slick camera work they'd gotten used to seeing on the news; it made
Roy a little seasick to watch.

For a while all you could see on the screen was the gray
of the water until the image of a girl, her arm around a
young boy, started to come into focus. Roy's heart jumped.

He turned away from the screen and blinked a few times,
as if his eyes were playing tricks on him. But now the picture of the girl and boy was perfectly sharp. His eyes were
telling him the truth. Roy didn't know what to do: shout
out; touch his fingers to the screen; keep quiet. For now, he
would sit with the others and watch.

Hanratty moved closer to the TV set and turned up the
sound. When, at last, Chuck Varne said something about
"WGUP's own Delores Taurus," he pulled out a pen from
his vest pocket and wrote something down on a paper
napkin. Hanratty spoke to no one in particular. "Torres.
Delores Torres," he said, pronouncing it with a Spanish accent. "I've seen her before. The girl's a natural." Roy came
close to correcting him. *Walker,* he started to say, *her name's
Delores Walker.* But he stopped himself.

Up until now, life had been pretty cut-and-dried for
Roy. He'd married young, he'd had some children; it didn't
work out and so he left. Boom, boom, boom, nothing complicated about it. He had no tolerance for complications or
for the kind of people who allowed them to dominate their
lives. So far, this philosophy—if you could call it that—
had worked just fine. He had a good job; he was well liked.
But even he had to admit that seeing Delores on television
plunged him headfirst into tangled thoughts.

They stayed at the café through the night until early the
next morning, while the rain came down like nails and the
wind screamed. Whenever the noise became particularly
loud, Lucy would screech back as if she were answering
some primal taunt. Nobody got much sleep. When the pie
ran out in the middle of the night, Rex whipped up some

oatmeal and another batch of coffee that tasted so bitter that the clowns took to spitting it at each other. Soon it became a game of who could spit the farthest, and the others became engaged. It wasn't a fair contest really, because Lola Lava Lips, the fire-eater, had a certain advantage. At daybreak, Carmen, the aerialist, started to sing "Here Comes the Sun." Rex joined in with his hollow bassoon voice. The midgets with their cupid voices chimed in, as did Lava Lips, though her voice was so hoarse she could barely be heard. By and by everyone was singing as they went through some of their favorite Beatles' songs: "Help!" "Rocky Raccoon," "Yesterday." Even Hanratty was tapping his fingers on the table and mouthing the chorus of "Yellow Submarine." Only Roy sat silent, chewing the end of a straw and staring into space. When the singing was finished, Carmen came over to him. "Hey, sugar face, you're some glum bunny today. One of the cats got your tongue?"

"No, I guess I'm just tired is all," he answered.

"Well, soon we'll get out of this rathole and you can give those pretty li'l pecs of yours a workout. Buck up," she said, giving his arm a little punch. She walked off, swaying her hips in a way that seemed odd to Roy for this hour of the morning.

News from the television said that the storm was dying down and moving out to the Gulf of Mexico. Hanratty stood up, still in his jacket, and banged a spoon on a glass again. "Decorum. Please, can we have some decorum? We can leave here now, but please be careful when returning to your quarters. Also, keep the animals tied up or caged at all times until the sounds are less extreme and we are sure they will not be startled and try and break away. You've been very cooperative, and I appreciate your patience." Hanratty always spoke to them as if he was addressing a group of tax lawyers. Nonetheless, his words brought them to their feet. They hooted and hollered and bolted out the door as fast as they could, except for Roy who stayed seated at his table.

When the room was clear, Rex came over. "What a mess," he said, looking at the dirty dishes on and under the tables. There was lemon meringue everywhere, and there were puddles of coffee from the spitting contest. "It looks as if the humans were caged and Lucy and her family took over the place."

"Yeah, it really is a mess," said Roy, looking around for the first time. "Tell you what, Rex, I'll help you clean the place up if you'll give me some advice."

"Sounds like a fair trade to me," said Rex, pulling up a chair next to Roy. Rex might as well have been sitting on a toadstool. His knees nearly covered his face, and he had to hunch over to listen to what Roy had to say.

Roy told him everything: about how bad things had been at home and how he'd felt he'd go crazy if he stayed; how he left his wife and two kids; how he drove south and now was starting all over. He told him about seeing Delores on television the night before and how he saw, for the first time, that they had some connection. A physical connection was how he saw it. He would have done the same thing—swum against a riptide—if he'd had to. She had his strength; or maybe he had hers. He wondered if he should try to get in touch with her.

"I haven't contacted her or anyone in my family in more than two years," he said. "Now, to come out of the blue just like that because suddenly she's on TV. I don't know. It seems wrong. Like I'm trying to use her or something. Besides, what... lemme see, how old is she now?" Roy started counting backward on his fingers. "What seventeen-year-old girl whose father walked out on the family would even want to see him again? No, never mind, it's not even a question. I'm going to leave it alone. That's that. Okay, Rex, let's clean this pigsty up. And I'd really appreciate it if we could leave this conversation between us." Roy stood up.

Rex put his hand on Roy's arm and pushed him back into his seat. "Whoa, hang on there one minute. What you did was very human. Heartless maybe, but human. Still, your child will always be your child. If you are lucky enough to have someone in this world that is of your blood..." Rex turned away without finishing that sentence. "You let her get away one time. Maybe that was a mistake and maybe she won't forgive you for it. But whoever's watching over you clearly wanted you to meet up with her a second time. I'm expecting there won't be a third chance. I guess that's all I have to say."

The two men stood and started cleaning the walls and floor in silence. When Roy was finished, he went over and shook Rex's hand.

"Thanks, pal," he said. "I'll let you know what happens."

Rex smiled his shy, broad smile. "Roy Taurus, aay?"

* * *

The previous day, Thelma Foote had been at her desk paying bills. The constant downpour had begun to make everything soggy. Even the invoices felt heavy and damp. As she studied the bills, she realized that although Delores was drawing more crowds to the park than they'd had in recent years, they were barely turning a profit: the pump needed replacing, the carpet in the theater was getting mildewed. It was always something at a place like this.

Weeki Wachee was small, and it relied on real live people for its entertainment. Maybe that was starting to be a problem. Over in Orlando, the Disney people were packing them in, using all the technical gizmos and wizardry known to man. And they had already bought up nearly forty-three square miles of cattle-grazing country—twice the size of Manhattan, or so she'd heard. How could little Weeki Wachee begin to compete? Not thinking clearly, she wrote out a check to the Florida Power and Light Company calling it the "Florida Lower and Plight Company." Funny slip, she thought, as she crumpled up the check and tossed it across the room into the trash can. *Damn, missed.* She used to be an ace shooter—and not bad at kickball or baseball, either.

She thought about the land that Disney was chewing up. That used to be land that couldn't be measured in miles. The pine forests and swamps had gone on and on, without anyone laying claim to them. It had been hard to imagine that it would ever be different until perfect concrete squares started replacing those familiar patches of land, and then shopping malls with more rug stores and discount shoe outlets than anyone could possibly need started sprouting up everywhere. But because she was used to being the oldest person around, Thelma tried not to tell stories that began, "When I was younger..."

No one can say I'm not modern, she thought, as she wrote out checks to *Cosmopolitan* and *Mademoiselle*, renewing the girls' subscriptions for another year. Lord knows, she'd relaxed her views on sex, telling herself, What do you expect when you put a bunch of young women in provocative outfits and have them waggle their tails underwater? She could always pretty much tell which of her girls were having sex and which were not. She knew that Blonde Sheila and the preacher were doing it like bunnies every chance they had, but what could she do? Unless one of her girls got pregnant, it was really not her business.

She even understood the commercial value of what Sommers was trying to do. Weather was a safe story involving no controversy. These days, with the whole Watergate shebang going on, it was one of the few things you could talk about without getting into a fight. Sure, having a young girl in a bathtub wearing a scanty costume was tawdry, but crassness seemed to be in vogue. Besides, it got people's minds off the really cynical stuff that was going on in Washington. She doubted that anyone gave her credit for understanding all that.

Damn, she was in a cross mood today. Clearly she wasn't the only one. Why else would the DJ on the radio station she was listening to have played "In the Wee Small Hours of the Morning" at five in the afternoon?

The next song he put on was one that she really liked: Janis Joplin, singing "Piece of My Heart." Thelma knew all the lyrics and belted them out along with the radio. She felt she had an affinity with Janis, maybe because she seemed like someone whom the world judged from the outside, never giving her inner self much of a chance. Thelma had taken it very hard when Janis died at twenty-seven.

When Thelma finished singing along, she checked her watch. Five fifty-eight—time for the six o'clock news. She switched off the radio and turned on the television, continuing with her check writing. As soon as she heard the teaser, "Live, from Belleair Beach, our weathergirl, Delores Taurus, will bring you the latest on Hurricane Claudia," she put down her pen. *Now he's gone too far,* she thought, dialing up Sommers on his private line.

"What the hell are you doing, sending her out on a story like that?" she shouted.

Sommers had Doug Perry, the producer, on the other line and was trying to have two conversations at once.

"It's a huge story," he said. "She was the perfect choice. Doug—the trees, the wind. Please!"

"She's not a reporter, Mr. S. She's not even a weathergirl."

"You're overreacting. No, not you, Doug. Mess the hair a little more."

"You can't go putting people at risk like this."

"Don't be ridiculous, she'll be fine. She's not as dumb as she looks."

Thelma was still on the line when Delores dropped her microphone and jumped into the ocean. "Oh Christ. You are a jackass!" she screamed down the phone at him. "Have you lost your mind?"

"Come in on her as close as you can," Sommers said to Doug. Then, to Thelma: "You wouldn't know a hot news story if it came up and licked you in the face, would you, Miss F.? Doug, where the hell is the kid? Find the kid!"

There was something frantic in his voice that made Thelma even more furious.

"I don't care if you get higher ratings than *All in the Family*. If one hair on that child's body is harmed, I promise you I will sue you and that ridiculous organization that calls itself a television station for every penny you're probably not worth."

"I don't see her," said Sommers, his voice getting small. "Where the hell is she? Oh my God, Miss F., I don't see her, do you?"

They both sat silently, staring at the blank screen. Sommers was the first to spot her. "Oh thank God, there she is." Then he shouted to Doug: "That's it! Keep it on the girl and on the kid. Come on in with them. That's it! That's it!"

Thelma watched as Delores and the boy came onto the screen. Just as the camera remained focused on Delores and the boy, so would she. She would stare at Delores until she was safely back to shore, holding the phone in one hand while pressing her other hand to the television screen.

She could hear Sommers breathing on the other end of the line—heavy, uneven huffs. They were both quiet as Delores swam her last strokes and stumbled to shore. Only when Armando wrapped the blanket around them did Sommers speak again. "How about that? Nice work, Doug."

"All I can say is, thank heaven they're all right," said Thelma.

"I'll be honest, I was sweating bullets over here," said Sommers. "Sometimes I think I really am a jackass. But it worked out okay."

"What if it hadn't?"

"A bridge we don't have to cross," he said. "Now our problem is that we have a gold mine on our hands. Do you understand that? I'm talking bigger than Mark Spitz."

"Mark Spitz?" Thelma said, walking around in tiny circles.

"Yes, I'm telling you, she is going to be huge."

Weeki Wachee at night looks as if the light of imagination has been switched off. Without the sun, the red bougainvilleas and lavender water hyacinths go mute. The amphitheater and outdoor pavilions are mere shadows, and even the clear, bottomless Springs can be overlooked as a puddle, a pond, maybe. Only the lamp in Thelma's office was visible from the highway, and, with all the rain falling that night, it appeared as a dim twinkle at best. Unless you knew it was there, right after the stoplight, you'd just keep driving down the road.

Sommers had said that Delores and Armando were heading back to the park. Thelma worried that Armando would miss the turn, that he'd get lost and panic, and was there anything worse than a frightened young boy driving around in a downpour like this? She'd best put on her rain boots and poncho and wait outside for them. It was the sensible thing to do.

For the next half hour, Thelma stood in front of the park, the wind blowing so hard that occasionally she had to hold on to a telephone pole to right herself. Rain seeped through her clothes and soaked her to the skin. The water in her boots was almost at her ankles. She thought of emptying them, but why bother? They would fill right up again, anyway.

Twice, cars pulled over to the side of the road. The first time, a man who was riding with a tiny dog in his lap asked her, "Little lady, are you in some kind of trouble?" When she said, "Oh no, I'm perfectly fine," he had answered: "Standing out here on a night like this don't seem so fine to me. Unless you is looking to get yourself killed." The second time, a woman with two identical girls in the backseat wanted to know if she needed a lift. "No, thank you," said Thelma. "I'm just waiting for someone." The woman didn't seem to hear her. "There's room for one more—where do you need to get?" she asked. Four eyes, round and bright as soup-can lids, shone at her from behind the woman. "That's okay." Thelma spoke louder. "I'm just waiting for someone." The woman shouted back, "Suit yourself, then," and drove away, the four eyes peering out the back window.

When Thelma finally spotted the WGUP van lumbering down the highway, she began waving her arms and ran onto the shoulder of the road. She even thought to take the hood down on her poncho so that Delores and Armando would recognize her. The van slowed down. She saw Armando's scared, tired face, and it struck her that maybe Florida shouldn't issue driver's licenses to anyone this young. She ran ahead of them into the parking lot to make sure that he found his way. When Delores got out of the car, barefoot and with salt caked on her face, Thelma had the unaccustomed notion to reach out and hug her.

She didn't, of course. "You need to go sit in the hot room and get the chill out of your bones," she said to Delores. "And you, young man," she said, shouting through the wind. "There's no way you're driving back to Tampa in this mess. You'll stay the night here. I'll put you up on the couch in my office." As they ran into the administration building, she noticed the thin frame on the boy and thought how easily he'd fit into one of her T-shirts and a pair of sweatpants. "I'll get a blanket and some sheets," she said, when they got inside. "Now get out of those soaking clothes before you catch your death of cold." Giving orders had restored Thelma's sense of order and authority. She understood those feelings.

Later that night, Thelma lay awake listening to the haranguing sounds of Hurricane Claudia. She thought about all that had happened that day and how frightened she had been. She thought she had constructed her life in such a way as to seal off fright. She wiggled her toes against the soft, clean sheets and luxuriated in the warmth and dryness of her flannel pajamas. She thought about Delores and all of her girls safe and asleep under this one roof. From some place inside her, she couldn't say where, she heard a familiar raspy voice. "Take it," it said. "Take another little piece of my heart."

Seventeen

ELORES BARELY HAD THE ENERGY to wash the salt off her face and brush her teeth. Even then, as she crawled under her blankets, she was engulfed by the taste and smell of the ocean, and by the time she fell into sleep, wrestling with her sheets, she was back in the water, fighting the currents.

Often when Delores swam in the Springs, a dolphin or two would shoot by her. Usually they came close enough so she could see a round black eye appraising her. Once, her fingers brushed up against one of the dolphins, and though it was only for a moment, she never forgot how strong and smooth it felt, like marble. There was life in that dolphin's eye and a hint of humor in its upturned smile line. If an animal can be said to be taunting, even flirtatious, then that dolphin was up there as one of nature's biggest teases. Delores often fantasized about what it would be like to grab hold of a dolphin's dorsal fin and hitch a ride. There was one dolphin that she thought she recognized as a regular, and she felt that it wasn't beyond reason to think that, one day, he'd just sidle up next to her and wait for her to hop on.

That night, as she bucked the waves in her sleep, she

was visited by a gentler dream. She was on the back of a dolphin, the one she thought she knew. She was holding on to his dorsal fin and they were flying through the water faster than the birds overhead. They were heading up the coast to New York to find Westie. She was aware of being propelled through the water by a force that wasn't her own. It felt like the tumbling-into-nowhere sensation that often accompanies dreams. It made her woozy, yet she gave herself up to it with relief and joy. She wished it would never stop, but abruptly it did. The dolphin disappeared, and when she went in search of him, all she found in the muck and tangle of seaweed was a small fish that glimmered like tinsel. She scooped it into her hands and held it to her chest. The fish wriggled and shimmied but she managed to keep it close. Eventually, the fish got smaller and smaller until there was nothing left of it but some drops of water. She kept trying to conjure up the dolphin again, but all her subconscious would deliver was a few grains of wet sand. When she woke up the next morning, she felt sad, but couldn't put a finger on the source of it. "You had quite a tussle going on there last night," Molly said to her. "What were you dreaming about?"

Delores shrugged. "You know. The usual water stuff."

By breakfast that morning, everyone knew about Delores's rescue of the boy. Someone had taped the front page of the *Tampa Tribune* on the door to the dining room. The headline, "Local Weathergirl in Heroic Rescue," was circled in red Magic Marker. The cook, a bulbous man named Curtis Braunschweiger, usually served grits and potatoes for breakfast. On this morning, he went out of his way to whip up a batch of pancakes with blueberry syrup to honor the occasion. Just before she was to sit down to breakfast, Delores got called into Thelma's office. Her mother was on the phone.

This time, her "hello" wasn't as bouncy as usual. "I just read about you in the *Daily News*," her mother said. "There's a picture and everything, although it's hard to tell if it's really you."

"It's me," said Delores.

"I'm not sure it was the smartest thing you've ever done, but it certainly sounded brave," said her mother. Then she dropped her voice. "Hon, I hate to rain on your parade. But it's about Helene. She's gone. She died two days ago. Up until three weeks ago, she was still taking care of Westie. Then a bunch of us in the building took turns caring for her. Frail as she was, she was quite the fighter. And remember the big globe in her living room? Westie loved to play with that thing. It's next to our TV set now. Oh my. Poor Helene. Poor Westie. And me? I'm up a creek here, trying to find someone to take care of him."

Delores heard her mother's voice getting tight, as if she might cry.

"Mom, how's Westie? Does he know what happened?"

"He knows Helene is gone forever. But, then again, so is everyone else in his life so it's not exactly new to him."

Delores hated when her mother jabbed at her like this.

"Gee, I wish there was something I could do." The words tasted like sour milk even as she spoke them.

"There's not much you can do, unless you know someone who's available for babysitting."

Delores said nothing.

Her mother continued: "Never a dull moment around here, I'll say that."

"Tell Westie that I love him and I'll see him soon, okay?" said Delores.

"Sure, I will. He's downstairs with the Hellers today. They have a girl around his age. We'll see. Okay, bye, hon."

"Bye, Mom." Delores hung up feeling guilty and annoyed at the same time. Poor Westie, poor Helene. She even felt bad for her mother, though she certainly had rained on her parade.

Delores came back to the dining room where she found that Blonde Sheila had saved her a place at the table. "He was watching you last night," said Blonde Sheila, rolling her eyes toward the heavens. "Who was watching me?" asked Delores, looking around the room. "You know," said Sheila, still staring skyward. "Him." Sheila had taken to wearing muumuus. Her body was sacrosanct, she said, a gift not to be squandered. Behind her back, Scary Sheila had told the others: "Sacrosanct, my ass. Her body is preggers."

Lester sat on Delores's other side. "Were you scared?" he whispered.

"Everything happened so fast, I didn't have time to be scared."

"In my opinion, it was a very brave thing to do," he said with a creak in his voice. "I don't know for sure, but it's not the kind of thing most people would do. I don't even know if I could have done it. My father says it's the most courageous thing he's ever seen a girl do."

"I guess no one knows how they'll act until something

happens," said Delores. "You don't think about being brave, or anything like that. You just do what you do."

Lester considered her words and was about to say something else, when Helen stood on her chair and started singing "For She's a Jolly Good Fellow." The others joined in, except for Sharlene and Adrienne, who came into the dining room together midsong. On this morning, they looked particularly funereal. Sharlene's hair was still wet from the shower. She'd taken to walking a few steps behind Adrienne, her shoulders slumped and head bowed as if her hair were leading the way. Adrienne wore a pair of old green thongs that slapped against the floor. There was a budding cold sore on the corner of her mouth. Neither of them even looked at Delores.

Adrienne rarely looked at anyone. When she first confided to Delores about her twirling debacle, she had said: "Once people laugh at you to your face, you always think that they're laughing at you behind your back. It's hard not to feel ridiculous." Delores had wanted to answer, "I know what you mean. I always feel at the verge of being found out." But those were during the days when she was still presenting herself as the daughter of entertainment professionals with "a little bit of French" in her, so she let Adrienne bare her humiliation and said nothing. It made Adrienne wary of Delores, since she assumed that her silence was a form of judgment.

Now things were even worse. Delores was popular, and it had been Adrienne's experience that the popular ones judged the harshest. It had been the girls in the Pep club who had come up with that dreadful nickname "Sparky" in the first place. If Adrienne wasn't going to acknowledge Delores, neither was Sharlene. The two of them sat in a corner of the dining room savoring their grudges and pancakes.

Thelma Foote stood with the rest of them and sang "For She's a Jolly Good Fellow." That morning, she'd been awakened by a phone call. She'd answered with an irritated "Thelma Foote here." A male voice had said, "My name's Roy Walker. I'm Delores's father." Her first thought had been: *oh no, not another one.* "What can I do for you?" she'd asked. But this wasn't the time to bring up Delores's father.

She continued singing with the rest of them, and when they finished, she clapped her hands to get their attention. "Okay, first a hand for cook Braunschweiger for these delectable pancakes." They all clapped, and Helen put two fingers in her mouth and made a loud, cheepy whistle. "And a big hand for Delores Taurus, whose Weeki Wachee spirit and bravery last night made us all so proud." Everyone clapped again except for Adrienne and Sharlene. "Oh, and let's not forget Delores's partner in crime, Armando Lozano."

Armando was still wearing the T-shirt and sweatpants that Thelma had given him the night before. His silky hair was shaggy and unkempt, and he looked around the room with the squinty eyes of someone just awakened from sleep. "Armando is an intern at WGUP," Thelma continued. "He was with Delores through her whole ordeal and drove her back here late last night. Although he is not a merman per se, he seems to me to be of that ilk. So let's make him welcome here, shall we?" The girls regarded Armando with nods and assessing eyes. He had full, kissable lips and smooth doe-colored skin. He was cute, and it was rare for a cute guy to be among them. Lester noticed the smile that passed between Armando and Delores. It was a little thing, but he saw how it made Delores blush, and how afterward, she looked down at the floor. Lester studied Armando. He had a nice complexion; that was for sure. But he had skinny arms and a narrow chest, and it gave him a stab of pleasure to think that Armando would never be able to hold his breath for two minutes underwater.

"There's one more thing," continued Thelma. "Because of Hurricane Claudia, the park is closed today. That means your time is your own. There'll be no chores and no practice." The girls banged their spoons against their glasses and let out cheers of "Yay, Claudia!"

Thelma folded her arms, put one foot against the wall, and leaned back. She was incapable of watching her girls and Lester without spotting areas that could use improvement. Sharlene had to do something with that hair. Lester's face was peeling from too much sun. Blonde Sheila still had that damn nun smile on her face and the demeanor of someone preoccupied with noble thoughts. Thelma preferred the old potty-mouthed Blonde Sheila with her stupid crotch jokes and obsession with other people's virginity.

If they ever did a mermaid version of *Hello, Dolly!* Helen

would be perfect in the lead role. No inhibitions there. Unlike that Adrienne. My, my, what a mess: always half a beat too slow, and so downtrodden—totally the wrong image for a Weeki girl. Delores needed to cut her bangs. Her feet were enormous, though probably they helped her to be such a fast swimmer.

These thoughts floated through Thelma's mind like paper scraps on a windy day, hovering around the stone that was weighing her down. Thelma knew from her own experience that, in life, there is always a moment that marks the divide between before and after. For Thelma, that moment came when Ann Blyth was chosen over her to star in *Mr. Peabody and the Mermaid.* As Thelma watched Delores talking with the other girls, casting glances at Armando, she realized these were her last moments of "before." She would tell Delores about the call from her father and his wish to be reunited with her, and the world that she had pieced together and forced into a whole would move off its axis just enough to make what was in place now all fall down.

Someone must have told a joke because they were laughing and shouting out things that were making them laugh harder. Thelma would wait until it got quieter, then she would pull her aside. She'd prepare her by saying, "I got a call this morning from someone who knows you. You haven't seen him in a while, but he'd like to see you. And the strange thing is, he's working right nearby." Delores would figure it out right away.

Thelma followed her plan. She asked Delores to come with her to her office and sat her down.

Delores stared up at her and repeated her words. "Someone who knows me called you?" she said, trying to eke out the logic in them. "I haven't seen him in a while, but he'd like to see me? And he works nearby?"

"Yes, exactly," said Thelma. "Surely you know of whom I'm speaking."

"Surely I have no idea of whom you're speaking."

"No need to get persnickety with me, young lady." Thelma's voice got clipped. "I am just the messenger here."

"Sorry. There've been a lot of surprises lately. I could do without another one. All I want is to be normal, even though at this point, I don't even know what normal is."

"It's your father."

"What's my father?"

"It's your father who called me. He's working nearby, in Venice. He saw you on television last night, and he wants to come here and see you."

Delores puffed out her cheeks. "Oh boy. What am I supposed to do with that?"

"You see him, I suppose. He is your father."

"What's he doing down here, in Venice?"

"Yes, well, that is the thing," said Thelma. "He's working at Hanratty's Circus."

"The circus? Now, that's funny," said Delores. "That's really funny."

She started to laugh. Thelma was struck again by Delores's teeth: they were huge and zigzagged all the way to the back of her mouth. Nothing an orthodontist couldn't fix, she thought.

Delores was laughing so hard now, there were bug-shaped splotches fanning out across her chest. "Omigod, the circus," she said, wiping the tears from her cheeks. "I don't know what to say. I'll come back later."

Delores left Thelma's office and walked over to the amphitheater. Inside, it smelled like wet wool and was as empty as a card store on the day after Christmas. She sat on one of the benches and stared at the Springs behind the Plexiglas. The storm had stirred up the bottom and, instead of its usual limpidness, the water was brown and cloudy. She thought about all that had happened in the past few days and got that tight feeling in her stomach again.

Lately, she'd had the sensation of having stepped outside of herself. She wasn't gone entirely, but sometimes she'd hear her voice and wonder who was speaking. She had no recollection of making a decision to swim out and save that kid the night before. There he was and there she was, and all she could remember was the water. Even now, she could feel every wave and the force of the current.

She continued staring at the muddy water and understood that she needed to go to the one place where she knew exactly who she was. Without bothering to change her clothes, she walked outside to the mouth of the Springs. She slipped into the water and swam, this time with the currents. It was colder than usual, and she became aware of debris floating by her: a tiny address book, a white tube sock, a heart-shaped pillow. She wondered if these things were discarded in anger, or simply neglected.

Did the people who dropped them believe that they would never see them again? Would they be surprised to know that, because of the storm, they had resurfaced? Sometimes things that seemed lost forever had a way of reappearing in the least expected of places. Like fathers who vanished, then showed up working at the circus.

Delores swam until her bones ached from the cold. She wondered where the dolphins and turtles went in a storm and hoped against hope that one of them would glide by her. She wanted a sign that they were okay, too, but she was shivering now, unable to stay underwater. She stepped out of the Springs and saw something moving imperceptibly along the shoreline. A rock, she thought, then looked again. It was a turtle taking shelter under a sweet pepperbush. For all she knew, it was the one she called Westie. As she ran back to the dorm, her bare footsteps in the mud took on a slushy cadence: *lost, found, lost, found, lost, found.* The sound of it, the thought of it, infused her with hope.

After she changed her clothes and dried her hair, Delores caught up with Thelma at her office. "I'll meet with my father," she said. "I'm curious who he is now. Believe me, there was nothing about the man I knew that even hinted that he would ever work at a circus. But, then again, he probably never thought I'd turn out to be who I am. And my mother! Well, you've met my mother. None of us were like this back home. One thing, though, when I meet him, will you come with me?"

"Of course I will."

"Thanks," said Delores. "That would be great. It's kind of scary, in a way."

Thelma figured that this wasn't the time to tell Delores that she'd gotten another phone call, this one from a very polite gentleman, a Mr. David Hanratty, the man who ran Hanratty's Circus. He also wanted to meet "the talented Miss Torres."

Eighteen

ROY WALKER WAS TOO AGITATED to sit still. He paced around his trailer. *This is how the animals must feel,* he thought to himself: *nothing to do but wait, nowhere to go but here.* Roy wasn't exactly an animal lover. He'd never owned a dog, or even a fish, and always regarded people who became overly involved with their pets as kooks. He certainly never expected to feel anything about these circus creatures other than that they were part of a job that needed doing. And yet Lucy and Nehru aroused in him feelings of compassion and protectiveness, which was more than most humans did. It touched Roy how unselfconscious Lucy was about her funny ears and loopy smile. She'd leap onto the furniture, hug you with those snaky fingers of hers, and dare you not to laugh. Lately, Roy stuffed his pockets with peanuts so that he'd always have them on hand. As soon as Lucy saw Roy coming, she'd swagger toward him, knuckles scraping along the ground, then swing herself up and coil around his leg, just high enough to reach into his pocket and pull out the treat. How could you not laugh at that?

But at this moment, Roy didn't feel up to Lucy's eagerness. He felt scared about the consequences of his phone

call earlier this morning, and he needed solace. Nehru the
elephant didn't need attention the way Lucy did; she
would just let Roy be. He walked to Nehru's cage and
stared down at the animal's leg. There was a large, rusty
shackle around it, tethered to a steel ball that must have
weighed five hundred pounds. Even though she was the
matriarch of the pack, Nehru looked worn-out and re-
signed, as if she'd given up any hope of breaking out and
living as she was meant to live. Roy knew that feeling. He
unlocked the cage door. The smell of straw and rotting potatoes lodged in the back of his throat as he looked up into
Nehru's shrewd and canny eye.

Sadness, my friend, it's as old as time and just as unstoppable.

Roy did not actually speak those words, but the thought
seemed to pass between them.

Roy dug into his pocket and found some peanuts to feed
Nehru. Nehru scarfed them down, then bent her shoulder
and head so that Roy could scratch her behind the ear. In
this way, they spent the rest of the morning: commiserat-
ing in silence.

The call came into Hanratty's office just after noon.
Hanratty picked up the phone and was surprised to hear
Thelma Foote asking for Roy Walker. "Miss Foote," he
said. "This is a pleasant surprise. But if I may ask, why on
earth are you calling Roy Walker when I'm the one who
called you earlier this morning?"

Thelma was quick to size up the situation and answered,
"He must have been calling me on another matter."

"But I can't imagine," said Hanratty.

"I'm sure in time it will become clear."

"Odd. But now that I have you on the phone, have you had time to consider my proposal?"

"In truth, Mr. Hanratty, Miss Taurus is exhausted. I thought I would wait until tomorrow to bring it up with her."

"Yes, I understand," he said. "So we'll talk then."

"Absolutely," said Thelma. "So now, could you please put Mr. Walker on the phone?"

Hanratty found Roy at the elephant cage. "I have a Thelma Foote on the phone," he said, disregarding Roy's intimacy with Nehru. "She would like to speak with you." Hanratty was far too polite to inquire how Roy knew Thelma Foote, but he knew something about eliciting information from people who weren't eager to give it. If a conversation stopped dead in its tracks, he felt no need to try to rescue it. He allowed the silence to linger between himself and the other person for as long as necessary. Inevitably, the other person would say things he ordinarily wouldn't, just to fill the uneasy void.

And so it happened with Roy Walker, though he refused to meet his boss's eye. Hanratty waited. Roy could feel the sweat roll down the sides of his neck. Briefly, his mind wandered. Why did his neck sweat so when he got nervous? He needed to say something. Hanratty was watching him. He couldn't just stand there and sweat. So he said the thing that weighed most heavily on his mind, the thing he had had no intention of bringing up with his boss. "I have a question for you, sir. Do you think that, by nature, human beings are forgiving?"

"I think that, by nature, human beings are self-protective," said Hanratty. "If it is in their interest to be forgiving, then they are. If not, then they are vengeful. I am fairly certain that being forgiving is not an innate virtue."

"I called Thelma Foote because that was my daughter we saw on TV last night—Delores Torres, or whatever she calls herself. Her real name is Delores Walker. I ran out on my family more than two years ago, and, until last night, I had no idea where my daughter was or what she was doing. I called that mermaid place this morning, and I asked Miss Foote if I might meet with Delores. I imagine she is calling me back with an answer. That's it. That's the whole story," he said, mopping his neck with a handkerchief.

Once again, a cloud of silence settled between them. Had Roy looked directly into Hanratty's eyes, he'd have noticed that he had the eyes of a man in overdrive.

This time, it was Hanratty who took up the silence. "Perhaps there is some way we could be mutually beneficial to one another," he said, in his tidy manner. "I've watched your daughter on the news. She has raw talent and hasn't realized even half of her potential. I can help her. Obviously, that would be a boon to you as well."

"Truthfully, I don't know if my daughter even wants to see me. How about I clear that hurdle first, and then we can talk?"

As he ran to Hanratty's office, Roy thought about the conversation he'd just had with his boss and wondered at its frankness. He thought about the crest of Nehru's head and about how his daughter was a famous performer. Although Roy Walker was no one's idea of an optimist, for one blinding moment, he glimpsed the assumption that all optimists have in common: that everything is possible.

All the while, Thelma Foote's irritation at having to be on hold while Mr. Hanratty fetched Roy had become so great that she'd nearly hung up several times. "In addition to everything else, I am now the secretary around here," she said out loud to no one. "I am certain that Dick Pope at Cypress Gardens would not play matchmaker to some dipsy-doodle circus performer and his estranged daughter. I have better things to do." By the time Roy finally picked up the phone, Thelma's voice was bristling with annoyance. "I have no time to talk," she said, "other than to tell you that your daughter will meet with you. Come to Weeki Wachee at noon tomorrow. That's when she'll be on a break. Ask anyone at the main gate to direct you to my office. Delores and I will be waiting there for you."

Grateful that he hadn't slid out of his daughter's life completely, Roy accepted the invitation without thinking about how he'd get to Weeki Wachee or, for that matter, what he'd wear. He worried that she might not recognize him. He'd lost a lot of weight—and hair. When she'd last seen him, he'd been a furious man. Now he didn't wake up angry every morning. He liked his work and the responsibilities that came with it. Had that changed the way he looked? Would she notice? Would she even care?

His thoughts raced: *Hanratty could give me a ride. No, I should be alone the first time I see her. On the other hand, if Mr.*

Hanratty's there, it might make it easier. Either way, it could be awkward. No, it will be awkward. I'll be lucky if awkward is all it is. Hmm, maybe I will ask Mr. Hanratty for a ride.

Delores showered and went to join the others. Most of them were sprawled on the modular couches. Adrienne and Sharlene sat cross-legged on the floor. Sharlene was looking down at something, her hair draped around her head like a tent. Johnny Cash was singing "A Boy Named Sue" on the stereo. Outside, the rain was tapering off and the sky was the yellow color of a healing bruise. Delores squeezed onto the couch between Armando and Molly. Her arms touched theirs, and she could feel the warmth of their bodies. "You smell good," said Armando. "Prell," she answered.

They spent the morning listening to music and exchanging stories about their pasts. Armando told the group that his parents were from Cuba and how every time he mentioned that he'd like to visit Cuba, his mother would look as if she might cry. She'd wave her hands in front of her face and say, "This is not for discussion. We are never going back there." Molly asked if any of them had ever been to a foreign country. Sharlene, of all people, looked up from the floor and said, "I was in Windsor, Ontario, once but I don't guess that counts."

Scary Sheila said that when she was about twelve, her family had gone for a week to St. Martin but they had to come home early when her father became infected by a rare bacterium called shigella. And Delores said that if she could pick anywhere in the world to go, she'd go to France. "My mother used to say she had a little French in her," she said. "That was only because she liked liver and, according to her, the French like liver."

Before she knew it, she had told them everything: about her mother and the fashion magazine; about Westie and about his babysitter who had just died; and about her father who had disappeared more than two years ago—although she couldn't bring herself to bring up the latest news about the circus. "I'm not who you thought I was in the beginning," she said, watching for their reactions. "But I am now. I really am."

"Christ, do you think any of us are who we said we were?" said Scary Sheila. "You don't really think I'll ever go back to the University of Florida, do you? First of all, they wouldn't let me back in even if I wanted to go. They told my parents I had a drinking problem. That was an understatement," she rolled her eyes.

"You want to hear about drinking problems, my old man was soused before he went to work every morning," said Helen. "Sometimes he'd be so desperate, he'd drink mouthwash."

"Okay, while we're telling true confessions, I've got one," said Blonde Sheila. "Right before I came down here, I caught my mother in bed with a neighbor from down the street. He was a nineteen-year-old hippie."

And then Lester spoke up. "When I told my father that I'd been hired as a merman here, he slapped me across the face and called me a queer. But I came here anyway."

Molly shot Adrienne a look. "And you thought you had troubles," she said, referring to the pyrotechnic baton-twirling travesty on the football fields of Zephyrhills High.

It was as if they were a big family, sitting out a rainy day together, telling their secrets. And, for that afternoon at least, they were all in the same boat: kids who had seen grown-up troubles.

Later that afternoon, Armando looked at his watch. "We'd better get back to the station," he said to Delores. "Sommers is going to think we drowned. Again."

"Shouldn't you change before we go?" she asked.

Armando had forgotten he was still wearing Thelma's shirt and sweatpants. "Oh God, I wonder if I still have any clothes," he said. "I guess I could wear one of the mermaid outfits."

"That'll never work. You're too skinny."

Armando flexed his muscles and in a tough guy voice answered: "Oh yeah? Well, there's more to me than meets the eye."

Delores laughed. He was anything but a tough guy. She liked that about him.

"C'mon, Mr. Muhammad Ali, let's go find you some clothes."

They walked across the lawn to Thelma's office. Thelma was sitting in her chair, her back to them, her Keds propped up on the windowsill.

"Knock knock," said Delores.

Thelma spun in her chair. She had the slack-faced expression of someone lost in thought.

"I'll bet I know why you're here," she said, pulling Armando's freshly washed khakis and sweatshirt from a drawer. It wasn't enough that she was matchmaker and secretary. Now she had to be laundrywoman as well. Thelma assumed that this effort, like so many of her others, would go unnoticed and unappreciated. But when she handed the clothes to him and said, "Here you go, young man, you'll be needing these," Armando bent down and kissed the top of her head. "You are an angel," he said. "An angel from heaven."

It had been years, maybe a lifetime, since anyone had kissed the top of Thelma's head. "An angel?" Her laugh sounded unsettled. "That's not the word most people would use to describe me."

"Then most people don't know you," he said.

Thelma blinked and looked at Armando as if he'd just spoken in a foreign language. She couldn't decide if he was really that nice or just an artful ass-kisser.

Armando ran off to change his clothes. "Nice young man," said Thelma, nodding as if she were agreeing with herself.

In the van back to the station, Armando and Delores turned on the radio just as Roberta Flack started singing her new hit, "Killing Me Softly." When she got to the part about "strumming my pain with his fingers," Armando cocked his ear toward the radio. "Kind of X-rated, those lyrics, don't you think?" he asked. Delores put her hand on his leg and kept it there until they got to WGUP. That's the kind of day it was.

If Alan Sommers had been moved or shaken by the events of the night before, he certainly had made a speedy recovery. Lately he had taken to wearing a gold chain around his neck; on this afternoon, he'd also left his shirt unbuttoned a notch or two lower than usual and he reeked of aftershave. "Hey, doll face," he said when he spotted Delores. "How goes it in the lifesaving business? The press has been hounding me all day. Wooh, all this publicity. We are on the map. On the globe. In the stratosphere!" He turned to Armando: "Get a good night's sleep, buddy?" He winked. "I'll bet you did." Then, just like that, the jocularity went out of his voice. "People," he shouted to the crew on the floor, "listen up. We've got forty-five minutes to go. I want tonight's show to be flawless. This isn't local television anymore. The entire world will be watching."

At around that same time, Roy walked over to the Giant Café. Hanratty was already there, seated at the counter with a cup of tea and a grilled-cheese sandwich. "Well, Mr. Walker, a rare privilege it is to be in your company twice in a day," said Hanratty, dabbing the corners of his mouth with a napkin. "Please, join me."

Roy sat on the stool beside him. "I'm going to see her at noon tomorrow," he whispered, sounding like a man who was being watched. "I thought maybe you'd like to come with me."

Hanratty was shrewd enough to know that Roy had no way of getting to Weeki Wachee without him. "How kind of you," he said. "Perhaps I can give you a lift."

"Yeah, that would be nice. Thank you."

Rex came over and took Roy's order: key-lime pie and a glass of milk.

As if in a movie, the three men looked at their watches at the same time, then stared up at the TV set.

"It'll be tough to compete with last night's act," said Rex. They all nodded, watching the camera zoom in on a grave Chuck Varne. As if he'd been eavesdropping, Chuck opened the broadcast with these words: "Last evening, we witnessed an extraordinary act of courage by a member of our own WGUP news team. Sent out to cover the damage caused by Hurricane Claudia, weathergirl Delores Taurus was standing oceanside at Belleair Beach when she spotted a little boy being dragged out into the roiling ocean. Without hesitation, Ms. Taurus threw down her mike and swam after the helpless child, all the while fighting against the forces of nature. Tonight, we will show you the footage of those frightening and treacherous moments that, fortunately for everyone, culminated in a victory at sea."

Again, they watched Delores's rescue and even though they all knew how it would end, Hanratty and Roy put down their food, and Rex blew a whoosh of relief through his cheeks when Delores and the boy finally landed on shore.

"Ladies and gentlemen," said Varne, "this is unprecedented television: the live drama of a miracle unfolding before your very eyes—for some of us, the very reason we got into this business in the first place." Moved by his own words, Varne had to clear his throat before he continued. "And tonight, we have an exclusive interview with Lee Alexander, the father of the young boy whom Delores Taurus rescued from the clutches of Hurricane Claudia. Back with you in sixty seconds."

When Chuck returned, there was a rail-thin blond man seated beside him. Lee Alexander had a short crew cut and a large Adam's apple that jumped up and down each time he swallowed. The camera crawled in on the man's face as Chuck continued: "Watching Delores Taurus swim out to rescue his six-year-old son Danny, Lee Alexander cut a silhouette of agony and desperation." Chuck paused as they showed a film clip of Lee Alexander standing on the beach watching the rescue. Indeed, his arms were folded in front of him and he was hunched over as if he were trying to keep his insides from coming out. Chuck continued: "Thanks to the valiant efforts of our own Delores Taurus, little Danny is safe at home tonight watching his dad on live television. Lee Alexander, welcome."

Alexander stared into the camera and swallowed hard. "Welcome," he said.

Everyone on the set worried that this would be tough going—everyone except Chuck, who had become an expert at putting words into other people's mouths.

"Mr. Alexander, it must have been harrowing to watch your boy being dragged out to sea. I can't imagine the feeling of helplessness and utter desolation that you must have felt. Can you tell us what it was like?"

Lee Alexander's mouth was dry as paper and his tongue

stuck to the roof of his mouth. "It felt as if the world was ending" (swallow). "Like my life was over. My family and I are so grateful. Really, that's all I can say."

Tears welled up in his eyes. His mouth twitched as he tried not to cry. The camera sucked it all up. Chuck, once again overwhelmed by the raw emotion of live television, wiped a tear from his eye. "Mr. Alexander," he said, in a cracking voice, "all of us at WGUP and in the greater Tampa area share in your happiness. God bless you and little Danny and the rest of the Alexander family."

Lee Alexander, with his bouncy Adam's apple, nodded to Chuck in a way that made clear that his ordeal had finally ended.

By now, it was six fifteen, time for another commercial break. "When we come back," said Chuck, his voice restored to normal, "we will bring you an update on Hurricane Claudia, and then the current weather from our resident heroine, Delores Taurus."

Roy and Hanratty sat up a little straighter. Rex, not knowing that Roy had told Hanratty about Delores, pretended that nothing unusual was happening.

After the commercial break, Delores appeared on-screen. "Tomorrow morning the clouds will clear and, by noon, we should have eighty-three degrees and full sunshine—good news for Roy Walker over at the circus in Venice."

No one at the Giant Café looked at anyone. Roy gripped the counter with both hands and thought that, if he were here alone, he would jump up and down and raise his fist triumphantly in the air. But since he wasn't, he sat quietly and scraped the last of the graham-cracker crust off of his plate. Rex caught Roy's eye and winked at him. And when the weather report was finished, Hanratty pronounced Delores Taurus "the real thing" before sinking his teeth into the rest of his grilled-cheese sandwich.

Nineteen

ROY AWOKE earlier than usual the next morning. Normally, he'd walk around his bed fifteen times, do his sit-ups and push-ups, then throw on his clothes, feed the animals and clean their cages, then come back to his room and shower. He always dressed by rote, wearing the same thing almost every day: a pair of khaki shorts, a white T-shirt, brown leather sandals. By now, he looked the way he looked, and staring in mirrors held no interest for him. But on this morning, after he returned from his chores and did his exercise routine, he took his time showering, then making sure to rinse the soap out of his hair.

The cold water set his mind racing. Delores had turned into a beauty. He'd never seen it coming. How would he talk to her? What would they say? Should he tell her about his affinity for the animals? Try to explain how trapped he had felt and why he had left? Apologize? He'd best be careful. She was clearly savvy—he hadn't seen that coming, either—and he didn't want to risk sounding corny in any way. He wanted her to know that he was comfortable in his life, happy, even.

He stepped out of the shower and wrapped a towel around his waist. The mirror on the metal bathroom cabinet was about the size of a plate, just big enough for him to give his face the once-over. He stuck out his tongue, stretched his lips, and studied his teeth and gums. He'd completely forgotten about the gap between his front teeth, the same way people with freckles never remember they're there. He ran his tongue over the space and let it linger for a while. He bent his head toward the mirror and studied his hairline. Had his forehead always been this big, or was his hair just receding? The rest of his hair fell like shingles around his neck; maybe he'd put it into a ponytail. Nah, he'd look too much like a hippie. Now he wished he'd allowed Carmen to cut his hair, as she had offered to do so many times, instead of cutting it himself. He caught the reflection of his eyes. How could he not have noticed that they were small and worm-colored and had puffy bags underneath them?

My eyes, thought Roy, *they tell the story more than any other part of me.* His tendency was not to look people in the eye, something that, in hindsight, probably made him look shifty and uncertain. Hanratty. There was a man whose eyes locked with yours. They commanded attention and made him seem firm and powerful. Roy would keep that in mind. He ran his hands across his stomach. No flab. That was the one thing he did have going for him: his physique. He didn't have an extra pound on him, and, between his exercise and all the physical work he did, he was as strong as ever. Working in the sun all day had also turned his skin the luscious golden brown of peanut butter.

The matter of what he'd wear was simple enough. He'd pick out the cleanest white T-shirt in his cubby and a pair of newish blue jeans. Of course he'd wear the Yankees cap. She'd probably remember that. Funny, to worry so much about impressing his daughter when, for the first thirteen years of her life, he had to admit, he'd hardly taken notice of her. Gail had once called him a self-absorbed SOB. At the time, he had had no idea why she'd said that.

As a boy, he'd been moved around from one unwelcoming relative's house to another, none of them having the desire or inclination to try to rein him in. Then he'd met Gail, who'd also come from a loveless legacy, and they'd recognized in each other the possibility of breaking the cycle. When she became pregnant with Delores, four months after they met, they decided to have this baby and get married. He would go to trade school and become an electrician. Everyone said he had the aptitude for it. They'd be a happy family. But after Delores was born, money was scarce. Roy dropped out of school and took a job at a grocery store. Gail barely had the energy, or interest, to make love when he felt like it. The more she loved the new baby, the more volatile he became. When he left, there was still the stain on the bedroom wall from a cup of coffee he'd thrown when she came home with a three-dollar pinafore from Alexander's she'd bought for two-year-old Delores.

He thought about these things as he slathered on shaving cream. He remembered how, as a very little girl, Delores sat on the toilet seat and watched, mesmerized, as he did this. Sometimes, he would put some of the lather on her cheek and pretend to shave it with the dull side of the razor. She would run her fingers across the smooth part of her face, then tell her mother that "daddy shaved me." See, there were some good memories. He hoped she remembered them as well.

When he finished, he splashed on some Aqua Velva.

At exactly ten a.m., Roy showed up in Hanratty's office. Hanratty had said he didn't want to take any chances getting caught in traffic. "A twelve o'clock appointment is a twelve o'clock appointment," he'd said to Roy. Hanratty was dressed in a tweed suit with a matching vest, a yellow shirt, and gold cuff links in the shape of a top hat. The two men, side by side, were a study in contrasts, like Skit and Skat, two of the clowns in the show. Skit was lean and wore raggedy clothes. He was forever "surprising" Skat by bopping him over the head with rubber mallets and squirting water into his face. Skat was plump and stodgy with a polka-dot bow tie and an oversized pocket watch. Though clearly smarter and better-dressed than Skit, Skat could never escape the antics of the more agile clown. Roy thought it wise not to mention the Skit and Skat comparison, but he was certain that Hanratty noticed it himself.

The two settled into Hanratty's Chevy Impala. Hanratty drove slowly, with both hands on the wheel, and kept lurching forward as if his body could help propel the car. They didn't speak, except when Hanratty said to Roy, "Have you thought about what you might say?" And Roy answered, "I've never known how to do that. I guess when the time comes, I'll just say whatever comes to mind."

As the two men were driving, Delores was finishing up her morning show, a revival of one of their classics, "The Wizard of Oz." She was playing the Wicked Witch of the

West, Blonde Sheila was Dorothy—"counterintuitive casting" is what Thelma called it. Delores would have only a half hour to wash off all the witch makeup and get ready for the noon meeting with her father. The logistics of it all preoccupied her, which was just as well, since it helped keep her anxieties at bay.

Nothing could keep Thelma's anxieties at bay. Everything about the prospect of meeting Mr. Hanratty and Roy Walker made her feel nettled. Being judged, making pleasant conversation, pretending to tolerate a man who'd walked out on his family: Thelma had organized her life so that she could avoid circumstances like this one. She'd figured out how to deal with Alan Sommers, but that was quite enough for her in the stranger department. She sat in the underwater booth, directing the show and fretting about all that was to happen. For a moment, she let her eyes wander to stage left where the witch's castle stood. Something was amiss. Right above the castle gate there was a bluish, mossy blob, something that had never been there before. Thelma squinted, slowly the realization of what she was seeing came into focus. "Goddam algae," she shouted. Her words would have fallen on deaf ears except for one thing: the microphone in her booth was turned on, so that everyone who was underwater heard exactly what she said.

They were just at the point in the play when Dorothy was about to pour water on the Wicked Witch and make her disappear. Thelma's voice echoed through the tank, and Blonde Sheila, hearing the Lord's name broadcast in vain, forgot her buoyancy and torpedoed to the surface. Without

Dorothy to dissolve her with the water, the Wicked Witch Delores had nothing to do but swim off to the side and hope that Blonde Sheila would reappear. Thelma had no idea what was going on. "Sheila," she shouted, "control your breathing. Get back down here. Delores, where are you going? Center stage, now!"

It was falling apart before Thelma's eyes. Blonde Sheila tried sculling to get back underwater, but her concentration had strayed so much that it was impossible. As she floated back to the surface, she said a little prayer: "Oh Lord, please know that it was not me who used your name in vain. And please forgive Thelma Foote. Algae makes her nutty as a fruitcake."

Unsure of what to do next, Delores swam to center stage and waited for Thelma to come up with something. Thelma shouted for the curtain to come down and the music to come up. "Somewhere Over the Rainbow" played as the baffled audience clapped politely and wondered what they'd missed.

Thelma stared at the empty tank before her. With "Jingle Shells" and *Mr. Peabody and the Mermaid* permanently replaying in her memory, she had always been waiting for the other shoe to drop. While Thelma agonized over her demise, Delores sat shivering in the hot room with Molly, who'd played the Cowardly Lion. "I hate Blonde Sheila," said Molly. "Just because she's born-again, she doesn't have to make *everything* about her."

"I felt embarrassed for her," said Delores. "And poor Thelma. Talk about trying hard—she gets the short end of everyone's stick."

"But Thelma brings it on herself."

"Yeah, but think about it, Molly. If she didn't do all this stuff, who would? I think she gets taken for granted a lot around here."

"So, Thelma's your new best friend?"

"No, but she is doing me an awfully big favor."

"Oh, and like you're not doing her a big favor?"

"No, I don't mean professionally. I mean personally she's doing me a favor."

"What's she doing?"

"I'll tell you something if you swear not to tell anyone," said Delores in a hush.

Molly drew an X over her heart. "I swear."

Delores told her about her father and the upcoming meeting. "I mean I haven't seen or heard from him for more than two years. I don't even know if I'll recognize him. And can you believe the part about the circus?"

Molly started to laugh. She put her hand over her mouth to stop it, but it was too late. "I'm not laughing at you, Delores, but honestly, you couldn't make this stuff up."

The incident during "The Wizard of Oz" had so rattled Thelma that she considered canceling the meeting with Hanratty and Roy. But common sense took the upper hand. *The girl needs to meet her father,* she thought. *This Hanratty fellow is an astute businessman, something that we sorely lack around here. Maybe this is opportunity knocking, not a sound I hear often enough.*

Buoyed by her own pep talk, Thelma rubbed talcum

powder into the dirt spots on her Keds and put on a fresh pair of khakis. She brushed her hair behind her ears and slipped into a windbreaker that had just come back from the cleaners. For this meeting, she was manager and agent. Easy, always easy, when she knew her place. She was the first to arrive at her office. She pushed three chairs together so that they would be facing her desk. It would give the meeting a form and a hierarchy, and it would make it clear that all discussion would be funneled through her.

By 11:57, she had cleared her desk of all papers. A few weeks earlier, a photographer from *National Geographic* had passed through and asked to take some pictures of the mermaids. One of the shots was of Delores underwater, looking at herself in a hand mirror while brushing her hair. The hair spread out in the water like a jellyfish and Delores wore a self-satisfied, somewhat taunting, smile. Lester had had the picture blown up to poster size ("A nifty photo for last-minute advertising if we ever need it" is how he put it) and now Thelma placed it behind her desk so that no one could miss it. At 11:59, Delores showed up wearing a floral-print wraparound skirt, a white cotton off-the-shoulder blouse, and a pair of straw-colored espadrilles. With her wet hair pulled back into a ponytail, she looked healthy and vibrant, like a girl gobbling up life with not a moment to waste. Thelma wondered if her father would notice.

At precisely twelve o'clock there was a solid rap on the door. "Come in," said Thelma, barely disguising the impatience in her voice. Hanratty walked in first, removing his hat and bowing excessively. "How do you do? I am Dave Hanratty. Miss Foote, I presume," he said, grabbing

Thelma's hand and gazing into her eyes. "Forgive me for
staring, but I had pictured someone less—ah, how should I
say this?—someone less modern. What a pleasant surprise."

Then he turned his attention to Delores. "And you must
be the courageous Delores Torres." He still pronounced it
with a Spanish accent, so it rhymed with "Suarez."

"Taurus. It's Delores Taurus," she said, trying to free her
hand from the vise of his grip. His eyes spilled into hers,
but she was distracted by a smell, a familiar, sharp licorice
odor. Sen-Sen. Her father. She smelled him before she saw
him. There he was, his hands cupped in front of him, as if
he were about to give someone a boost, and his eyes small
and shifty, as always. Yes, she remembered—that, and how
watery they often were. He looked different, though he
still wore his ratty old Yankees cap. Stronger. Definitely
tanner. More relaxed, maybe.

Roy Walker assessed his daughter. Had she always been
this imposing? She was beautiful, achingly so, in her
strength and assurance. All eyes were on him as his silence
filled the room. Delores stepped into the discomfort by
sticking her face in front of his and slowly waving her
hand back and forth. "Hey, do you remember me?"

"You related to Delores Walker?" he asked.

"Who wants to know?"

"Her father." He winced as he said it, not sure if he still
had the right to claim her that way. He took off his hat and
bowed his head. She noticed the bald spot. That had not
been there before.

Thelma slapped the palm of her hand on her desk.

"Okay, enough of all that," she said, impatient with Roy's inability to look his daughter in the eye. "None of us have any time to waste, so let's get down to why we're all here. Hanratty, you look like a man of purpose. What brings you to Weeki Wachee?"

Hanratty cleared his throat and moved forward in his chair. "Two evenings ago, we, along with everyone else in the area, watched with riveted fascination as Miss Taurus— have I pronounced it correctly?—made her valiant rescue. As a circus impresario for nearly thirty years, I have developed a keen sense for recognizing talent and charisma. It was instantly obvious to me that Miss Taurus possessed more than her share of both. At the time, I was unaware that her father was in my employ—what a great coincidence. When Mr. Walker told me that Miss Taurus was his daughter, it came to me right away that there was potentially a symbiotic relationship between Hanratty's Circus and Weeki Wachee Springs. It almost seemed preordained, if you believe in such things. Anyway, at first I thought that Miss Taurus could become one of the Hanratty acts, but that didn't seem substantial enough. With all the shenanigans going on up in Orlando, I asked myself: what could we bring to the table that they couldn't? How can you outshine a multimillion-dollar theme park with all the modern gadgets and hijinks that money can buy? And the answer came to me, pure and simple. Human beings, live animals: everything we do is real."

Hanratty knew when to pause, when to raise his voice, how to hold a crowd. Even the usually irascible Thelma Foote couldn't take her eyes off of him.

"While we're all aware of Miss Taurus's talents, her father, Mr. Walker, is not without his gifts as well. I have seen him with the animals, the elephants especially, and I can tell you he has a very personal and special relationship with them. Miss Foote, you have created a wildly successful attraction underwater. Wouldn't it be a boon to your business to develop a spectacle as well?"

Thelma ran her fingers over her lips before she spoke. "Mr. Hanratty, what you say is not without merit. But my first concern is for the girls, and I wouldn't want to do anything to distract from their show."

"Of course," said Hanratty, nodding.

"Then again," she continued, "anything that increases awareness and business is always a plus in my book."

"Let me ask you this: how deep is Weeki Wachee Springs?"

Delores and Thelma exchanged quizzical looks.

"The Springs are forty-five feet at their deepest," answered Thelma.

"Good," said Hanratty, then paused for a few moments. He made eye contact with everyone in the room before completing his thought. "I'm sure you all know that elephants love to swim. They give themselves showers with their trunks. And it naturally cools them down, because water gets trapped in the wrinkles of their skin and evaporates slowly. Here's another thing. They swim with their mouth below the surface of the water and use their trunks much like a snorkel. In fact, there are many who believe that the elephant is the next of kin to the manatee. Some coincidence, huh?"

Thelma heard the excitement growing in Hanratty's voice, and it made her anxious. She began picking at a spot on her windbreaker, where there was a flaw in the fabric.

Hanratty fixed his gaze on Roy, who was looking down at his hands, which he was rubbing together. He hadn't been aware that his boss had picked up on his relationship with Nehru.

"I'm sure among all of our creative efforts, we can figure out a way to have the elephants and the mermaids interact in the water in such a way that would draw crowds from all over the state. All over the country, even."

Delores rolled her eyes. First that jerk Sommers makes her sit in a bathtub on television, now this yo-yo has her swimming with elephants. There was no way that was going to happen.

Thelma finally spoke up: "Elephants and mermaids. Honestly, Mr. Hanratty, I think you're taking this a little too far. Even for a circus impresario."

Roy lifted his head and stared into Hanratty's shoulder as he said, "Nehru's nearly forty. That would be asking an awful lot of her."

Then Delores spoke. "I'm the one who's supposed to get into the water with the elephant. Does anyone care what I think? I'm not a huge elephant fan. In fact, I think they're kind of creepy. I'd just as soon stay underwater and leave the elephants on the land."

Hanratty closed his eyes. "You can't see it, can you?" he said, sounding as if he were in pain.

It was true. Only Hanratty found joy in the far-flung possibilities.

"Don't you get it?" he asked. "The mermaid—half animal, half human—and the elephant, the grandest creature in the animal kingdom. It is mythic in its proportion. The mind's eye will take in the magic; it's our own dullness and cynicism that turns it away."

Thelma rested her chin on her thumbs and held her hands prayerlike against her face. Hanratty's frustration was palpable to her. Usually it was she who saw what others were too lazy or unwilling to comprehend. It touched her how much he cared. She and Hanratty were cut from similar cloth but for one thing: he was a true showman. She aspired to that, but she knew that her talent lay in being a shrewd businesswoman and a good manager. She thought about Alan Sommers, who seemed so slight in comparison. Sommers was a marketer, a man who understood what was commercially viable. But Dave Hanratty, he was the real thing. She realized that, until today, she had never met anyone like him.

Roy was lost in the worry that his job was at stake. He could care for the animals and do what was required around the circus. But Hanratty was talking about a performance, a performance that people from all over the country might come to see. He would be working with his daughter, with whom he'd not shared even a single word in two years. Already he had done things beyond his wildest dreams. What more would be asked of him? What more could he ask of himself?

But it was Delores, now mesmerized by Hanratty's words, who began to see what he saw and relish the possibilities.

Where she was strident a few moments earlier, she now spoke as if waking from a dream. "It wouldn't just be the elephant and the mermaids," she said. "There are the turtles and the dolphins and..." She paused, finishing the sentence to herself. "This could be the greatest thing that ever happened here!"

Thelma imagined the headlines in the papers and the pictures they would run. Attendance would increase, as it had after "The Merfather." Maybe she could finally afford to rebuild the amphitheater, never mind the pump. After all of the years that she'd struggled to keep Weeki Wachee going, this stranger who had suddenly walked in the door could pin this place permanently on the map. *If I were a more sentimental person, I would weep,* she thought. But there were the practical issues to consider.

"Supposing that this could happen," she said, "what would we need to do to house elephants on the premises? Where would they stay when they were not swimming?"

Hanratty waved his hand as if he were brushing aside crumbs. "These are details we can attend to. The real question is: how do we make this as spectacular as it can be?"

There were ten elephants in Hanratty's Circus. Roy knew that since Nehru was the matriarch of the group, whatever she did the others would follow. Then a thought, as ridiculous as Lucy herself, leapt into his mind. He had often seen the reckless and adorable chimp riding on the back of one of the elephants. Suddenly, he saw a flotilla of elephants and dolphins and manatees and mermaids. If Noah were putting together an ark in Central Florida, this

would be it. Hanratty, he realized, was encouraging everyone to go beyond their boundaries. Anything was possible. For a man who'd given up everything because he'd felt
suffocated and trapped, this was as thrilling as landing on
the far side of the moon.

The four of them sat looking at each other in silence, all
of them imagining possibilities they had never imagined
before.

Lost in the tapestry, Delores closed her eyes; when
Hanratty clapped his hands together, she nearly jumped
out of her skin. "That's it, now you're with me!" he shouted.
"Have they ever seen anything like this up at Disney?
Anywhere else in the world? I think not."

They filed out of Thelma's office, still daydreaming. Roy
Walker was the one who broke the silence as he said to his
daughter, "This certainly ain't the Bronx."

Later that night, when Roy went to the Giant Café for a
cup of coffee and a piece of pie, Rex asked him how it had
gone with his daughter. Roy chewed as he thought about
it, then swallowed hard. "We never really talked. Hanratty
came up with some fantastic scheme for combining the
mermaids and the circus and we were all so overwhelmed
by it that the conversation never turned to anything else.
Before we knew it, they had to do a show and we had to
get back here and that was that. Here's the strange thing,
Rex—she and I may end up working together."

"Sometimes it's more about doing than talking," said Rex.
"If you're going to work with her, well then, that would be

the way to let her know who you are, to get to know each
other again."

When Molly asked Delores how it had gone with her father, Delores told her that he was smaller than she'd remembered. "When I was little, he was always flying off the
handle, fighting with my mom. He seemed scary and so
much bigger to me then. He's actually a little guy with a lot
of muscles. He was shy around me. He wouldn't say anything, even when I said something stupid like, 'Hey, remember me?' But then, this guy who's his boss, Mr. Hanratty,
came up with the most amazing idea and we all kind of got
swept up in it. Even Thelma."

Delores told Molly about the elephants and the mermaids in the water. Then she paused. "Here's something I
thought about, and you have to cross your heart and swear
to God that you won't tell anyone. I'm secretly hoping that
somehow Westie can be part of it. Maybe he could come
down here for a while, or something. We could teach him
to swim. He could be in the show. My mom's always com-
plaining about how hard it is to raise a kid by herself. Who
knows? Maybe she'd even like the idea."

The whole time Delores talked, Molly never looked up
from the shirt that she was ironing. Even when Delores
said, "You think I'm off my rocker, don't you?" Molly kept
her eyes fixed on the shirt. "Not really," she said.

Twenty

WHEN THE CALL came from her mother, Delores was out at the Springs working with the elephants. For the past three months, Wulf the elephant trainer had taught the elephants to swim downstream in formation: Nehru in front; two behind her; three behind them; and four at the end. Despite their heft, the elephants had taken happily to the water, sometimes squirting it through their trunks. They had learned how to swim with the mermaids around them and didn't seem fazed by the occasional manatee or turtle that joined the procession. In order to house the elephants at the Springs, as Hanratty had decided they should, some of the woods in the back of the park had been cleared and an Elephant House was being built. It was to be a large cement structure with overhead fans and big openings, so that it would be airy and cool in even the most desperate heat.

Roy followed the progress of the Elephant House avidly, eager for its completion. There would be room for the elephants to wander, which meant no more shackles. Nehru's freedom felt personal to him, and he did what he could to convey to her that it was close at hand.

Sometimes the little sayings from fortune cookies put into words feelings he had trouble articulating himself. He'd tuck them into his wallet or slip them into his pocket and it could be months, even years, before he'd find them again. Just the other day, he'd found one in the back of his Dopp kit that said: *The things that are the most precious are not the things we own, but the things we keep.* That was exactly how he felt about Nehru. Of course he didn't own her, but he felt it was an honor to be her keeper.

Delores would watch her father with the elephant, how he leaned in close to her and murmured things that only the elephant could hear. Nehru had a peculiar stance—knees bent as if she were lurching forward. It seemed as if the two of them might fall into each other. This morning, Delores had pointed them out to Wulf: "They look like they're telling secrets," she said. Wulf was German and, by nature, practical. "*Ach* no. Nehru came from India on a boat. She was packed in the container very tight—this is why she stands in such a way." Maybe he was right, but Delores saw what she saw and it gave her a pang to realize how at ease and intimate her father was with the elephant.

The sight of Adrienne running toward her momentarily distracted her. Adrienne ran like a girl, hands flapping in the air. She was so out of breath, she couldn't complete a sentence. "Phone call. Thelma's office," she panted in her reedy voice. Delores climbed the sloping hill toward the office. It was one of those days in early August when, even if she had tried to run, the punishing sun and humidity would have pushed back at her. By the time she picked up the phone in Thelma's office, the sweat was dripping down her arms. The last thing she felt like doing was talking on the phone.

"Hello," she said flatly.

Her mother didn't bother with a hello, she just launched right into what she had to say.

"Listen, hon, I need help. I could really use you to come up here for a few days. Between the jobs, and trying to find babysitters for Westie, I just can't cope. Just a few days so at least I could find someone for Westie."

"Sure," said Delores, already filled with dread. "I haven't been home in ages."

That night, Delores sat in between Lester and Molly at dinner. She pushed her meatloaf from one side of the plate to the other, finally giving up trying to eat.

"You okay?" asked Molly.

"I don't know, I guess I am," she answered.

There was so much that wasn't being said right now. She hadn't told any of the others, except Molly, that the short, quiet guy who took care of the elephants was her father. Every day, she saw her father, and still they hadn't spoken. That was ridiculous. If he wouldn't initiate it, she would. But good grief, what was she supposed to say?

In her preoccupation, Delores hadn't noticed how Lester had been watching her. She could hear concern in his voice when he asked, "Wanna go sit out on the rock? It's pretty out there this time of day."

"Good idea," she said, looking at the clock. "I have a half hour before I need to get to WGUP. Let's get out of here."

They climbed onto Lester's rock and sat silently watching the sun set. The past few weeks the temperature had been steadily in the midnineties; the humidity, the same. It was the kind of heat that got inside you and festered and Delores was beginning to dread her weather reports, describing "sizzlers" and "scorchers" night after night.

They sat in silence until Delores turned to him. "I have something to tell you that I hope you won't tell anyone else for now."

"We don't tell each other's secrets, remember?" he said.

"Okay then, here goes." She told Lester the whole story about the circus, and how her father was the short, stocky guy who cleaned up after the elephants.

Lester did a double take. "The guy with the baseball cap? That's your father?"

"Yup, that's him," she said.

"The one who's built like an Airstream? Holy cow! I mean, you're hardly built like an Airstream. Well, you know what I mean."

"In any case, the woman who took care of my little brother died," Delores said, and then whispered: "Breast cancer. And I promised my mother," she continued, "that I'd go up there for a few days and help out, which I'm really not looking forward to. Except for one thing. And you've really got to cross your heart and swear to God not to tell anyone what I'm about to tell you." Lester nodded solemnly.

Delores told him her idea to bring Westie back to

Weeki Wachee, just for a little while. As she spoke, she studied his face, waiting for him to laugh or raise an eyebrow or do something to betray how her words struck him. "You think I'm nuts, don't you?" she asked, when she had finished.

"No, I don't," he answered. "I think you're the boldest person I've ever met."

"You are so great," she said, leaning over and kissing him on the cheek. "So, you really don't think I'm crazy?"

Lester's face reddened. Delores thought about how Scary Sheila had called him "Lester the Lobster" behind his back. She had thought it cruel at the time, but it did make sense.

"Well, while we're on the subject of crazy," said Lester, "here's a really crazy idea. Why don't I come up to New York with you? I've never been to New York. Plus, I've got a birthday coming up, so this could be the perfect present for me. My father's been bugging me to 'widen my horizons.' That's what he's always saying, 'Being a merman is not an occupation for a young man. You need to widen your horizons.' Going to New York would certainly do that, don't you think? I don't know, maybe you think it's a bad idea. Of course, if you do, I won't come." Lester looked away, so as not to read any rejection on her face.

"New York in August," she said. "It can get as hot as here, only the air gets trapped and there's nowhere for it to go."

"You forget, I like the heat."

She remembered the first time he'd told her about how he was counting on the sun to cure his acne; he'd confided in her as if he knew she'd keep it to herself. And then he'd told her all about Thelma's history at Weeki Wachee. She'd never repeated a word of that, not to anyone. Lester was a true friend. He was on her side and meant the best for her. She couldn't even count on one hand the number of people in the world who made her feel safe the way he did. He'd probably even be nice to her mother. It wouldn't be so bad to have him come along. It might even be fun.

Her mother had called her and told her how cheap the airfares were that time of year. There was a 10:20 Delta flight out of Tampa that would cost thirty-five dollars. The more she thought about it, the more she thought how Lester might be the perfect buffer between her and her mother.

"The airfares are pretty cheap," she said. "You could stay with us—I'm sure my mother won't mind. It's not real fancy, to say the least." She gave a little laugh.

"I'd like that," he said.

She shook her head and told him to book the 10:20 Delta flight for the day after tomorrow. She hadn't the slightest idea what would happen once they got to New York, but the wave of relief that came over her was enough for the moment.

Since her father had shown up four months earlier, Delores hadn't known what to call him. "Dad" was too intimate; he didn't feel like a dad to her. It was too strange just to call him "Roy." So she resolved it by calling him nothing. Whenever she wanted his attention, she'd say "Umm," until he realized that she was addressing him. On the morning before she was to leave for New York, Delores went down to the Springs just as Wulf and her father were taking the elephants to the water. She walked behind him saying "umm" for a while before he noticed her.

"Good morning," he said, then kept walking.

She caught up with him. "When you have a minute, I need to talk to you."

He looked toward the ground, took off his sunglasses, and wiped them with his T-shirt.

"Right now?" he asked.

"Pretty soon."

"Walker, over here with the bucket. Now!" snapped Wulf. Delores could see her father get tense. She worried that there'd be a scene like so many she had witnessed at home. Her father looked down at the ground and kicked something in the grass. "In a half hour, at the snack bar," he whispered to Delores, before doing what Wulf had asked.

Thirty minutes later, she was sitting at a wooden picnic table drinking a Tab when he came up and sat across from her. Between his Yankees cap and his wraparound sunglasses, she could see only the bottom third of his face but she knew without seeing them that his eyes were not meeting hers.

"Don't you think it's odd that we haven't talked about anything but elephants since you've been here?" she asked, as he sat down across from her.

"What else is there to talk about?" he asked, with a hint of a smile.

"That's a joke, right?"

"Really, I don't know what to say."

"Hmm," she played with her hair. "How about why you left us."

He turned away from her and looked toward the water.

"I thought you'd take me with you. Then, when you disappeared, I thought you'd send for me. Here I am, more than two years later, and I'm still waiting. You could have at least written to us, or called. Sometimes we thought you might be dead or something. But the worst thing was that after a while, we didn't even care."

He rested his forehead on his knuckles. She saw him swallow, and for a long while he said nothing, as if he were trying to digest her words. Finally, he looked up and turned toward the Springs where Wulf was working with the elephants. "Nehru," he said. "She's sweet, don't you think?"

Delores shrugged, and thought: *That's it?*

"The thing about elephants is that they can be so gentle, but they can also get so angry that they destroy and kill anything and anyone around them." He took off his sunglasses and cleaned them again with the bottom of his shirt. "Your mother and me, we were always fighting, about money mostly. She'd tell me I was stupid, that I did everything wrong. And our *personal* life..." He put special emphasis on the word *personal*. "Well, no need to go into details about that, but when you don't have at least that, it can make you feel like you are nothing, a nobody."

He stopped talking and used Delores's napkin to wipe the sweat from the back of his neck. She nodded. "God, she can be such a nag sometimes," she said.

"Sometimes it would really get to me," he continued.

"The thoughts I had. I can't describe them, but they were ugly. I was afraid that I'd do something I couldn't take back, something really bad.

"And then, do you remember the night I left?"

"The night of the liver?" said Delores. "How could I forget that?"

"Yeah. I went out and had a couple of beers, then drove to the Chinese restaurant to get some food. It was dark out. I stopped for a red light and there was this family crossing the street right in front of me. The wife was wearing a brown wool coat. I remember that, it was very windy. I couldn't make out her face, but she was small and I guessed she was very pretty, and the sleeves were too long for her, which made her look even smaller. The husband put his arm around her to protect her from the wind, and he held her close like she was a teddy bear. She was pushing a carriage with a baby about West's age in it, and their daughter, who was a little younger than you were then, was holding her father's hand. They seemed happy, as if they were one piece instead of four separate ones—or so it seemed to me." He stopped talking and shook his head. "I'm talking too much," he said.

"You?" She laughed. "Never."

He closed his eyes and clasped his hands in front of him. "This awful feeling came over me, like I was going to step on the gas and run them down, all of them. I could feel what it would be like to do it, could feel the bumps underneath the tires, could hear the cracking sounds. I got so scared that I turned off the ignition. When the light changed, I was still sitting in the car with the ignition shut down. People were honking, and I guess I was crying or something because some fellow pulled up next to me, and he asked me if I was all right. I finally got myself to the Chinese restaurant. While I was waiting for my food, I thought about what I had just done—or not done. I stayed at the restaurant a long time. I was too scared to get back in the car. I drove home real slow thinking about that family, about what it must be like to come home to them. By the time I got to our house, I had this fantasy that she—your mother—would be happy to see me, that maybe you'd all be happy to see me. Well, if you remember how it was, just the opposite was true."

The awful memory of that night made Delores wince. "Yeah, there was a lot of screaming and food throwing, I remember that," she said.

He nodded. "West and your mother were crying. You yelled at us that we were both crazy, and she and I had an awful fight. That's when I shoved a fistful of the Chinese food into your mother's face and she smacked my hand away. There were bad thoughts racing through my head, things that I might do. I said to myself, Roy, you are acting like a crazy man. If you don't get away from here, surely you will hurt someone, or even worse."

"You mean like you'd kill us or something?" Delores sat up straight.

"I'll tell you this," he said. "That night I saw how a man can cross the line, if you know what I mean. I never want to see that possibility so clearly again." He shuddered as he said this. "I had to get out of there, so I got back into the car and started driving south, the same way we did when we went to Florida. That's how I ended up here, and then I found this job."

"But you didn't even write or call or anything. Even if you hated Mom and wanted to kill her, what about me and Westie? We didn't do anything wrong."

"How could I explain this to you or West? You were just kids. So I took the coward's way out. To tell you the truth, I don't like myself very much. The best I can do is to try and make up for it in the way I live now. It's a quiet life. I like it; I like working with the animals and, for the most part, people leave me alone. I'm not as angry as I used to be. Don't you see? If I wrote or called you, there was the chance I'd get dragged back there. I just couldn't do it, couldn't go back. So I stayed hidden. And now look what's happened?" He threw his hands up in the air, the way people do when they check to see if it's raining.

"Yeah, what's happened is that we had a father, then we got used to not having a father. Now he shows up and what are we supposed to do? Pretend that we have a father again? Oh, and by the way, we call him Westie, not West," said Delores, her voice flat. "He walks now and he looks a lot like you. Weren't you a little curious about how your children were growing up?"

"Yeah, always," he said. "But I guess not enough to risk it."

That was how it was. Her father, with the bulky arms and flash-flood temper, was a scared, guilt-ridden man trying to make up for what he'd done by sweeping up animal shit and taking orders from people like Wulf.

He took off his sunglasses and stared at his daughter staring at him. Whoever she thought he was, he knew that he had just scrambled the picture. Did she understand what he was trying to say, he wondered; would she ever forgive him? He squeezed his eyes shut a few times, then wiped under them with the back of his hand.

"The silver dollars . . . ," he said.

"Yeah, I found them. I used some of them to get down here. I never told Mom about them. I still have a bunch left over. You want them back?"

"No, what would I do with them?"

"Did you leave them for me and Westie on purpose?"

"Wish I could say I did, but honestly, I'd been collecting them for years."

"Why?"

He smiled for the first time since they'd started talking. "I liked how heavy they were. Money should feel like money—something with purpose, not just a flimsy piece of paper. I collected them for years. Money for a rainy day. I guess that rainy day came around."

"I guess," she said.

He looked at his watch. "Gotta go," he said.

"Sure," she said.

They got up from the picnic table. She still didn't have it in her to call him Dad or Roy.

"Umm, good-bye" was the best she could do.

Twenty-one

ON THE FLIGHT from Tampa to New York, Lester wore a blue suit, a white button-down shirt, and a red tie with blue stripes. When Delores asked him why he was so dressed up, Lester said, "My father says you should dress for an airplane ride the way you'd dress for church."

"Have you ever been on an airplane?" she asked.

"No, never. Have you?"

"Nope, this is my first time. But obviously, I've never been to church, either," she said, looking down at her tie-dyed shirt and denim bell-bottoms.

The stewardess came around and offered them a drink. Lester chose hot chocolate, Delores ordered a Tab. The drinks arrived on separate little trays, each with a cocktail napkin and chocolate-chip cookie wrapped in cellophane. They exchanged smiles that said, "Can you believe this?" and unwrapped their cookies. Lester took a sip of his drink, which was so hot that he spit it back into the cup. Then he looked up at the nozzle over his head that was hissing out a stream of cool air. He held his cup underneath it. The cold air blew into his drink causing the hot chocolate to spray over the sides of the cup like a fountain.

It splashed onto Lester's face and all over the front of his white Oxford shirt. At first, he seemed stunned, so Delores began dabbing at his shirt with her napkin; a ribbon of chocolate dripped onto her arm.

"Willy Wonka," said Lester, referring to one of his favorite recent movies.

"Augustus Gloop," said Delores, remembering the name of the boy in the movie who nearly drowns in chocolate before being spit out by one of the candy factory's machines.

Lester started laughing; Delores started laughing. Lester never laughed with the others because it turned out that when he did laugh he made a kind of braying sound. Delores laughed wide open for once, baring her overbite.

That laugh was the most eventful thing that happened between them on the airplane. Delores soon lost herself in the newest issue of *Teen Girl*, and Lester pulled out a paperback, *To Kill a Mockingbird*. Delores glanced over and noticed how small and jammed together the type was. "You read a lot of books?" she asked, interrupting him. He looked up at her. "Yup. That's what I do when I'm not working." She didn't know anyone who read books. Lester was what her mother would call "a queer duck." That's not exactly how she'd describe him, but he was different— she'd give him that.

Later, she interrupted him again. "So, you sure you don't mind sleeping in Westie's room? It's small, I mean, it won't be the most comfortable place in the world."

"You've seen me sleep on the rock. It can't be smaller than that, can it?"

The size of the room was the least of it. "You've never really met my mother," she said.

"No, but I saw her when she was at the park. I thought she was pretty—kind of looked like you." Lester stared down at his book again.

His comment gave Delores pause. Why should she bother telling him that her mother was a phony, and a whiner, and an egomaniac? Let him find out for himself. When she had called home to ask if she could bring Lester, her mother had made a harrumphing sound. "How do you like that?" she'd said. "My daughter, coming home with a strange man. That'll really give the neighbors something to talk about." The way she said it made Delores wonder if the neighbors already had other things to talk about.

There was a crowd of people waiting at the gate, but it wasn't hard for Delores to spot her mother. Even without her craned neck, she was tall. She could make out the top of Westie's head next to her and could see how she held his hand in hers. Westie seemed to have grown a lot since she last saw him in April, and it crossed her mind that he might not recognize her. But the moment he saw her, he tugged at their mother and started yelling: "Dores, Dores."

Delores ran toward them and scooped up Westie. His bare arms and legs were sticky and warm, and he smelled like vanilla. She held him until he started wriggling to get free; even then, she hesitated before putting him down. The image of her father standing head to head with Nehru flashed into her mind. Then she realized that her mother was standing behind Westie, waiting to be greeted. Kissing wasn't a Walker family tradition; they were genetically inclined to back away from each other and avoid eye contact. But Delores felt effusive in that moment, maybe even wanted to impress Lester a little. So she leaned over, gave her mother a smacker on the cheek, and said in a chipper voice: "Hi, Mom. It's great to see you."

Her mother, encouraged by this show of affection, threw her arms around Delores and called her "my gal." Then, she extended a hand to Lester and said: "You must be Lester Pogoda. I've heard so much about you."

They took a taxi to the apartment in the Bronx. Taking a taxi was an extravagance that her mother treated herself to only on special occasions. Having her daughter come home, with a boy no less, was one of those occasions. She sat in the front seat with the driver; Lester and Delores sat in back with Westie squeezed between them. Gail tried to make conversation, but every time she'd say something, Delores would holler "What?" until finally she gave up and they all sank into their own thoughts.

Lester was staring out the window at the concrete buildings and deciding that he already didn't like New York. The people in the airport looked pale and agitated. In Florida, everyone was brown and red; their faces were animated. The people here looked washed out and exhausted. So did the buildings. And what trees there were sagged under the weight of their withered leaves. There was humor in the sun colors of Florida: the burning yellows, screaming corals, pulsing greens. There was nothing humorous about this place: it seemed just a monolith of gray concrete. So far, New York was certainly not for him.

Gail was worrying that she'd make a fool of herself in

front of Lester. Between the magazine and Watergate, she should have plenty to talk about; that wasn't the problem. She had views about these things—it was a shame about that nice man John Mitchell having to resign; and Martha, what a chatterbox—but she wasn't used to giving voice to them, particularly in front of strangers. This boy was just a kid, though. He seemed perfectly nice and not bad-looking.

Delores was staring at her mother in the front seat. She looked good. The makeup she wore gave her face a kind of glow, but it was more than that. Even the way she held herself was different. She was no longer stooped. Now she sat upright and walked with purpose. If she were someone else's mother, Delores might even think she was pretty. She thought about her father, how much more relaxed and peaceful he looked now, and she wondered how it was possible for two people to write misery all over each other the way these two people had done.

Only Westie's chatter filled the car. Mainly, he kept repeating, "Dores, I want to swim with turtle," until Delores said to him, "Westie, do you want to go back to the Springs and see the turtle?" He just kicked his legs against the back of the front seat and kept talking about the turtle. "I brought you a present," said Delores, reaching into her duffel bag. She pulled out a gray stuffed animal with brown buttons for eyes. "Do you know what it is?" she asked. Westie studied the toy. "Babar," he said. "That's right," said Delores. "Babar. He's the biggest animal in the world. He's bigger than this taxi, bigger than a horse. Maybe as big as a barn."

Westie took hold of the toy and squeezed its trunk. "I know a real elephant. Maybe I could introduce you to her sometime," she said. His eyes got round and wide, and he waved the elephant up and down. "Babar, Babar," he said excitedly.

"Delores," her mother turned around. "Don't go filling his head with make-believe. He's got enough of real life to deal with."

"Mom, believe me, the elephants are the least of it." She thought ahead to the conversation they would have to have about her father and the circus and Weeki Wachee, and for the life of her, she couldn't quite see her way to the other side of it.

The apartment was smaller and more dingy than she remembered. Nothing except Helene's globe was new; nothing had been replaced. Only the food stains on the walls had been painted over. After they put away their suitcases, they sat around the kitchen table drinking fruit punch, a little recipe her mother had picked up from the magazine, and egg-salad sandwiches. Westie sat on the floor in front of them playing with his new elephant.

"So, Lester, what would you like to do in our fair city?" asked her mother in her cheeriest voice.

He wanted to answer, "Not much, to tell you the truth," but there was so much expectation in her voice, he knew enough to say more. "The usual stuff: the Empire State Building, the Statue of Liberty, Macy's department store." His father had suggested he take a look at Wall Street, that maybe he'd be inspired by all the men who went to work there in suits and ties every day. But that held no interest for him.

"You know, I'll bet you'd really like Orchard Beach, which isn't too far from here," said Delores. "We could take Westie."

"No siree Bob," said her mother. "Absolutely not. Westie's going nowhere near that beach."

"But Mom, why not? He *looves* the water," Delores could hear a whine rise in her voice.

"How do you know he *looves* the water?"

"When you were in Weeki Wachee that time, I took him swimming. He really liked it." She started to tell her about the turtle, then stopped herself. "Why are you so against him learning how to swim?"

Her mother clicked her tongue against the roof of her mouth, then took a deep breath. "I'll tell you why," she said. "Because having one mermaid in this family is quite enough. I have other things in mind for Westie."

"Oh, like what?" Delores shot back.

"Something a little less cheap than wiggling his ass at some second-rate amusement park."

Delores, startled by her mother's comment, had the impulse to say the meanest thing she could think of. She wanted to blurt out that she understood why her father had walked out, that her mother was a real bitch who didn't care about anyone but herself. She could hear Blonde Sheila saying "bitch," coming down hard on the word and making it sound solid and authoritative. Maybe if Westie hadn't been there, she'd have said it. Instead, she snapped back: "You may think that what I do—what we do—is cheap, but I'll tell you this: I love my job and I'm really good at it. When I'm in the water, I get to be a real sea creature. That's an honor, to be one of them, and nothing you say can take that away from me. And, by the way, do you make it a habit to use words like 'ass' in front of Westie?"

"Don't you dare talk to me about being a mother. At least I am here, which is more than I can say for Westie's sister or father."

Blonde Sheila's voice was in Delores's head now, and later she'd tell Lester that that was what made her say what she said next.

"I've been in touch with Westie's father. I know where he is. I know more than that actually. He's got this whole other life. It sounds crazy until you see it, but in his own kind of pathetic way, at least he's trying."

"You've seen him?" she asked.

"Yeah, I've seen him. He works right near me. In fact, right now he's kind of working with me."

Her mother seemed to be pulled across the table by Delores's revelation. Her face got hard and white, and her body caved in. Delores had just answered the question she'd asked herself earlier. This was how one person wrote misery on another, and she immediately wished she could erase her words.

"It's a long story, Mom," she said, her voice becoming softer. "You're really not going to believe it." Delores told her mother about the circus, Mr. Hanratty, the elephants. She said she believed her father was sorry for leaving them and, in his own way, was trying to make up for it. "I think he thinks he'll never be forgiven, but he sure tried hard to make me understand why he did it."

"I'm not really interested in why he did it," said her mother. "Though I do think it's pretty strange that he left one circus to join another. I'll say one thing about that man, there's nothing predictable about him." Color came back to her face, and she sat up straight. For a few moments, mother and daughter reclaimed their family, laughing and reveling in the strangeness of one of their own. Then her mother grew angry again, breaking the spell. "He was a coward to leave us the way he did. I'll never forgive him that. If you want to think that he's trying to make up for it, then that's your business. But don't expect me to buy into it just because you do. You're a big girl now, and I can't stop you from choosing him. But don't ever forget that that man, your father, walked out on you and your baby brother."

They both looked down at Westie, then across the table at Lester. Lester? Amid the bedlam of the friendly fire, they had completely forgotten that Lester was still in the room.

"Westie," said Delores, "let's take Lester to your room so you can show him your toys." As Westie led them to his pile of toys, Delores spotted the puppet right away. He was lying in the corner with a heap of other dolls. His skirt was wrinkled and covered with brown stains; his head was turned toward the wall. She picked him up and began examining him for cracks or scratches. The rhinestone tear was gone from his cheek. "Otto," she whispered. He lay lifeless in her palm. She placed him on her hand. Westie was showing Lester his train set. Delores brought the puppet to Westie. "Westie, didn't you promise to take care of Otto? Look at him; he's filthy." Westie ignored her. For so long, she'd needed Otto to make her world whole; now no one seemed to need him anymore. As she placed him back on the pile of dolls, Delores saw that there were dustballs and a couple of toys strewn under Westie's bed. What a mess!

Later that evening, after Delores and Lester came back from seeing the Empire State Building and Macy's, they walked into the apartment as her mother was talking on the phone. Her mother's voice, which to Delores seemed overly flirty, drifted toward them. "Oh, Bert, you are too much," she was saying, as she wrapped the telephone cord around her little finger.

Oh my God, she's talking to a man, thought Delores. *That's just great. She probably parades men in and out of here like some backstreet whore.*

The following morning, after talking with some potential babysitters in the neighborhood, her mother went back to work at the supermarket, and Delores and Lester took Westie to the Statue of Liberty. Even Lester was moved by that sight, the lady in the harbor welcoming strangers with empathy in her unblinking eyes. New York was like Weeki Wachee in that people came because they'd be accepted here. People who couldn't go anywhere else made this their home and, like the people at Weeki Wachee, they formed a family defined by their otherness.

On the morning of their third day in New York, Delores decided to call Molly.

"How are rehearsals going?" asked Delores.

"Pretty good," answered Molly. "Slow. You know how Mr. Hanratty is—we have to do everything over about a hundred times. So how's it going up there?"

"We're doing fine up here. Lester's been great. My mother's the same—for better or worse." She told Molly about Westie's messy room, her mother's cursing, the men she was sure were coming and going. "Let's just say she's not going to win the Mother of the Year award anytime soon."

There was dead air on the other end of the phone. "Molly, you still there?" asked Delores.

"Yes, but I have something to tell you. I heard that Armando's doing your job."

"What? At the TV station?"

"Yeah, he's doing the weather," said Molly. "Well, I don't think permanently," she said. "But I just thought you should know."

Somehow, the news about Armando didn't surprise Delores. There was something about him that was too good to be true. He was too everything: too handsome, too polite, too smooth. Too ambitious.

Delores tried to keep her voice even. "Listen, I really have to get off the phone now."

"Yeah, sure. Well, good luck with Lester and your mom."

Later that night, Delores was waiting when her mother got back from her cleaning job. Lester and Westie were asleep in his room, so it was just the two of them. "Can I get you a Tab?" asked Delores, as her mother plopped onto the couch, took off her shoes, and rested her bare feet on the arm of the couch. Her mother often complained about how hard she worked, but now, looking at her red and swollen feet, Delores could feel it viscerally. "Mom, you know what you need as much as a Tab? You need a pedicure. And lucky for you, one of the things I've learned in my career as a *cheap* ass-wiggler is how to do pedicures. So go soak your feet for a few minutes and I'll get my tools."

Delores pulled a cosmetic bag from her duffel while her mother stood in the bathtub and let the cold water run over her sore feet. When she came back to the living room, Delores was waiting with the Tab and polish. "You get comfortable and gimme those," she said, patting her lap. Her mother lay back and closed her eyes while Delores massaged her feet with moisturizer.

Strange, this sudden intimacy. When there were fifteen hundred miles between them, her mother became a cartoon figure, someone she could parody in a few short sentences. But this close, it was more complicated. She saw things in her mother that reminded her of herself: how hard she kept trying even though the odds seemed stacked against her, how much alike they looked. They both had the same big, strong feet. She thought about her father and how he had ended up at the circus, while she was at a tourist attraction not even twenty miles away; about his affinity for the elephants and her own for the turtles and dolphins. She was connected to these people in the most primal ways, yet she knew so little about them.

She patted her mother's feet dry with a towel.

"I can't remember the last time I felt taken care of like this," said her mother.

Delores wondered if this was true.

"*Oh, Bert, you are too much.*"

As she shook up a bottle of Pinky Pink polish, she tried to sound casual as she asked: "Mom, who's Bert?"

"Oh, Bert." Her mother raised her hand then dropped it again. Her eyes were still closed.

Delores waited. "So who is he?"

"Just a friend."

"What kind of friend?"

"A friend friend!"

"Is he a friend that Westie knows?"

"What is this, *What's My Line?* He's a friend, that's all you need to know." Her mother sat up.

"Don't move, or you'll smudge," said Delores, grabbing her by the ankle. "Okay, forget about Bert for a moment. What about getting a sitter for Westie? What will you do when we leave?"

"I'm trying to find help—what can I do? Maybe your friend Lester would like to stick around and babysit."

"Very funny." Delores kept polishing.

"Why not, he's kind of cute."

"Seriously, Mom, you're having a tough time, aren't you?"

"That is an understatement," said her mother, her eyes welling up with tears. "Westie's a sweet boy, but he's a handful. And with no male authority around, I worry . . ."

"Look here, you like the color?" asked Delores, blowing on her mother's pink toenails.

"Pretty. You do nice work, hon."

Delores opened a bottle of sealer. "Listen, Mom, I have this idea. Let me finish before you say anything. Seeing as I'm making pretty good money, and I work at a place that's always filled with young people, well, I thought that maybe Westie could come down to Weeki Wachee and stay with me for a little while. Not long or anything, a few weeks maybe. Just think about it. He'd be outdoors every day, there'd be lots for him to do. He'd never be lonely, and there'd always be someone around to watch him."

"What are you saying, Delores?" Her mother's voice was clotted with anger.

"Just that you could use a break, and maybe Westie could come down and be with me for a little while." The pungent smell of sealer filled the room.

"What kind of a mother do you think I am?" She pulled her feet off her daughter's lap and sat upright. "I know you're a hotshot star down there, so maybe you've forgotten about your mom back home. Well, let me refresh your memory. My mother left us when I was two years old. I was a teenager when I had you. My husband walked out on me. Then you up and go to Florida to do this mermaid thing, leaving me alone with your baby brother. And now you want to take *him* from me 'for a little while'? Do you have any idea how that makes me feel? Where would that leave *me* in all this? Does anyone ever consider *my* feelings? Tissues. Where are the friggin' tissues?" She wiped her eyes with the back of her hand.

"Here," said Delores, giving her mother some of the cotton balls in her bag. "Now, can I say something?"

"No, let me finish. I work pretty damn hard to keep

my life going. To keep my dignity. I know you send me money every month, thank you very much. But frankly, I am sick of everything always being about you. I have a life, too."

"Yeah, well, I see how your life is, I see exactly how it is."

"You see nothing, young lady. You see exactly what you want to see. If you are saying that I am a bad mother, then you have no idea what a bad mother is. I'm still here, aren't I? I have sacrificed a helluva lot to make a home for that boy, which is more than I can say about you or your beloved father."

If she got derailed right now she might never find her way back, so Delores kept her anger inside. "You're right," she said. "Which is why I want to help out. This wouldn't be forever. And it could be really good for you. You could quit the job at the supermarket. Maybe you could even do some more work for your friend at the magazine—Avon, or whatever her name is."

"Avalon," said her mother pointing to the cotton balls. "I need more of those." She wiped her nose and dabbed her eyes. "There is one thing. Avalon has said a couple of times that, if I could find the time, maybe the magazine would pay to send me to secretarial school to learn typing and shorthand. She says they need more trained clerical help. But that's ridiculous. What am I talking about? Am I going to send a three-year-old to live with a bunch of mermaids, a bunch of freaks? No, no, that's crazy. Westie stays with me and that's that."

God, her mother was the most annoying person in the world. She really brought out the worst in her. Delores thought about Dave Hanratty and about what he might say in this situation. "If you had some time off from taking care of Westie, you *could* go to secretarial school and learn some real skills. You'd never have to take any stupid job just because it's there. You'd earn good money. Don't you see? You'd get to call the shots. This could change every-thing."

Her mother sniffled as she listened.

When she finally did speak, her voice was nasally and girlish. "That part makes sense. The part about sending Westie with you, that part's just nuts. Lemme sleep on it."

Her mother yawned. "It's getting late. I need my beauty rest. Want to keep me company while I set my hair?"

Delores sat on her mother's bed, watching as she took little pieces of hair, twirled them around her finger, then clipped them with metal pin-curlers. When she finished, she wrapped a blue hairnet, babushka-style, around the construction site atop her head. "And you think I'm a freak?" Delores couldn't contain herself.

"Takes one to know one," her mother said and laughed.

Delores smiled weakly. "So you'll think on it, on all the stuff we talked about."

"Yeah, we'll talk tomorrow. Sleep well. And don't do anything I wouldn't do," she winked and nodded toward where Lester was sleeping. Delores rolled her eyes and went off to the pullout couch in the living room.

When she got up the next morning, she found her mother already sitting at the breakfast table with a cup of coffee in one hand and the Yellow Pages resting on her knees. She'd taken the hairnet off and the pin-curlers out but hadn't yet combed out her hair. As she leaned over the phone book, hair pieces fell over her face like party streamers. "So lookee here," she said, poking her finger at a little ad in the middle of the page: *Jump-Start Your Career Now*, it read. *Learn All the Clerical Skills You Need to Be a Professional. The Marcie Breitman Learning Center.*

"Grab a pencil, hon, and write down this number. This one seems to be close by." Delores wrote down what her mother said, then asked: "Does this mean you've made up your mind?"

"About what?"

"You know, about Westie coming to Weeki Wachee, and all that," she said impatiently.

"We'll cross that bridge when we get to it. I'll call some of these places, and then let's see where we're at."

This was better than nothing, thought Delores.

"What are you kids going to do today?" asked her mother, pushing a curl off her forehead.

"Mom, why is your hair like that? Why didn't you just comb it out?"

"You know, sometimes I'm glad you left home. I really don't need a critical seventeen-year-old watching me all the time. But if you must know, I don't think it's right for a man—even your cute young friend in there—to see a woman with her hair set. So I took out the pin-curlers in order to be presentable, but then wanted my coffee real bad, so I didn't bother to do the rest. Is that all right with you?"

"Yeah, it's fine with me. Only you look a little like George Washington."

The conversation might have gone downhill fast had Westie not called from the bedroom. Delores tiptoed in to get him. Lester was still asleep on his side; he'd thrown off his covers and she could see his bare shoulder. It was tan and muscular and reminded her of the wing of one of those giant ospreys that flew over the Springs. She was still in her slippers and robe, and she paused as she was about to pick up Westie, who had the sour odor of a morning child. In the dappled light that seeped through the crevices of the Venetian blinds, it would have been the most cozy, natural thing in the world to run her finger lightly down Lester's back, just as a way of saying "How are you?" Only the presence of her mother in the other room stopped her. Lord knows if her mother saw that, she'd never hear the end of it.

Delores took Westie into the kitchen and cuddled him in her lap as they sat at the table, across from her mother with her bizarre George Washington–do, still skimming the Yellow Pages. How long had it been since there were this many Walkers in the apartment? In the Walker home?

"Home" was a funny word, thought Delores, warm and empty at the same time. When she thought of home, she thought of towels on the bathroom floor, toast crumbs spilled on the kitchen counter from the morning's breakfast, half-finished sentences shouted from room to room. A dull ache filled Delores's stomach. It was that same sensation that had gnawed at her on those cold Sundays when she'd lock herself in the bathroom to drown out the sound of her parents' fighting. Only this time, the feeling that was snaking up inside her wasn't hers. She felt it for her mother, imagining what it would be like for her to sit in this home by herself, so quiet and alone.

Her mother looked up from the phone book abruptly, as if nudged on the shoulder by her daughter's thoughts. "Well, hon, I'd love to chat. But I don't have all day. Some of us work for a living."

"I know, Mom, but there's one more thing I've been meaning to tell you."

Her mother stiffened, as if awaiting a blow.

"You know the back of your closet, where you keep your old fox stole and stuff?" Delores continued. "Go look behind that, there's something there for you."

"Now?" asked her mother.

"Yeah, now's a good time," said Delores.

Her mother went to the closet and came back holding the Crown Royal bag half filled with coins. "Where did this come from?" she asked, holding the bag away from her.

"Dad collected them. Didn't you know that?"

Her mother shook her head, as if trying to rid it of an old memory. "No, not really," she said.

"Well, they're for you."

Her mother seemed embarrassed and clearly wanted to move off the subject. "So, what are your plans for today?" she asked.

Delores's old friend, Ellen Frailey, had said she would pick up her and Westie and Lester and take them to Orchard Beach for the day. So Delores was only half lying when she said, "Oh, Ellen's going to drive over."

Her mother scraped back her kitchen chair. "It beats me

how that friendship has survived. She probably has all these fancy Riverdale friends by now. Well, you are a novelty, I will say that."

And just like that, all of the sympathy Delores had been accruing for her mother that morning went out the window and down the sewer right in front of their apartment on the Grand Concourse in the Bronx.

As they rode toward Orchard Beach in Ellen's Toyota, Delores and Lester savored the briny fish smell of the water. They'd been on land for four days now. To them, that was akin to drowning, and although the soupy water of Orchard Beach was not comparable to the crystalline Springs, just the sight of it felt restorative. They spread their blanket on the beach, anchoring each corner with a shoe. Ellen had greeted Delores with a big hug when they first saw each other. "You are more gorgeous than I remembered," she'd said when she walked into the apartment. She'd picked up Westie and told him what a big boy he was, then thrown her arms around Lester and told him how happy she was to meet him. Delores was relieved that Ellen hadn't changed all that much, even if she did have a lot of fancy new friends.

When they got to the beach, they settled on the blanket for about two minutes before Delores shot Lester a look that said, "Let's go in." She asked Westie to dig the biggest hole that anyone had ever dug and said she was sure Ellen would help. Then she and Lester ran down to the beach, dove in, and swam for a while. Lester came up beside

Delores. "Wanna put on a show?" he asked. "Here?" she answered. "Why not?" he said. "I'll bet none of these people have ever seen live mermaids before." She glanced toward the shore where ladies were going into the water only waist-deep so as not to mess their hair. Couples with kids were sitting on blankets eating sandwiches and potato chips. Two older couples were playing cards. "Bet you're right," she said. "Let's do it."

The saltwater stung their eyes, but they hardly noticed. They thrust themselves into swanlike forward leaps, keeping their arms, legs, and heads back as they swam forward; they spun pinwheels; they flew into a Weeki Wachee maneuver, the knee-back dolphin, doing backflips with one leg straight and one leg bent. From the shore, they looked like a pair of sharks who'd suddenly slipped into town, their swift motions cutting sharp angles in the surf. By and by, a crowd gathered. Delores spotted Ellen and Westie. Ellen waved and gave her the thumbs-up. She picked up Westie and he waved, too. Lester went through his dance sequence from "The Merfather." Some of the ladies waded in up to their shoulders so they could get a closer look. Delores and Lester moved smoothly and quickly in every direction, making startling turns, melting into the ripples, and seemingly never coming up for air. Nearly half an hour went by before they finished. When they finally stood up and walked toward shore, the crowd applauded. Delores overheard one woman say to another, "He's a real hunk, isn't he?" She was pointing at Lester.

Later in the afternoon, Delores took Westie for a ride on her back, just as she had done a few months earlier in the

Springs. "Hang on, buddy," she yelled, as she rode the waves out to where the water was calmer. This time, there were no turtles, just clumps of seaweed and an old beer can. As she dried him off, she asked him if he liked the water. He stuck out his tummy and nodded his head. "Yes," he said. "I like it a lot."

She rubbed his hair dry and said, "Westie, can you keep a secret?" Again he nodded.

"Mommy doesn't know we came here today. This is just between us, so let's not tell her, okay?"

Sensing that this was part of some great adventure, he nodded solemnly, then pulled her by the hand. "Swim," he said. "I want to swim."

"Would you like to come back to Florida with me? You could swim every day. You could see the turtles."

Westie considered her offer for only a moment. "Okay, I'll come."

"Are you sure? You'd have to leave Mommy for a while. But I would be with you every day. Maybe you could also meet an elephant."

Westie nodded again. "Yes, I can see the turtles and elephants."

Delores hugged him. "Okay then. This is another secret, just between us. Promise?"

"I promise," he said.

Twenty-two

*H*OW CAN THE *Marcie Breitman Learning Center help you to achieve your goals?*

No one had ever concerned themselves with Gail Walker's goals before, and it made her heart skip to think that someone actually did now. The true answer was not something she wished to write on her application to the Marcie Breitman Learning Center, so instead of saying *I want to be somebody and not always feel as if I am disappearing,* she wrote: *I want to learn the skills I need to become a professional.*

Out of desperation, she'd convinced herself that an opportunity like this only came around once. The magazine had agreed to pay two-thirds of the $450 tuition fee; those silver dollars would cover the rest. Avalon said she knew for a fact that there was an opening for the secretary to the marketing director at *Cool,* and that, with a degree from the Learning Center, Gail would be the perfect candidate.

Gail tried to imagine it: a job where she didn't have to stand on her feet all day; a job where she'd get paid enough to buy clothes and wear something other than her cheap uniform. She'd quit the supermarket job. She wouldn't wake up each morning dreading the day ahead. She'd stop being an embarrassment to her daughter and herself. Delores had promised her that Thelma Foote would help with Westie. What an awful, severe woman she was, Gail thought, but she seemed efficient and responsible. Westie would be taken care of, that's all that mattered. She judged herself a bad mother for thinking that it would be okay to send her three-year-old child away from home, but she could flip that argument and argue she was a good mother for wanting what was best for him. So yes, she told Delores that Westie could go with her to Weeki Wachee. She'd call Thelma Foote on Sunday, when the rates were cheaper, and make sure she thought it was okay. What was the big deal? He'd be outside all day, not cooped up in this stinking apartment. There'd be other kids around. And besides, this was only temporary. He'd come home as soon as she got her certificate.

Delores knew enough not to wallow in her victory. Had her mother even suspected that this is what she had been dreaming about, she'd take it back fast, if only out of spite. So Delores spoke to her only of the practicalities: the clothes he'd bring, the airline ticket she'd buy. But alone with Lester, she pirouetted merrily around him. "I can't believe it. Westie Walker is coming to Weeki Wachee." She giggled. "Say that three times in a row: Westie Walker of Weeki Wachee."

Lester ran his hand over his cheek, pausing to let his fingers flutter over a new zit. "Uh, I don't mean to be a downer," he said, "but what are you going to do with Westie once you get him there? I mean, where will he sleep, and what'll he do while you're working?"

She froze in place. "Well, Lester Pogoda, you certainly *do* know how to bust a gal's bubble, don't you?"

"I'm sorry," he said. "It's just that . . ."

"It's just that, you're right," she said, finishing his sentence. She'd thought about how wonderful it would be to have Westie at Weeki Wachee, but she had never fully considered the logistics of what would happen if he actually came. "I suppose he could sleep in the dorm with me. I'm sure Molly wouldn't mind."

"What about the rest of them?" asked Lester.

Delores pictured the other girls: how they walked around the dorm naked; how freely they talked about having their periods and the jokes they made about the bloodstains on the sheets. Even with Blonde Sheila gone pure, there was still plenty of talk at night about virginity, sexual intercourse, and blue balls, whatever they were. And what if it turned out that Blonde Sheila really was pregnant?

Delores and Lester stared at each other, as if they were teetering on either end of the same thought: of course the dorm wasn't the place for a little boy. But if not the dorm, where would he stay? Maybe the whole idea of bringing him down there was a little crazy to begin with.

"Thelma," she said. "I'll call Thelma. She'll know what to do."

Knowing that her mother would be reassured if she knew that Thelma was in on the plan, Delores had lied to her mother about Thelma's willingness to help out. Now, as she waited for the long-distance operator to connect her, she could feel panic churning up her stomach.

Thelma picked up after the first ring. "Yes, what is it?"

"Hey, it's Delores."

"Oh, hey, how are you-all doing up there?" She sounded as if she was doing something else, which made Delores get to the point fast: "I've convinced my mother to let my little brother come live with me for a little while. So he's coming back down with us. Thing is, I'm not sure exactly where he'll sleep. You know, stuff like that."

Silence.

Delores envisioned Thelma picking a thread off her windbreaker. She could feel her peevishness before she heard it.

"Are you out of your mind, bringing a little kid down here? I'm running a business, not a day care center."

"Yes, but I thought that..."

Thelma wasn't listening. "Have you told Mr. Chatty about your brilliant idea?"

"Who's Mr. Chatty?"

Thelma sounded embarrassed. "Oh, it's just a little nickname I made up for your dad. Anyway, what does he think about all this?"

"I haven't told him yet."

"If you're going to hold the Walker family reunion down here, don't you think he ought to know?"

"I wanted to talk to you first." Delores sounded as if she might cry.

"How do you envision this? What do you think the kid will do all day?"

"He loves the water," said Delores. "I'll teach him how to swim. Who knows, maybe he'll become the world's youngest merman. That wouldn't hurt business, would it?"

"I'm sure there are laws against hiring three-year-olds."
Again a pause. "This is ridiculous. No, I can't allow this. It's
out of the question."

Thelma slammed down the phone. Delores tried to hold
back her tears.

Lester shook his head. "She didn't buy it, I guess."

"I don't know what I'm doing," Delores said, her voice
trembling. "This is the dumbest idea I've ever had."

"Call her back," he said. "Tell her you need her help."

This time the phone rang three times. "Yes," said Thelma.

"Look, my mom is exhausted," said Delores, still close to
tears. "She can really use a break. Besides, I miss my
brother. I don't want to come back without him."

"Are you threatening me, young lady? Because if you
are, it won't wash with me."

Delores hadn't meant it as a threat. "No, not at all, honest. Look, I really don't know what I'm doing. I'm really
scared. I know this sounds like a crazy idea; it's just that
Westie's growing up so fast, I don't want to miss any more
of it."

Thelma heard the longing in Delores's voice. She remembered that wanting something so badly and not getting it could shift a person's point of view forever. Here she
was with the power to give this girl the thing she probably
wished for more than anything else. It was too late for her
to rewrite her own history, but Delores was young: her history was still being written.

"Let's talk about this," said Thelma, settling into her desk
chair and pulling a pen and legal pad from her drawer. "For
starters, we can get a cot and have him sleep in the dorm

with you While you're working, he can be with some of
the other girls. We're going to have to ask Mr. Chatty to
pitch in. How do you think he'll feel about that?"

"I don't know," said Delores, "but I know that Lester said
he would help out, too."

Thelma went on: "Food: you'll pay for his food and
clothing. And you have to promise me this: if he gets
homesick and wants to go home, you've got to let him go."

Delores paused. "I promise."

Thelma wrote everything down on her notepad. Fifteen
minutes later, she put down her pen and groaned. "This is
probably the worst decision I've ever made, but you can
bring the damn kid down here on one condition. I'm going
to tell the others. If they say no, then the party's over. If
they say yes, then we'll try it for a little while and see. Just
call your father and tell him about your harebrained
scheme."

Delores flushed with relief. "Oh God, thank you. I'll call
Mr. Chatty tonight."

Lester gave her the thumbs-up. She made a mental note
to leave her mother ten dollars for the long-distance
phone calls. Lester sat on the floor with Westie, who was
watching cartoons on television, while Delores went into
Westie's room, where her mother had already started packing up his belongings. "I'm sorry, but he doesn't have a lot
of summer clothes," said her mother. "Don't worry about it,
Mom," said Delores. "There's plenty to choose from down
there."

Her mother seemed not to hear her. She held up a red-
and-blue-striped T-shirt. "He's so little," she said, staring at

the handkerchief-sized garment, then turned to Delores. "When you buy, buy big. He's growing like nobody's business."

"I know, I will," she said, folding the last of his shorts. Her mother lowered the lid of the suitcase. "Wait, just one more thing," said Delores, stepping over to the pile of dolls. She dug out Otto and straightened his skirt. She wrapped him in one of Westie's pajama bottoms, then stuck him in one of the side pockets of the suitcase, alongside Westie's favorite Tyrannosaurus, and snapped the latch shut.

Delores knew her father got off work by five, so she waited an hour before calling him at Dave Hanratty's office. Hanratty answered the phone crisply: "Hanratty's Circus, Spectacular and Amazing. Hanratty speaking." Thelma could certainly learn some phone etiquette from him.

"Hi, Mr. Hanratty, this is Delores Taurus. I was hoping to speak to my father."

Hanratty couldn't have sounded more delighted if it was P. T. Barnum roused from the dead.

"Well, well. This is a special treat. How lovely to hear from you, Miss Taurus. Just one moment, I'll go find him."

As she waited, she wondered how she would explain to her father about Westie. Maybe she'd start by saying that life was full of surprises, but here he was, living among elephants and chimps, so he probably knew that. She'd just have to figure it out as she went along. Seconds later, he picked up the phone.

"Hello," he said with no affect.

"Oh, hi, umm. It's me. Well, I guess you know that. I

have some news. My mother, umm, your not-really-wife-anymore, and I decided that it would be a good idea for me to bring Westie down to Weeki Wachee for a while. You know, for a change of pace for everyone." She paused, waiting for him to speak, but he didn't.

"I just wanted to tell you so it won't be a shock."

"Okay then."

"That's it? Do you have anything to say about it?"

"Not really."

"Okay then," she said. "See you in a couple of days."

"Right."

She stared at the phone before returning it to its cradle. *Mr. Chatty*, she thought. *Now there's a man who should never have had children.*

They'd agreed Gail would not go with them to the airport. "It's too hard," she'd said, her eyes filmy with tears. So on the morning they were to leave, they got up at six to take the subway to Grand Central Station in Manhattan, where they would catch a bus to the airport. Delores was just taking the cereal from the cabinet when her mother came out of her bedroom wearing her favorite red-and-white-checked blouse and a pair of white pants. Her hair was neatly combed and she'd put on lipstick and some dusty-blue eye shadow. She walked slowly to the kitchen table, never taking her eyes off the floor.

"You look real nice, Mom," said Delores.

"I don't want him to remember me as some hag," she whispered to Delores. "Look here, I'm going to make some pancakes. Hand me the milk, hon." Her voice was flat, absent its timbre of anger. She seemed frail and wan against the colorless light.

The four of them ate breakfast in silence. When it was time to go, Gail put her hands on Delores's shoulders. "I can't believe we're doing this," she said. "When I spoke to Thelma Foote yesterday, she said we'd try it for a while. Just a while. And remember, if he gets homesick, home he comes." Then she picked up Westie, and nuzzled her head into the softest part of his neck. She took deep breaths as if she were trying to ingest his smell. It embarrassed Delores to hear the creaking sounds coming from her mother's throat. After a long while, she let Westie down. "You'll like Florida," she told him. She patted Lester on the back and smiled a pencil-thin smile.

"Mommy," cried Westie. "Mommy is coming with us."

"Mommy's not coming now," said Delores, leaving her sentence in midair.

Her mother turned around and walked over to Westie. She knelt beside him and said, "Mommy's staying here for now. But you'll see Mommy very soon."

"No, Mommy, you come with us. We'll stay in a hotel." He began to cry.

Gail managed to keep her voice steady: "Tell you what, when you get to Florida, Delores will buy you a big box of cupcakes. You can eat one cupcake a day, and by the time you finish the box, Mommy will come down."

"We're going back to the turtles. Remember the turtles?" said Delores. "Remember how we talked about the elephants and how you would get to swim every day?"

"No. No turtles. Mommy comes, too."

Gail stood up. It was important to her that Westie not see her cry. "You go now," she said, turning away from them and walking back into her bedroom. She sat on her bed, trying not to hear Westie's wails as Delores and Lester led him down the hall. *Only a monster would let her child go motherless,* she thought to herself. *What kind of a person am I?*

Twenty-three

*T*HE FIRST NIGHT Westie spent in the dorm, he cried himself to sleep. In between sobs, he'd say, "Mommy, I want my mommy." The more the girls tried to comfort him, or sing to him, the louder he cried. He calmed down only after Delores promised to take him to the elephants the next day, but by then he was also exhausted.

The following morning, Delores and Westie walked down to the Springs, where they found her father waist-deep in the water next to Nehru. He was murmuring to Nehru, who appeared to be bending down so she could hear him. Delores watched for a while before hollering: "Hello. Umm, hello." He turned toward her and she pointed down at Westie. "Look who's here."

Westie stared at the man in the water who, though he looked remarkably similar to him—short and round, like a hatbox—was a complete stranger. Roy stared back, all the while stroking Nehru's trunk. At one time or another, most children with siblings wonder if, should they all be drowning, whom their father would save first. Most probably wouldn't answer: the elephant. Delores thought back to their conversation of the week before, and how he'd said:

"I like working with the animals and, for the most part, people leave me alone." He looked at peace there, in the water with Nehru. She'd never thought about peace, and what it was. But if he felt about Nehru the way she felt every time she swam in the Springs, then that was peace. That was home.

Her father whispered something to the elephant, then climbed out of the water. He crouched down on his knees and stared into Westie's face. "Well, well," he said. Had he noticed the gap between Westie's two front teeth? Just like his gap. "Well, well," he said again, a grin creeping over his face. Westie squinted and moved a step closer to Delores.

"Westie, do you know who this is?" she asked. "This is your father. Your daddy," she said, knowing full well that just because you call someone your daddy, doesn't mean you feel it. "Daddy," she said again. Even saying the word made her feel peculiar, though for all Westie cared, she might as well have said: *This is the man in the moon.*

Roy scanned the boy with his eyes. "So, young man, how do you like it here so far?" His voice, too loud and too singsong, betrayed his discomfort with children.

"We just got in last night," said Delores. "He bunked with me in the dorm and was a big hit with the girls, weren't you, Westie? We're going swimming later. Westie likes to swim."

"So, young man, you like to swim?" asked her father.

He was clueless; he had no idea how to talk to anyone, much less his own son.

Delores tried to move the conversation along. "Westie's never seen an elephant before. This is his first," she said.

Roy pointed to Nehru. "She's big, isn't she?"

Westie nodded, his eyes filling with the sight of the creature.

"Would you like to meet her?" asked Delores. Westie looked up at her with a "Can I really do this?" expression on his face.

"Go on," she said. "Nehru's real nice, you'll like her. Your dad will introduce you."

"You think?" asked Roy, under his breath.

"It'll be fine," she said. "Take him."

Roy went to lift up Westie, who held on to Delores's legs. "It's okay," she said to him. "He's going to lift you up so you can pat the elephant." Westie tentatively disengaged himself from Delores's legs.

Roy scooped the boy into his arm and waded back into the water. Westie looked like a cub snuggled against his father's broad, tan chest. *He's so pale and new,* thought Delores, and it made her wonder when people started to look used up. With his free hand, Roy patted Nehru on her chest. He urged Westie to do the same. Tentatively, Westie poked at the animal with one finger. He poked again and again. Roy took his hand and held it up so he could pat Nehru's flank. Nehru bent her head and Roy whispered something Delores couldn't hear. The elephant sucked in some water and squirted it out her trunk. Westie giggled as the spray rained down on him. Contained within the arc of the spray was a perfect, fleeting rainbow. Now her father and Westie were splashing water back at Nehru. As they did this, Delores had the bizarre notion that maybe Westie might become comfortable with Nehru, Roy with Westie, and that maybe even the four of them could eventually add up to something that resembled a family.

Before she went off to the television station that afternoon, Delores asked her father if Westie might stay with him until early evening. At first, he hesitated, saying that he'd have to run it by Wulf. Then he considered what it might be like to bring Westie to the Giant Café after work. They'd eat hamburgers and key-lime pie. He'd introduce him to Rex, and if Mr. Hanratty came by, he'd stand up and say, "Mr. Hanratty, I'd like you to meet my son, West Walker, though we call him Westie now." He'd take him back to his trailer to show him where he lived, and if there was time, they'd visit Lucy.

"Yeah, that'll be okay," he said to Delores. "I'll take the kid."

The air-conditioning in the van breathed out warm air. It was so hot that, from time to time, Thelma and Delores would have to wipe the steam off their sunglasses. Thelma claimed she had better things to spend her money on than air-conditioning. Yet when Delores tried to open a window, she got annoyed. "I'm not paying to cool down all of Florida," she said, yanking on one of her driving gloves. So Delores sat as still as she could, feeling the sweat under her arms and down between her breasts.

They drove in silence for the first half of the trip. Then Thelma began talking as if they'd been in a conversation the whole time. "I must say, I used to have respect for Mr. Sommers, but over time I've come to think of him as something of an ass." She kept her eyes on the road. "That nice man who runs the Giant Café has been setting up his new café at the Springs over the past week. Rex is his name, and I'll tell you this, he's a real gentleman, something you don't see very often."

Delores jumped in: "Did Sommers give Armando my job?"

"No," said Thelma. "He just put him in your spot while you were gone."

"How do you know he didn't give it to him for good?"

"Oh, he'd never do that. Right now Sommers is golden. And it's all because of you. He's not going to do anything to change that."

Ever since her trip to New York, Delores had been thinking a lot about her television job. Her mother had called her "cheap," and Delores couldn't dislodge the word from her brain. And now that Westie was here, did she really want him to see her sitting half-naked in a bathtub on television?

"I'm tired of the bathtub thing. And besides, it's not dignified." She cocked her head as she said *dignified*. She'd never used that word before.

Thelma glanced at Delores. "The thing about dignity is that it's more how you feel than how you look. If sitting in the bathtub humiliates you, then I would be the first person to tell you not to do it. People like us hold our dignity inside, and let the rest of the world judge us however they want. It's humiliation that's unbearable." She banged her fist against the horn and shouted "You stupid louse" to the blue Dodge that had just cut her off. She went on· "You know Rex, the man I was telling you about? He's almost eight feet tall. People stare and say stupid things to him all the time like 'Hey, big fella, how's the air up there?' He's always very respectful, no matter how insulting they get. Eventually, they come around to liking him just for him, and he never lets on that they've made witless fools of themselves. That's what I call dignity."

When they pulled into the parking lot at the studio, Thelma reached across Delores to put her gloves in the glove compartment. "Whatever you decide to do, I'll stand behind you," she said, not wanting to make any more of it than that.

They rode up to the eighth floor where they headed straight to Sommers's office. His receptionist greeted them with a big hello, then buzzed her boss. "Fishgirl is back," she whispered, then giggled over something he said. "You betcha." She hung up. "Have a seat, doll. Thelma, he'll be just a minute."

When Sommers finally called them in, he was sitting on his couch, his arm around the back of it. He was staring out the window and chewing on a Fig Newton.

"So how was the Big Apple?" he asked Delores, still looking out the window. "Makes this place look like some rathole in the middle of nowhere, doesn't it?"

"I like it here," she said.

"Well, don't get too used to it. You and I aren't going to spend the rest of our careers in this swamp, I'll tell you that."

Delores took a seat across from him. Thelma sat on the other side of the couch. "What about Armando?" asked Delores. "Is he going to spend the rest of his career in this swamp?"

Sommers threw back his head and laughed extravagantly. "She slays me, she really does," he said to Thelma.

She caught a whiff of stale onions, then said, "Delores isn't trying to be funny."

"Oh, I know what she's getting at," he said, turning to Delores and raising a finger. "He subbed for you when you were away. I told you before you went to New York that I'd take care of who would fill in for you. Right before you left, he came to me and said that our viewers tune in to see Delores Taurus, not just any mermaid. He said that no one could replace you, so we shouldn't even try. He suggested we do something very straightforward and simple, then said he would like to try it. I figured, what the hell? He's good-looking, he's got that ethnic thing going and a great head of hair. He did a couple of dry runs and was good. His timing was *perfecto*. Says he learned from the best."

"Hmm," said Delores, scowling.

A wormy smile crept across Sommers's face. "You worried that your cute boyfriend's gonna steal your job?"

"He's not my boyfriend."

"You've got that right. You know that your little friend plays on the other side of the street, don't you?"

"What do you mean?"

"Excuse me, Mr. S., but this conversation is completely inappropriate." Thelma sat up and put her hands on her knees.

"Oh, come now, Thelma. Everyone knows that Armando likes boys."

Delores suddenly felt light-headed and had to grip the sides of the chair to steady herself. "I don't understand."

"It's okay, child, nothing for you to worry about." Now Thelma was glaring at Sommers, who didn't seem to notice.

"Would you like me to spell it out for you?"

"No, not really," said Delores.

She remembered the night after the hurricane when they were driving back to the studio. Roberta Flack had come on the radio and he'd said something about her song being "X-rated." She'd put her hand on his knee and he'd just sat there, didn't react or make a move. She remembered thinking that it felt no different from resting her hand on a stack of books.

"I don't want to do the weather from the bathtub anymore," she said.

Thelma leaned forward while Sommers tried to dig a piece of the fig cookie from between two molars. Not bothering to take his finger out of his mouth, he said something incomprehensible.

Delores and Thelma exchanged looks, and Delores thought about what Thelma had said earlier about dignity and humiliation. The news about Armando, Sommers mocking her to her face, this was the kind of humiliation Thelma was talking about. Unbearable.

"Now I don't understand," said Sommers.

"No more bathtub. End of story. That's all she wrote," said Thelma.

Sommers took his finger out of his mouth. His face reddened to the color of clay. "Are you telling me what you will or won't do?" he shouted at Delores.

"Yes, I guess I am," she said, not believing that she'd just talked back to him like that.

Thelma nodded at Delores, encouraging her to continue.

"Do you have any idea what you're saying, who you're talking to?" he was still yelling.

"I do." She brushed her bangs off her face with the back of her hand.

Everything about Sommers—his wiry hair, rat-a-tat speech, jerky motions—bespoke a man whose fuse was about to blow. Delores could picture what it would be like when he finally exploded: fragments of his tiny, sharp teeth; shreds of his expensive shirts; bits of Fig Newton sinking into the shag carpet and splattering against the ceiling-to-floor windows.

He turned to Thelma. "To what do you attribute her sudden change in attitude?" he asked, trying to contain himself.

"Ask her," said Thelma.

"To what do you attribute . . ."

"I heard you," said Delores, gaining confidence. "It's just that I have a job to do and I do it pretty well. But how can anyone take me seriously if I'm doing it in a bathtub?"

"You're a star," he said. "I made you a goddam star. Do you know how many girls like you would give their eyeteeth to be where you are?"

"If I may say, I think it's the other way around. I think Delores has made you a star," said Thelma.

Sommers bit down on his ring. Beads of sweat bubbled up on his upper lip. Maybe he'd gone too far.

Delores had never known what it felt like to be repelled by someone until this moment. So searing and absolute was her contempt for him that it bordered on pleasurable. Something deep inside of her went cold, and her words, when they came, were crisp and brusque.

"I'll wear a green, fitted dress that suggests a mermaid. I'll keep the stupid stuff about it being a rainy day for Mr. and Mrs. Jones's twenty-fifth wedding anniversary. I'll even have my hair wet and slicked back if you like. But that's it. No bathtub."

"Not a bad compromise," said Thelma, folding her arms in front of her chest.

"So that's what it will take to keep you on the team?" asked Sommers, sounding relieved.

"That's it," she said.

"Wet hair, eh? That's a nice touch. Wish I had thought of it myself." His compliment was meant to breach the gap that had just been hollowed out between them. Although Delores smiled, they both knew that something had changed.

Part Three

Twenty-four

$\mathcal{T}$HE AQUA ZOO would be the first of its kind—
Dave Hanratty wasn't interested in anything
that wasn't—and it would change everything that had
come before it. The colors of the Springs, the familiar
navy and white, had now become aqua and palm-frond
green. The Giant Café had been redesigned in the shape
of a carousel, with a bright blue-and-green metal roof.

Over the past three months, boastful new signs had
sprung up along the roads nearby promising things like:
THE GIANT CAFÉ: THE BIGGEST AND BEST FOOD IN THE WORLD and
THE AQUA ZOO: SPECTACULAR AND AMAZING BEYOND YOUR
WILDEST IMAGINATION. Even the gift shop bragged about
NEVER BEFORE SEEN TREASURES FROM EARTH AND SEA. Its inventory, which had always been skimpy, now overflowed with
stuffed blue elephants and yellow chimpanzees with green-
and-blue-striped swim trunks sewn on their little bottoms.
There were packets of magic flowers that sprang to life
when you put them in a glass of water, and wooden pop
guns with the words *Aqua Zoo, Weeki Wachee Springs* decaled
onto them. The decals went on everything Hanratty could
get his hands on: seashells, umbrellas, sun visors, coloring
books, and boxes of taffy and pecan delights. There were

bins filled with licorice, button candy, gumballs, and all kinds of chocolate treats. The faithful could buy banners and bumper stickers and big, glossy books with colored pictures of all the animals. Of course there was the mermaid inventory: little dolls stitched by hand, with red yarn for hair and with tails made out of sparkly material, and, for the overly zealous, full mermaid costumes to be spun to order by Barbara and Bobby Wynn, the finest, and only, mermaid tailors in the world.

Hanratty's genius was his ability to create a buzz months in advance of the actual opening without anyone having an inkling of just why they were so excited. As soon as he found out that Delores's mother worked at *Cool*, he began sending her envelopes filled with press material about the Aqua Zoo, "just in case your mother might be interested." He posted billboards on Route 50 that read: FLORIDA LIVE, LIKE YOU'VE NEVER SEEN IT BEFORE; WANT PLASTIC DUCKS AND MICE? KEEP GOING EAST. FOR THE *REAL THING*, TURN AROUND AND HEAD WEST; FLORIDA FAKE OR FLORIDA WILD? YOU CHOOSE. All had the Weeki Wachee logo of a mermaid silhouetted against a clamshell, the words *Weeki Wachee Springs*, and the site's address. They were just the kind of provocative messages that would pique a person's curiosity. The folks at Disney protested wildly, but what could they do? These were America's highways, and even *they* didn't own them.

A master of psychology, Hanratty was mindful of the pride and solidarity that uniforms engendered. Even before the Aqua Zoo opened, he made everyone at the Springs wear green camp shirts with blue elephants lumbering over their breast pockets, aqua Bermuda shorts, and white tennis shoes with white socks. No one protested except for Thelma who, with some trepidation, told Hanratty that she was not a clown and therefore saw no need to dress in costume. "Of all people, Thelma, I thought it would be you who would embrace what I am trying to foster here," Hanratty had replied. "You and I are kindred spirits, what they call old souls, don't you think? I have always savored the understanding we have between us. But if you don't want to wear the uniform, far be it from me to cause you discomfort. I value your friendship and partnership far more than I do your dress." By the end of the conversation, Thelma had agreed to the shirt and the aqua pants—only hers would be full-length—and, of course, she retained the option of wearing a windbreaker, even if it did have a blue elephant over the left breast pocket.

One afternoon, as she and Rex were going over purchase orders for new silverware for the café, they got to talking about Hanratty. Thelma said she thought he was some kind of a genius, though she couldn't really get a grip on who he was. Rex said, "He's a man who wears his head on his sleeve and keeps his heart to himself. He is quite conscious of creating his own mythology, and so he will act with his head despite his heart's inclinations. That's good for us."

Rex had a way of setting things straight in her mind. She'd never thought about anyone consciously creating his own mythology. But, of course, that's exactly what Hanratty was doing. A man like that doesn't construct an empire and leave his ego behind. *Fine,* she thought, *let him do it. Just as long as my girls and the Springs are okay, let him build whatever empire he wants.*

What everyone would always remember about the summer before the opening of the Aqua Zoo was the smell in the air. It was sweet, like maple syrup. There was no explanation for it, other than that optimism and anticipation give off their own sweet aroma. So who's to say that the trees and the air weren't intoxicated as well? Even Roy, who normally kept his head down and went about his work, now had reason to talk to people. Thelma and Delores decided that, after a brief time living in the girls' dorm, Westie would be better off sleeping on a cot in his dad's trailer at night. Although he spent most of the daytime with Delores, the constant presence of a little boy on the campgrounds made everyone a little nicer, a little more playful.

The clowns let Westie ride around in their cars with them and taught him how to make rude, honking sounds whenever he lifted his leg. The acrobats taught him how to do cartwheels and to fold himself up into a heap the size of a sand castle. Because Lucy and Westie were roughly the same size, the chimp thought nothing of grabbing the boy by the hand or rolling him onto the ground. And to think that Roy used to worry that Westie would become a mama's boy.

Dave Hanratty had never known a kid like Westie. He liked that he was squat and stubby like his father, and he

seemed regular in the way that children of circus perform-
ers aren't. Often, he would ask Westie's reaction to things
to gauge how they would work in the show. One afternoon, they sat down by the Springs together as the clowns
rehearsed a new act. The clowns would squirt the elephants with water from their seltzer bottles until the elephants would get so put out, they would dunk the clowns
with their trunks. Hanratty watched Westie's reaction. "Do
you like it when the elephants dunk the clowns?" he asked
Westie. "No," said Westie, who seemed scared by the
power of the elephants. "It's stupid." Later, when they
changed the act to the elephants squirting water back at
the clowns, Westie laughed so hard he had to lean forward. Hanratty knew the act would work.

Like his sister, Westie couldn't seem to bring himself to
say "Daddy." The best he could do was "Doy." "Doy, watch
this," he'd shout, before jumping into a pile of hay. "Doy, I
need a hamburger." "Doy, let's go see Nehru." "Doy" was so
much more than Roy had ever hoped for that, at times, his
heart would jump at the sound of the special name.

At night, Delores and Roy would tuck Westie into bed.
Westie would sometimes cry and say he missed his mom.
Delores would reassure him that she would come to visit
soon, but often, exhausted by his misery, he would cry
himself to sleep. The boy had such a sunny nature, it tore
at Roy's heart to see him so sad. One night, Roy got the
idea that if he read to Westie at bedtime, he'd get distracted and have less time to fret.

He had no clue as to what kinds of stories children
liked, nor could he think of any adults who read books.

When he happened to mention this to Rex, Rex told him, "There's one book that I've read over and over since I was a boy, and each time the story reads in a way it never did before. It's called *The Jungle Book*. It's a children's story, really, but I never get tired of it." Rex told Roy it was about a boy, Mowgli, who was chased into a wolf cave by a tiger and brought up by wolves.

"Sounds scary," said Roy.

"Not so," said Rex. "He makes friends with the animals in the jungle and gets to know them not as a little boy would know an animal, but as one animal would know another. Tell you what. Borrow my copy and read him a story about Mowgli, the little boy. See how he likes it." The next day, Rex handed Roy a brown paper bag. Inside was an orange book with a worn cloth cover and a painting of a little boy in a loincloth surrounded by a bear, a panther, and two wolves. The book was heavy, but the type was big and the lines had thick spaces between them. Roy held it in his hand as he would a can of baked beans. That night, he and Delores began to read to Westie about Mother Wolf and Father Wolf, and Tabaqui the jackal, and Shere Khan the tiger, and how, one night, Father Wolf went out to investigate a rustle in the bushes:

> He made his bound before he saw what it was he was jumping at, and then he tried to stop himself. The result was that he shot up straight into the air for four or five feet, landing almost where he left ground.
>
> "Man!" he snapped. "A man's cub. Look!"
>
> Directly in front of him, holding on by a low branch, stood

a naked brown baby who could just walk — as soft and as
dimpled a little atom as ever came to a wolf's cave at night.

The Jungle Book became a nightly ritual. Roy and Delores
took on the voices of the different animals, with Delores
hissing to impersonate Kaa the python, or speaking in a
high child's voice when reading Mowgli. Roy growled
when he imitated Baloo the bear, and made the deep hollow sounds of a tuba when he was Hathi the elephant. The
book became the common language between Roy and his
children. Roy and Delores took to calling Westie "Little
Brother," the name the animals called Mowgli, and Westie
began calling Nehru "Hathi."

All families have their codes and their funny secrets.
This wasn't much, but Delores always liked the part when
Baloo teaches Mowgli to speak the words "We be of one
blood, you and I" in all the languages of the different ani-
mals. Despite all that had happened to the disjointed
Walker family, this much was true.

Gail Walker sat in her cubicle outside the marketing director's office at *Cool*. Her diploma from the Marcie
Breitman Learning Center, still new and crisp, was tacked
up on her bulletin board above her desk. The certificate
was next to a note from Marcie Breitman herself that read:
*You, Gail, are a people person. Just remember to keep your sunny side
up and your nose to the grindstone, and you'll knock 'em dead.* It infused her with confidence and a sense of purpose. Today
she was charged with finding someone to construct one

hundred crossword puzzles whose clues would lead to the words "The solution is Cool"—favors for an upcoming event in September. She had already spent the morning calling around at party-supply stores and various puzzle companies. So far, no luck, but Gail wasn't discouraged. This was her job. She was earning ten thousand dollars a year and she had her own chair with a gray, cushioned back and metal armrests. She wiggled her toes, feeling the soft leather that lined her strappy white sandals. Avalon worked just one floor up, and, by the end of the month, Westie would be back home living with her. *Not bad*, she thought, smoothing the pleats of her white Dacron skirt. *Not bad at all.*

These days, she was allowing herself the extravagance of a daily long-distance phone call. Every night at six thirty, just after she'd get home from work, she'd dial up Dave Hanratty. Westie would be waiting to speak to her. On this evening, Hanrattty bypassed his usual greeting, "Hanratty's Circus and Aqua Zoo, Spectacular and Amazing," with "Hello, Mrs. Walker, how are you tonight?"

He asked her about how she was doing on the new job, what was in the next issue of *Cool*, and the type of audience it was targeting.

Since this was her first real business conversation, Gail tried her best to sound confident and authoritative. "*Cool* is a high-end fashion magazine with a circulation of close to five hundred thousand," she said. "The demographics are women, twenty-five to forty-five, with a household income of thirty thousand or more."

"I'll tell you my intention in asking you these questions," said Hanratty. "On November sixteenth, we will introduce the most spectacular live show ever performed in these United States. It will feature mermaids and chimps and elephants and much more, and I can tell you this: no one has ever seen anything like it. In addition, there will be an impressive array of people here from every walk of life. Without tipping my hand any further, let me just say that it would behoove *Cool* magazine to send a photographer and a reporter to our opening ceremony. Were this to happen, I would be honored to bring you here as my personal guest—hotel and airfare included. Think about it. Perhaps you'll have an answer when you call tomorrow. Just one moment, there's a young man here who is eager to speak with you."

Westie told his mother about his day. "We swam with the elephants," he said. "Delores and Lester and me are going to the movies on Saturday, and we read the part about Mowgli and Bagheera." As they had in every conversation for the past two weeks, Mowgli, Hathi, and the panther Bagheera populated most of his conversation. Gail noted how his vocabulary was growing daily. By now, he was speaking in paragraphs. It made her sad that she wasn't there to watch him say all his new words. She knew she should be happy to hear the excitement in his voice, yet it was painful to imagine the three of them there without her. She never asked Westie about his father, but every time he said "we," she knew exactly who he meant.

First thing the following morning, Gail ran upstairs to see Avalon. She told her all about the Aqua Zoo. "Dave

Hanratty's known for stopping at nothing to attract a crowd," she said, trying to sound as if he were a casual acquaintance. "Do you think the magazine might consider covering it?"

"Hmm, mermaids, chimps, elephants," said Avalon. "You know, there has been talk around here about doing a mermaid winter-fantasy story, now that we have connections." Avalon winked at Gail. "Maybe this is the moment. Okay, I'll bring it up at the story meeting tomorrow."

"That would be great," said Gail, trying not to get her hopes up. "By the way, have you ever heard of this book called *The Jungle* something or other?"

"Umm, *The Jungle Book?*"

"Yup, that's it."

"It's famous. Talk about your chimps and elephants, this guy literally wrote the book on them," said Avalon.

"Maybe I'll pick me up a copy after work," said Gail, who couldn't remember the last time she'd set foot inside a bookstore.

Twenty-five

THERE WAS A MOVIE playing inside of Hanratty's head, which no one was privy to except for Hanratty. When people spoke to him now, he seemed to look past them, absorbed in words they could not hear. At odd times, he would burst out laughing or move his lips as if repeating something overheard. The details of his behavior became the subject of speculation: the ubiquitous yellow legal pad that he carried at his side the way a traveling salesman might clutch a Bible; the dozen or so colored pencils that were jammed into the inside pocket of his jacket; the way he'd snap his fingers and then jot down notes, or draw diagrams with arrows and arcs and cartoon versions of different animals on them. No one ever got close enough to decode his drawings, but Scary Sheila observed that each color seemed to represent something or somebody in his plan.

The Aqua Zoo was what was playing in Hanratty's head, the big picture that only he held of how the show would come together. He had told each of them how he envisioned his or her part, and he expected each to build from that blueprint. Two deeply tanned dolphin trainers, Sally-Ann and Tucker, had been brought up from the Seaquarium in Miami, and Hanratty told Lester and Delores that they would be working with the trainers and some dolphins. "Sally-Ann and Tucker will take your work to the next dimension," he told them. "I want you to stop thinking of yourselves as merpeople and start thinking of yourselves as dolphins. Just remember: there are no boundaries."

Early each morning, Delores, Lester, Sally-Ann, and Tucker would board a motorboat and go out to the middle of the Weeki Wachee River where Sally-Ann and Tucker would teach the other two strange whistles and hand signals that would breach the world between them and the dolphins. The idea was to have the dolphins get comfortable enough with Delores and Lester so that they could touch them, ride them even. Sally-Ann and Tucker taught them to mimic the dolphins' movements, to leap in the air, to arch and sway as though they, too, had dorsal fins.

Hanratty spent most of his time with Wulf and the elephants, just watching and taking notes. Sometimes, Roy would bring all the elephants into the water. Hanratty would observe how the elephants naturally followed behind Nehru. He would have one of the clowns sit on the elephants' heads, just so they could all get used to it. Hanratty liked having Westie around at rehearsals, at first because he used the boy as a barometer, his giggles and fidgeting prompting more scribbles on Hanratty's pad. After a while, though, he saw how at ease Westie had become with Nehru. She seemed to view him as another young calf and became protective of him around the other elephants, and even around the clowns. "You and Nehru are friends, aren't you?" he said to Westie one morning.

The boy looked up at Nehru, who was looking down at him while chewing on some long grass stems. "Nehru is my friend," he said. "I like her." Hanratty patted Westie on the shoulder. "That's excellent."

Thelma, of course, was in charge of the mermaids and their routines. All she knew was that Hanratty had asked her to choreograph "a routine for a world where animals were the humans and humans were things that occupied the air and filled the waters." As he said those words, he rushed to write them down on his pad, then continued: "I can tell you this, your girls will be used to their full advantage. I am considering how to maximize all of their talents."

Thelma knew she was no Dave Hanratty, but she was beginning to understand how he operated, how he pushed away all constraints and barriers and was unfazed by the impossible. She began to take notes as well. Thelma had already lost Delores and Lester to Hanratty's schemes, and she'd be damned if she'd let him come up with anything for the rest of her girls. She watched her girls swim and considered how she could "maximize their talents."

Two weeks before the opening, Hanratty brought in an engineer from Georgia Tech named Oliver Turch, a tall man slightly stooped, as if he'd hovered over too many textbooks. Turch was there to help figure out how all the elements of the show would come together so that there would be no collisions and no surprises, other than the ones Hanratty had planned. The most memorable thing about Oliver Turch was that he was the only person who ever said no to Dave Hanratty. For years to come, Turch would dine out on stories about the man who invented the Aqua Zoo. "Get a load of this," he'd tell his buddies. "He wanted to know if it was physically possible to have dolphins jump in formation over an elephant's head. I had to convince him that if he flew in penguins from the Bronx Zoo, they'd be dead in the heat within two hours. I had to tell him ix-nay on building a floatation device that could hold one elephant while another towed it down the river." Then Oliver Turch would shake his head and say, "Of course, that guy is now a famous millionaire, and now I'm teaching high school in Valdosta, so what do I know?"

No one knew what to make of the Aqua Zoo. Those who saw it with their own eyes couldn't stop talking about the dolphins who took to the air with Delores and Lester riding on their backs, or the aerialists, like fireflies, who skittered across high wires that stretched from one side of the Springs to the other. Those who read about it were captivated by the pictures of a little boy riding down to the Springs on the head of an elephant. The *Orlando Sentinel* dwelled on the little puppet that the boy held in his hands: "Its rhinestone tears picked up the glimmer of the sun and shot it back to the water," the reporter gushed.

The local news shows kept showing footage of the opening number: a magnificent white Arabian horse, carrying a woman with short champagne-colored hair and wearing a bright red gown, galloping toward the crowd. The woman turned out to be Peggy Lee. She sang "It's a Good Day" like ice cream melting, and there was no end to the shots of the audience swaying to the sultry rhythm of her song. It didn't take long for someone to figure out that Peggy Lee had starred in Disney's animated hit *Lady and the Tramp*. And here she was, appearing in a rival attraction in Central Florida. The news shows had a field day with it.

Armando Lozano, who was covering the pageant for WGUP, talked about the midgets riding on turtles and the clowns and elephants having water fights. "This is a show that will go down in Florida history," he boomed. And he was right. People started to call Dave Hanratty a genius— what else could you call a man who had mermaids standing on elephants and twirling batons that were blazing at both ends? The press took to calling him Mr. Florida, and the sobriquet took hold.

For weeks afterward, the crowds on Route 50 were headed west toward Weeki Wachee, not east toward Orlando. Rumor had it that the day the *Tampa Tribune* had run a front-page rave about the Aqua Zoo with the headline "Live Magic at Weeki Wachee," Walt Disney himself had walked into a conference room filled with theme-park executives, slammed the newspaper down on the conference table, and said, "Why don't *we* have anything live around here?"

It was nearly dark before Gail made her way to the elephant house where Roy was washing down Nehru, and Delores and Westie were sitting on a bench nearby. Westie was the first to notice his mother. As he stood up to run to her, he dropped Otto, who was on his lap, onto the sand.

"Mommy," he shouted. "Mommy's here." Delores watched her father's eyes shift down to the floor as her mother stepped closer. She moved toward her mother warily, wondering if she'd come to take Westie home. "Hi, Mom," she said. The two women held each other by the elbows and drew their heads together, as if they might kiss. Delores's hair was still wet from the show, and Gail's makeup was fresh and skillfully applied. Afraid they'd rub off on each other, they didn't kiss.

Gail was first to speak. "That show was the most amazing thing I've ever seen," she said. "I've already called Avalon and told her about you and the dolphins, and Westie—oh Westie, you were such a big boy, and so brave on top of that elephant."

"I wasn't scared," Westie said, still flushed. "I was so high up, but I wasn't scared at all." As Westie went on about Nehru and the other elephants, Delores studied her mother. She was wearing a short, sleeveless magenta dress that emphasized her big breasts and went well with her black hair. She wore her hair up in a twist and a pair of sandals made out of see-through plastic. Very va-va-va-voom, in an Annette Funicello kind of way, she thought.

Just then, she saw her father glance up at her mother. Gail must have noticed as well, because her body stiffened and she stood at attention. "Hello, Roy," she said. "Hello," said Roy, still not looking her in the eye. "You look nice."

"So do you," she said.

The four of them stood in a knot of silence: Mr. Chatty and the three Walkers.

This is the best it will ever be, thought Delores. But she was not going to let that weigh her down on this day.

She picked up Otto and dusted him off. She had used her remaining silver dollars to have his skirt remade and his face repainted and he looked as he had when she first got him.

"Hey, Little Brother," she said, handing the puppet to Westie. "I have an idea. Let's go."

They walked down to the Springs and sat down on the shore next to a rubber clown's nose that someone must have lost earlier in the day. Westie took off his shirt and they both pulled off their shoes. Delores waded into the water; with the sun down, it was cooler than usual and she splashed some on her wrists and then on her face. "Don't forget to hold on tight," she said, as she crouched down.

Westie held Otto in one arm and wrapped the other around Delores's chest. He climbed on her back and they floated on the surface like that for a while. Delores thought about the last time they had swum together like this, and how light—almost weightless—Westie had felt then. Now he was substantial; she could feel his strength in the way his feet gripped around her ribs. They really were of one blood, she and he.

"Come on, Westie," she shouted, just before she dove under the water. "Swim. Let's swim away."

Maybe a turtle swam with them, but maybe not. By then it was too dark to be sure of anything.

ACKNOWLEDGMENTS

My world is a saner, happier place because of Kathy Robbins. I am grateful to Elisabeth Scharlatt for always knowing what needs to be done, and to Brunson Hoole, Cheryl Nicchitta, Liz Maples, and everyone else at Algonquin for their care and fine work. Rachelle Bergstein at the Robbins office asked tough questions and made brilliant suggestions. I can't wait to read her novel.

Barbara Wynns of Weeki Wachee Springs is the real thing, and I am indebted to her for all of her help. Becky Okrent, Danielle Perez, and Kathy Rich cheered me on and gave me great advice.

Lisa Grunwald has taught me invaluable lessons about friendship and about writing. This novel and I are immeasurably enriched by having her in our lives.

Great husbands do not necessarily make great editors, but in my case they do. This book would not exist without Gary Hoenig.